Stefan Malmström is a former ne[...] Sveriges Radio and Swedish TV4. Tod[...] and author. At a young age, Stefan w[...] Scientology in Hässleholm, a small town in southern Sweden. *KULT*, his first book, is based on his experiences in the cult. Stefan lives in Karlskrona in Sweden with his family.

KULT

Stefan Malmström

Translated by
Suzanne Martin Cheadle

SILVERTAIL BOOKS • *London*

This edition published by Silvertail Books in 2019
www.silvertailbooks.com
Copyright © Stefan Malmström 2019

1

The right of Stefan Malmström to be identified as the author
of this work has been asserted in accordance
with the Copyright, Design and Patents Act 1988.
A catalogue record of this book is available from the British Library.

978-1-909269-93-4

Night on our earth now has fallen.
Shimmering starlit, sheen!
Our small worlds wander so distant.
Darkness so endless seems.
Darkness and depth and the dusk hour,
Why, why do I love them?
Though the stars wander so distant.
Earth is still our human home.

Erik Blomberg
Translated by Linda Schenck

1.

Luke's hand shook as he tried to put the key in the lock. Something was wrong. So wrong.

"Just open the door!" screamed Therese, Viktor's ex-wife, standing behind Luke and on the verge of hysteria. It was eight-thirty on Monday evening and they were outside the door of Viktor's apartment on the third floor of Alamedan 30 in downtown Karlskrona.

Luke swore to himself. The key wouldn't go in.

"You must have given me the wrong key," Luke said. "It doesn't fit."

Therese grabbed his arm and tried to take it from him.

"Give it to me. I'll take care of it."

Luke jerked his arm away.

"No, I'll do it," he snapped, feeling instantly guilty for the sharpness of his tone. It wasn't fair to speak to Therese like that. She had every right to be beside herself with worry. Viktor should have arrived with his and Therese's four-year-old daughter Agnes at Luke's for dinner two-and-a-half hours ago, at six o'clock. Luke started trying to call Viktor on his cell phone when he was an hour late, but he didn't answer. An hour later, Luke was worried and he decided to leave his cabin on Björkholmen and head to Viktor's apartment, a five-bedroom, 3,000-square foot place in a spectacular brick-and-granite building. Viktor, Luke's best friend, had lived there since he divorced Therese three years earlier.

When Luke came up to the third floor, he heard music playing in Viktor's apartment and assumed he was in there with Agnes. But the door was locked and when Luke rang the bell no one opened it. After ten minutes of ringing and pounding, Luke realized he was going to have to call Therese as she had a spare key.

Therese answered after four rings, and there was a lot of noise and talking in the background. She was at a work party and grew both irritated and nervous when Luke asked if she could come with her spare key. She had left Agnes with Viktor around five o'clock, at which point everything seemed normal. She promised Luke she would come with the key as soon as she could.

As soon as the call ended, Luke pushed the elevator button to send it

I

down so Therese wouldn't have to take the stairs. Ten minutes passed before he heard the elevator running. It stopped at the right floor and Therese stepped out—wearing full make-up and party clothes.

"I should never have agreed to shared custody," were the first words out of her mouth. "He can hardly take care of himself. How in the hell could he take care of a child, too?"

"Now he's ruined the entire evening for me," she continued while giving Luke the key. "We're celebrating the biggest order in the history of the company and were just about to sit down to eat. A three-course meal. He's definitely going to have to pay me back for this."

Now it was a few minutes later, and that calm anger happened had been replaced by pure, primal panic. Luke had never seen a mother terrified for the safety of her child before, and it was as powerful as any emotion he had ever witnessed. It made him even more desperate to get into the flat quickly.

Luke examined the key. At first he thought it was one of those keys which worked whichever way you held it, but now he realized he might be holding it upside down. He turned it quickly and it slid in all the way. He twisted it and heard the latch click open. Luke shoved open the heavy door and the sound of the music hammered against his eardrums. It was jazz.

Strange, he thought. Viktor doesn't like jazz.

He turned on the light in the hallway and entered the stylishly minimalist apartment. Viktor hadn't spared a dime when he divorced Therese and bought the place. He tore out nearly everything. New kitchen, new bathrooms, refinished floors, fresh paint everywhere, a complete renovation. He hired a local interior decorating company and gave them free license. It cost a fortune, but if anyone could afford it, Viktor could. The floor in the foyer was composed of black and white marble squares in a checkerboard pattern. White walls, a narrow black bureau under a painting by Blekinge artist Kjell Hobjer of a large red fish, covering almost the entire picture, set against a bright blue background.

Luke's thoughts were racing with questions but no answers. Was the gas stove leaking? In his mind, he saw Viktor and Agnes lying passed out in their beds. But he didn't smell gas. It smelled clean. Viktor hired a cleaning lady who usually came on Sundays.

Damn strange, Luke thought. Completely dark in the apartment and jazz playing loudly. So unlike Viktor.

"Viktor!" Luke called into the apartment as Therese pushed passed him, threw open the door to Agnes' room, turned on the light, looked in and then continued into the apartment. Luke also looked into the room. The bed was empty, and the comforter lay on the floor. The pink pillows and stuffed animals rested in a neat row on the petite red armchair. The book of princess fairy tales, which Luke read for her last Saturday night, lay on the nightstand.

Luke hurried towards the gigantic living room. The computer, the source of the music, was on. He saw Therese stop in the entrance to the living room. She screamed and disappeared into the room. A second later, Luke halted at the same spot and saw Therese leaning over Agnes, who lay in her nightgown on the pale grey sofa. She had thrown up and looked like she was sleeping deeply.

Luke turned his head and went completely cold when he saw Viktor—hanging lifeless from a noose on the bathroom door.

2.

Luke ran to Viktor and lifted him as he pulled him sideways so the rope would slide off of the top of the door. The rope had been tied around the door handle on the other side. Viktor's cheek pressed against Luke's when he lifted him down, and the thought occurred to him that this was the first time he had felt Viktor's cheek against his. They usually hugged when they hadn't seen each other in a few days, but never cheek-to-cheek. This was the first time. And Viktor's cheek was cold.

"What the hell have you done, Viktor? What have you done?" Luke's voice trembled as he quickly laid him down on the parquet floor. Luke caught the scent of urine as he clumsily tried to release the noose around Viktor's neck and looked into Viktor's eyes. He saw no sign of life in them. He tried to feel for breath and find a pulse in his neck but found none. He made a few awkward attempts to blow air into Viktor's lungs, but he soon gave up. There was no response. The realization that Viktor was dead instantly brought back memories from Luke's time in the Devil's Rebels and with Johnny Attia's gang in New York. It was fifteen years since he last saw death.

"Luke, she's dead!" Therese's crying turned to screams and Luke rushed to the sofa. He pushed Therese, who was performing CPR on Agnes, out of the way. He leaned over the girl, placed his mouth close to Agnes' nose and felt the faintest movement of air.

"She's breathing," he said.

Luke pushed the coffee table away with his foot, lifted her down onto the pale turquoise Ikea rug and began to blow with all the strength in his lungs. After a moment, he began pushing with both hands on her chest. He passed his mobile phone to Therese after the first thirty compressions.

"Call an ambulance! Now!"

He leaned down and continued blowing and pushing in turns. He realized that he might crush her tiny ribs if he wasn't careful, and he eased up the pressure of his compressions. He looked into her face while he pushed, hoping to see some sign of life.

"Come on, Agnes," Luke begged. "You're going to make it. Please."

Luke looked quickly up to Therese. She sat paralyzed, his phone in her hand. Luke realized that she wouldn't be able to say anything comprehensible and took his phone back.

"Keep pushing. Thirty times. Then mouth-to-mouth," he said to Therese, standing up and dialing the number. A woman answered immediately.

"I need an ambulance. As quickly as possible. Alamedan 30. There are two people here, one's dead and one is a little girl who's still breathing."

"Could you please repeat that? Not as quickly, and try to speak more clearly. I need to know your name, too," the dispatcher said.

When Luke was stressed, his American accent tended to grow stronger, making it hard for Swedes to understand him.

"Luke Bergmann. We need an ambulance. Hurry, for god's sake! There's a four-year-old girl who's going to die!"

"Okay now, you've got to try to calm down so I get the right information. Take a deep breath and then tell me your location, both street address and city."

Luke clenched his teeth. He took a deep breath and tried to speak slowly.

"The address is Alamedan 30 in Karlskrona. Two people. One is dead. The other, a little girl, is dying and she's definitely going to if you don't send a goddamn ambulance. Now!"

"Can you tell me what happened?" the woman asked.

"Does it matter?" Luke asked stubbornly. "I don't know what happened. We came into the apartment and this is what we found."

"I can't just send an ambulance without first getting an idea of the situation. I have to be sure this is real and that it's truly an emergency."

Luke lowered his voice, trying to project fear rather than anger.

"I promise you this is real. Please."

The woman fell silent for a couple seconds.

"I'm sending two ambulances."

Therese was crying and blowing as instructed. Agnes lay as lifeless with her long, blonde hair spread out around her head and her white nightgown against the aqua-colored rug. Therese's tears had dampened Agnes' beautiful face. Luke thought how pretty Agnes was, how stunning she would be when she became a teenager. He and Viktor talked about it as recently as Saturday evening. Agnes was watching her favorite show on TV, *Anki and Pytte*, and was laughing so unabashedly at the clever little duck that Viktor and Luke interrupted their dinner preparations to stand and watch her.

"That girl is going to have trouble with boys when she gets to be a teenager," Luke said to Viktor.

"It's more like they're going to have problems with me," Viktor answered.

Luke's smile abruptly disappeared. He folded his arms. "And me," he said.

A little later, the phone rang. Viktor went into his home office and asked Luke to put Agnes to bed, which he gladly did. She ran her little finger along his muscular, tattooed arm and asked why he didn't wash better. Luke's heart melted even more when Agnes then took off his black knit cap and started to curl her fingers into his thick, black hair as she trustingly fell asleep in his arms.

"Agnes! Please, Agnes! Breathe! Please!" Therese gasped after having attempted to blow life into the little girl's body for the fourth time. Agnes lay with her mouth half-open and her eyes closed, her long, fine eyelashes pasted to her skin. She looked like she was sleeping peacefully. But this time she might not wake up again.

Luke's anger towards the ambulance dispatcher dissipated and was replaced with a chill that took a tight hold on his insides. Luke whispered a prayer to himself, to a god he didn't believe in.

Let Agnes live. I'll do anything. Just let her live.

Where in the hell were those ambulances? He looked towards the bathroom where Agnes' father, his best friend, lay dead. The jazz music increased in intensity and drowned out the sounds of Therese's struggle to bring Agnes back to life. An electric piano and a guitar were vying for who could play the most notes per second.

What boring music, Luke thought, beginning to feel sick at the same time as his legs started to shake. He had to silence the noise. He walked on quivering legs to the computer, and pressed mute. On the table stood a small, flame-colored jar with the cap off and a white powder in it. A glass with a grainy fluid in the bottom stood next to it. A half-eaten Marabou milk chocolate bar lay on the floor next to the table. He noticed a faint whiff of chocolate when he performed CPR on Agnes. Luke heard sirens in the distance.

"Luke! She's not breathing any more! Agnes, no!"

Therese screamed in confusion and took Agnes into her arms where she sat on the floor and rocked frantically back and forth. Luke knelt down and held her and Agnes tightly.

6

3.

"If I say it's 1787, what sort of mental image do you get?"

The guy asking Jenny this question was named Peter. He was 25 years old, six years older than Jenny and, as of six months ago, a graduate of the MBA program at Lund University. He wore a brown corduroy jacket, a red scarf around his neck, glasses, and a moustache. Aristocratic, like an English dandy. A completely different style to the other guys Jenny knew.

Jenny graduated from high school in Karlskrona with top grades a half-year earlier. Now she was working at a café, taking a sabbatical year from her studies and intending to begin her university studies the next fall.

She sat wedged into a newly-purchased, bright red IKEA couch in her boyfriend Stefan's sister's modern apartment on Kungsgatan in central Ronneby. Victoria was turning 23 and had invited a few friends over for cake. She was going to have a larger party later in the month.

Peter sat sunken into an armchair across from the couch, holding a cigarette elegantly between his index and middle fingers. Empty dessert plates and coffee mugs sat on the coffee table. They talked a lot about politics, which was totally uninteresting to Jenny. The bourgeois coalition had won the election and broken the string of three Social Democratic governments. Just that day, conservative politician Carl Bildt assumed the role of prime minister. Now, Peter thought, Sweden was on the right track again.

Through the impressive Pioneer sound system, Whitney Houston's velvety voice enveloped them: *I'm your baby tonight.*

Stefan, Jenny's boyfriend, sat to her left, and on her right was Stefan's older sister Viktoria. Of the eight people in the room, these were the only two Jenny knew. The last time she sat on a couch with Viktoria was a month earlier, at the siblings' parents' house for coffee on a Sunday. It was the first time Jenny met Stefan's mother and father, and the atmosphere was tense. Viktoria decided to try to lighten the mood. Suddenly she gave a start, leaned away from Jenny, pinched her nose, laughed, and said, "Ew, Jenny! Did you fart?!"

It was so incredibly mean of her! Jenny felt like sinking through the floor. Her lame protests were pointless. She blushed all the way down her neck and knew that everyone thought she had passed gas.

So this was the second time within only a few weeks that she was sitting on a couch, blushing. The question Peter asked her made everyone fall silent and turn their attention to her. Damn that I always blush! she thought. As long as she could remember, she thought it was awkward to be the center of attention. Standing in front of the class and giving a presentation was torture, despite the fact she knew she was pretty and one of the best students in the class. When the teachers returned exams and announced the results aloud, a custom in Swedish classrooms, she was almost always the one who earned the most points, and it was just as awkward every time when she heard her name and everyone looked at her. The flush came like clockwork. It got so bad that sometimes she blushed even before the exams had been returned, blushing purely at the thought that she might soon blush.

All the friends looked at Jenny. Her thoughts whirled around in her head. She felt pressured and nervous. So, naturally, she blushed.

"What do you mean?" she asked.

Peter smiled at her.

"Well, think about this year, 1787. And try to get a picture, some mental image connected to this year."

Jenny hesitated, feeling like she had to respond.

"Women in beautiful dresses," she said. "A ball." She giggled and looked at Peter.

"Okay," Peter smiled. "Where are you, then?"

"I don't know."

Peter didn't give up.

"What thought popped into your head when I first asked the question?"

"Hm. Paris, maybe?"

"Great! Where in Paris? Do you see any buildings?"

Jenny closed her eyes now. She took the first image that appeared in her mind.

"A palace. Versailles."

"Good, Jenny! Who are you at the ball?"

"Me?"

"Yes. Do you see yourself? Who are you?"

Jenny took her mug and sipped a little tea to give herself a moment.

"I don't know. One of the people dancing, maybe?"

"Describe yourself."

Jenny closed her eyes again. On the inside of her eyelids, she saw a great ballroom, many people dancing around in ornate 18th century clothing. She saw a beautiful young woman in a white gown laughing and dancing.

"I'm wearing a totally white ball gown. Big hair, it must be a wig. Pearls in my hair and a mask on my face."

She fell silent, a bit surprised by the detailed nature of what she just said. She had an idea where it came from, though. They read about the French Revolution in school last year. She was fascinated by Marie Antoinette's fate and borrowed a book about her from the library. It was so quiet in the room, you could hear a pin drop.

"Who are you?" Peter asked quietly.

"A noblewoman at the court," the answer came with lightning speed. "My duty is to calm the queen. That's my job." She smiled and looked around at the others. They smiled back.

"Wonderful!" Peter said. "There may be a reason that you saw that particular image?"

He leaned towards her. The music had stopped, and the room was silent. He asked, "Might it be that what you just told us about is a memory and not something you imagined?"

Jenny glanced around the room. They looked back at her with interest. Clearly, this type of discussion wasn't out of the ordinary for them. She turned towards Peter.

"That I lived a past life as a noblewoman in Paris, you mean?" She gave a laugh. "Yes, maybe it is. But it could also be because a few months ago, I borrowed a book from the library about Marie Antoinette."

"Why do you think you were interested in her?" Peter responded quickly.

There might be a point to what he was saying, she thought. She was truly interested in that historical era. When she read the book, she felt the desire to live in that setting, wanted to be part of it. She liked the thought of having lived at the palace in Versailles. And she was drawn to the idea of past lives.

"A lot of people around the world believe in reincarnation," Peter continued, leaning forward and extinguishing his cigarette in the heavy marble ashtray. "There are over a billion just within Buddhism and Hinduism. Who says that Westerners are right?"

Jenny nodded.

"Not everyone has lived such an exciting life as you seem to have," said Max, one of the guys. "I was your average poor, lousy farmer in Skåne in the late 1700s."

Everyone laughed and the rest of the evening was filled with laughter, more talk of past lives, and loud discussions about the quality of Nirvana's music and whether Mikhail Gorbachev should get the Nobel Peace Prize now that he was dead. Jenny was happy around these people. Despite being so much younger than they were, she felt like they respected and were interested in her. They were smart, pleasant, and not only focused on themselves. She wasn't used to that.

It was already 11:30 before Stefan and Jenny left the apartment and went to the bus stop to take the last bus to Karlskrona.

"Those are pretty exciting friends Viktoria has," Jenny said.

"Yeah, they're cool," Stefan said. "It's really interesting, all that stuff about past lives."

"I have a hard time accepting it," Jenny said. "But the images that came to me grew so incredibly clear the more he asked. What if we are souls and just jump from body to body? I really want to believe that's true."

They walked silently for a moment. They arrived at the bus stop and stood there to wait. The bus would be coming in five minutes.

"How does Viktoria know them?" Jenny asked.

"One of the guys, Max, is an old friend of Viktoria's from elementary school," Stefan answered. "I think he's the one who first got to know the rest. Most of them are from Karlskrona, but a few went away for college and have now moved back home. My sister said that some of them are part of some sort of religious movement that believes we all have these past lives. Scientology, it's called. It's not about Jesus and Christianity, that sort of thing. I think they're just interested in this reincarnation stuff and with getting better at communicating. Viktoria isn't really into all that, but she likes the people a lot."

"Me, too," Jenny said.

"Yeah, I noticed," Stefan said, smiling and laying his arm around her. "Did you think Peter was hot?"

"Idiot," Jenny said. "It's not like that." She looked away so Stefan wouldn't see her blushing.

4.

Early Wednesday morning in Hogland Park. One and a half days since a father and his four-year-old daughter were found dead in an apartment eight hundred yards from the park. The sun was cautious. A quiet morning fog swept over the city, which was built on thirty-three islands. The fog prevented the sun from reaching all the way down to the few early-bird souls who left their houses on the largest of the islands, Trossö Island.

One of them was Luke Bergmann. He didn't care in the least whether the sun was shining or if it was storming. He didn't notice.

He was sitting on a bench in the park, looking at a small bag recently placed in his hand by a pusher. The bag contained relief. Possibly death, but above all, sweet relief. That was what he wanted.

For sixteen years, he resisted the urge. Since he fled to Karlskrona he had not fallen down that hole even a single time. The urge had subsided, but it was always there.

In his pocket was cigarette paper, Rizla brand. The pusher also gave him a box of matches. He had everything he needed.

In his mind, he saw himself thirteen years ago when he smoked for the first time. It was the same day his mother died from a heroin overdose. He still remembered the feeling. Liberation. A warmth in his core that released all anxiety and angst and made the panic go away.

After that, he stuck to marijuana. It was enough. The other guys in the gang took everything they could get their hands on; crack, ecstasy, heroin, alcohol. But Luke didn't.

He picked up the cigarette paper and rolled, twisting up the top. He refused the mouthpiece and didn't want to have any tobacco mixed in. The sun began to spread its warmth. A group of young people in orange overalls working summer jobs were picking up garbage near the playground. Luke weighed the joint in his hand.

The first night after Viktor's and Agnes' deaths, he hadn't been able to sleep a wink. He lay there, tossing and turning. Sweating. He couldn't tear his thoughts away. He spent the second night in a kind of purgatory between sleep and wakefulness. Dozing. Dreaming nightmares filled with death. The same theme every time. The first guy he killed in a gang fight on Troutman Street in Brooklyn twenty-four years ago—a sixteen-year-old black kid from the Black Stabbers—came running at him. Wide, staring, drugged eyes with a meat cleaver raised over his head. Luke watched as the sharp edge of the cleaver approached his face. He was paralyzed, waiting for the blade to split his forehead. He awoke in the moment of death, convinced it was all over. In his confusion, he jumped up out of bed to run away and when he became fully conscious, he was panting, his pulse racing.

Two young guys in overalls with black garbage bags in their hands approached the bench where Luke was sitting. He stuffed the joint into his pocket and got up. He decided to go home and smoke it there.

On Tuesday, he called Åsa Nordin, his boss at Ekekullen, and told her what had happened and asked to take a few vacation days. Ekekullen was the group home in Rödeby for teenagers with a history of criminal activity and drug abuse where Luke just started working. Previously, he worked for eight years at a similar home in Listerby outside Ronneby. Amanda, his ex-wife, called the same day. She heard what had happened and was crushed. She also knew Viktor well and had met Agnes a few times. Luke hadn't talked to anyone else in two days.

It took him fifteen minutes to walk home to the little cabin on Björkholmen where he lived. It wasn't big, and it had low ceilings. The shipyard workers who lived there in the late 1600s must have been pygmies. Luke, who was almost six feet six inches tall, hit his head on the beams more than once in the beginning, but he soon learned where he needed to duck. He fell in love with the little cabin the second he stepped into it for the first time four years earlier. It was as far as you could get from Williamsburg in Brooklyn where he grew up. His landlord had outfitted it with a jacuzzi, modern kitchen, woodburning stove and a fantastically beautiful little patio. And then there was the best feature: it included a private dock and rowboat just 50 yards from the front door. He discovered how peaceful it was to row and loved going out for a lap in the evenings when the weather was calm. Sometimes he took his fishing pole with him and brought home a pike or a perch to fix for dinner.

Luke went into the bedroom, took out the joint and matches, and set them on the nightstand. He looked at the large black and white photo of himself in a wrestling pose from one of the competitions he was in. The photo was framed on the wall behind the bed. He was nineteen years old when the picture was taken and tried so hard to look tough. So ridiculous. He would take it down as soon as he found the energy.

He was hungry. The joint would have to wait. He hadn't eaten in two days. He went out into the kitchen, his thoughts spinning around in his head. He opened the freezer, took out a frozen dinner, and put it in the microwave.

Luke and Viktor were close friends for ten years. They met six years after Luke came to Sweden, through their wives who worked together as teachers at a secondary school in Karlskrona.

Both couples were childless, unlike most others their age, and they started to hang out together. Luke and Viktor took an immediate liking to each other. Although Luke had lived in Karlskrona for several years, he hadn't got to know many people. In the beginning, he spent all his time learning Swedish and trying to acclimate to Swedish society. When they met in 2004, Luke was commuting 50 miles to Jämshög where he was in his last semester of his education as a social services assistant.

He had never had a friend before who felt so easy and comfortable to talk to, despite that they seemed so diametrically opposite. Viktor was extroverted, social, and curious about other people. Luke was a lone wolf, quiet, and could be interpreted as sullen. Viktor had to fight to learn anything about Luke. Many conversations passed before Luke told him a secret only his ex was privy to before: his past included a life of drugs and crime in a gang in Williamsburg and a job as a guard for the Israeli mafia in New York, as well as the flight to London in 1997 where he fell madly in love in Amanda from Karlskrona who was working there as an au pair. The move to Karlskrona, his Swedish courses, adult education classes and then his education as a social services assistant in Jämshög. Viktor was fascinated by Luke's personal journey and more than anything wanted to know about the therapy Luke had gone through. They spent an endless number of hours talking about the differences between various forms of therapy.

2008 was a terrible year for Viktor. He and his wife Lotta tried to get pregnant for several years and they finally found out they were. They were going to have a baby. But at the same time, she started having vision trouble and terrible headaches. It turned out to be a brain tumor. She and their unborn child died only four months after the diagnosis. Viktor was crushed, went into a deep depression, and was only saved by meeting Therese a few months later. Therese was nine years younger, a vision of beauty, and Viktor fell deeply in love. After three months, Therese was pregnant and they got married half a year later, at the very end of Therese's pregnancy. Then came the next blow. When Agnes was only six months old, Therese told Viktor that she didn't have feelings for him anymore, that she realized she still loved her old boyfriend and was going to go back to him. She took Agnes and moved out. It was too much for Viktor. He went immediately to the emergency intake of the adult psychiatric center. This time, the depression was even deeper, and it took Viktor months of crisis therapy to return to himself in any recognizable form.

Luke's own marriage broke up a year before Viktor's, after Amanda became tired of the fact that Luke was more involved in drug-addicted teenagers than in her. Besides, she wanted to have children, too, and when Luke refused, she gave him an ultimatum. He had to choose: children or a divorce. Luke had been clear from the start that he didn't want children. He chose divorce. So when Viktor ended up in his second great crisis, Luke had plenty of spare time. He literally moved in with Viktor and helped him by making sure he got to have Agnes every other week. Luke was convinced that Agnes was the primary reason Viktor found any joy in life again. Viktor loved his little daughter more than anything else. Now they were both dead.

While Luke ate the microwaved, tasteless chicken dinner, he thought about the two images burned into his mind: one of Viktor hanging from the bathroom door and the other of Agnes lying lifeless on her back on the turquoise rug. And he pondered the same thing he had been thinking since Monday, namely how could Viktor have taken not only his own life, but also that of Agnes? If he was capable of doing something so awful, how could Luke have missed the signals? Viktor was in an unusually good mood on Saturday evening. He talked about his trips to Russia and how he was heading to Kaliningrad again. He had something big on the way, the details of which he didn't want to share. Was it only to hide his true plans? Why in the hell didn't he say anything, if that was how he was feeling?

Luke was furious when he thought about it. But he also knew he could never understand people who took their own lives. Who knows what's going on in the head of a person who has decided to do something so irrevocable? Why had his friend hidden these destructive thoughts? Why didn't he confide in Luke?

Luke looked at the clock. It was nine in the morning. He went back to the bedroom and looked at the joint. He wondered if he should contact Viktor's therapist the next day. He wanted to understand why.

He decided he was going to do it, after he talked to the police. Someone from the precinct had called him and asked him to come on Thursday afternoon to read through his witness statement and to answer a few more questions about what happened. Luke hoped the therapist would be able to meet him after that. He had to do this, for Viktor's sake. He took the joint and the baggie filled with green leaves. He went to the bathroom, emptied its contents into the toilet, and flushed. Back in the kitchen, he took out a large unopened bottle of Captain Morgan from the pantry, sat at the kitchen table, and started drinking. He could ensure a grand stupor without plunging into complete darkness.

5.

His balls were itchy again. That always happened at night, and it woke Thomas Svärd up every time. He rubbed the skin between his thumb and index finger and drew his fingernails over it in turns. It felt good. But after a while, he got worried that he would scratch the skin until it bled and then it would only be painful.

He turned on the lamp, pulled down his boxers, and looked. He saw a faint redness and wondered if it was from the scratching or if he had a fungus. The stump of what was once his cock hung there, a little flap of skin a few centimeters long. He still felt sick when he looked, so he tried to ignore it.

But he couldn't. At times he managed to forget about it, but now thought that was just him in denial. Over the past few weeks reality sunk in. It was gone. He would never fuck again. Never again feel the pleasure of penetration. Never again have an orgasm.

The shitty part of the misery was that the horniness remained, and just as strong as before. He especially felt it in the mornings. He often dreamed about fucking, reliving those moments with the children, and woke up horny. But now he couldn't release it.

It was insanely cruel. It would have been easier to be rid of the whole package, both his horniness and his cock. In fact, if he had got rid of the horniness he would have an easier time, even if it would have made life a little less worth living. But being rid of the instrument that gave him so many wonderful experiences was probably the worst punishment anyone could have subjected him to. The worst torture.

When it bothered him the most, he felt like a lion in a cage. He had to move, and walked around restlessly, trying to force himself to think other thoughts. Uncomfortable thoughts. One thing that often worked was to think back to the bathtub incident from when he was twelve. A year or so earlier, he realized what happened when he pulled the skin at the end of it up and down. It was a complete surprise. He sat on the toilet and pulled on his wiener. It felt good. He started to pull more quickly and the pleasant feeling grew stronger. Suddenly, something white squirted out from the tip and landed on the rug. He must have made some sort of sound because his mom knocked loudly on the bathroom door, wondering what he was doing. He panicked and tried to wipe up the white stickiness with toilet paper.

When he opened the door and came out, his mother looked inquisitively at him. But she didn't know what he'd done. The next time, he was lying in the bathtub and started pulling again. Suddenly, the door opened. He forgot to lock it. Mom came in and saw what he was doing and flew into a rage. She went and got a pot of boiling water and poured it over his erect penis. He luckily had time to sink down a bit in the water, but a lot of it splashed on him. He screamed loudly from the pain, but she just took hold of his wiener and squeezed. She looked crazy-eyed as she frothed at the mouth and screamed, "This is the damnation of man! You will go to Hell if you do that!" She then forced him to read the Bible every evening for three weeks. After every reading, she hit him to "beat the evil out of him".

It began sometime around then, and really got going just a few weeks later. Patrick, the neighbor boy, was fourteen years old and set up a tent in the forest. They were playing Cowboys and Indians, and afterwards they gathered in the tent. Patrick ordered Susanne, who was twelve years old, to take off her pants and underwear and lay on her back. There were five of them looking on as Patrick took off his pants and boxers. Patrick had developed a little hair around his cock and Thomas remembered how he stared when he saw it. It was the first time he had seen anyone else's erect cock. Long and pointy. Patrick took hold of it and laid on top of Susanne, who just lay there, completely silent. Then Patrick started humping. But he was interrupted when they heard voices approaching.

Even cut short, the event made a deep impression on Svärd. The young girl's smooth vagina, completely free from disgusting black hair. The pointy spear that approached and entered. That was when he understood what this tool should be used for.

He sat up in bed, set his feet on the dirty rag rug, lit a cigarette, and looked at the clock. 12:30 at night. He had to piss. He stood up and walked the two yards to the bathroom. He opened the bathroom door, turned on the light, and went in. Since the attack a year ago, he couldn't stand to piss anymore. It sprayed wildly in every direction. The doctor did the best he could, but all that was left of his urethral opening now functioned in much the same way as a sprinkler on a warm summer day.

The bathroom wasn't large. Built sometime in the middle of the previous century, it was at least fairly bright and nice. But it was tight and he had got used to backing in. It was completely tiled and the showerhead hung on the wall behind the toilet. When he showered, the whole bathroom got wet and he had to spend fifteen minutes wiping up afterward. There can't have been more than one man at a time in this damn bunker, he thought.

He got up and flushed. He went out into the main room, sat at the rickety little table, and turned his laptop on. He needed to fill in his account for the next assignment and so he logged into SexNordics BBS. He went into his galleries and saw that he had some messages. An idiot from Dallas who claimed that his latest Sandra picture was fake. He probably studied her birthmarks and decided that it wasn't the right girl in the picture. At the same time he was asking for a picture of Sandra when she was younger; thirteen-year-olds were too old for his taste.

Svärd pondered this. He earned serious money from the Sandra pictures but realized that he needed to change things up. Demand for the 4 to 6-year-old range was increasing. There were crazies who were ready to pay up to a hundred dollars for a picture of a naked four-year-old in sexy poses. He went quickly through the other messages and swore to himself. Not one single fucker who wanted to shell out; just idiot freeloaders who didn't care about watermarks over the image and who wanted to praise him for his fine collection.

He logged on to his bank webpage and checked his account balance. $303.91 was all he had. Damn, that's hardly enough for a flight, he thought. Have to get more money.

He spent an hour finding suitable preschools on Kungsholmen in Stockholm; there were over twenty. He went to every webpage to see which ones were open in the summer and surprisingly enough, seven were. He formulated a letter of interest for a substitute teaching position and sent this along with his falsified diploma from Linné University and a false CV to all seven. He used his old fake name, Gustav Thordén, and was almost sure that some of them wouldn't bother calling around and checking that it was all true. Even if they did call, it would be nearly impossible for them to get hold of anyone over the break. And if they were desperate for staff, as he hoped, then they might just skip that part of the process completely.

Afterwards, he went to the weather website and checked the forecast for the following day. Sunshine and hot as hell all of Thursday. Vacation time. The local playgrounds would be full of families with small children. He closed the lid of his computer and crawled into bed with a faint smile on his lips.

6.

"Then I want you to fly home to my mom. Check what she's wearing and fly back here and tell me what you saw! Hantverkargatan 17A, third floor. You can find it, right?"

Jenny gasped quietly. She felt a reluctant admiration that a soccer player nicknamed "Pidde" dared to challenge Peter. She looked at Pidde, who was looking intently at Peter. He wasn't joking any more. His cheeks had developed a red hue over the past few minutes. His voice had risen considerably. His tone had hardened.

Pidde's actual name was Per Johansson and he was the star of Karlskrona AIF, the city's soccer team. He was friends with Affe, who was on the way to joining Scientology—a little half-hearted for now, but it would come. Pidde was popular among the city's youth. He studied to become a teacher at the college in Växjö. He was smart and attractive and had amazing promise as a soccer player. Not a terribly common combination among the city's soccer players. Jenny liked him but thought he could have left his Palestina shawl at home that evening. She knew he was doing it to be provocative. She heard the others talk about him being a communist. Communism wasn't popular among the Scientologists, that much she understood.

Affe played junior league soccer with him and was given the assignment of trying to interest him. That was the strategy: to get people who were popular, smart and locally famous in the movement, then others would follow. The idea came from Celebrity Center in Hollywood, which the Scientologists had successfully led for over ten years. They were successful in recruiting Jenny's favorite star, John Travolta, who was the first really big international star to become a Scientologist. Jenny almost fell out of her chair when Stefan told her. John Travolta! And last year, Tom Cruise joined the movement. That was big. If those two were part of it, there must be something about it that was really great, she thought.

This evening, they were having coffee at Peter's in his apartment on Vallgatan. They were celebrating Peter reaching the Scientology state of OT

III, Operating Thetan Level III. That was three levels above the first auditing level, which was called "Clear," and meant he could now leave his body and act in the physical world without it. It felt a little creepy, Jenny thought. What if he were suddenly at her house when she was going to shower, or flying around in the night in their apartment?

Candles in candelabras stood on the floor, a large Buddha head of walnut watched from the antique bureau, an impressive crystal chandelier hung like a dimmed sun over a round Art Deco-style coffee table with curved legs. The room was like an antique shop, a museum of vanished gallantry and the Swedish bourgeoisie that invaded Blekinge in the late 1600s.

On the coffee table stood black currant tea and sandwiches, Robinson's blackberry marmalade, and Peter's favorite spread, a soft French cheese called "The Laughing Cow". Madonna's "Like a Prayer" came through the stereo speakers. Ten people were sitting in the small living room. Some were sitting on the floor, the rest on the brown leather couch and in armchairs. Jenny and Stefan felt like they were part of this group now. The first evening in Ronneby was followed by several late evenings over coffee. Jenny learned a lot about the ideas surrounding Scientology during these evenings. Peter, Mikael, Fredrik, Maria—they were all so pleasant, smart, and cool. They opened up a whole new world for her.

This was the first time anyone dared to deny it. To question. The room fell quiet after Pidde's challenge. Stefan leaned over and turned down the volume of the music. Jenny was looking forward to hearing how Peter would handle it. She didn't think Pidde stood a chance. Everyone's eyes turned to Peter.

Peter looked intently back at Pidde. He smiled.

"Why should I? I don't need to prove anything to you. This ability isn't something we play around with. It should be used for more important things."

Pidde looked around the room at the dozen guys and girls there. He threw up his hands.

"But there are a few people here, I think, anyway, who might be a little doubtful whether you or your soul or whatever you want to call it can leave your body. Or that there's a soul at all, for that matter. Now you have the chance to convince us. Go on and check so I can call my mom later and see if you're right."

Peter leaned back on the brown leather couch, lifted his cup and took a small sip of his tea before he answered.

"So you don't think we have a soul? Do you think we're just wandering piles of flesh that satisfy our primal needs for a few trifling years and then we're buried and become earth again?"

He set his teacup down and many in the room smiled. Jenny heard this formulation before. She liked it.

Pidde didn't give up.

"Don't change the subject, Peter. Go on now so that you get it done. If you do it and you're right, I promise I'll sign up and start working for you tomorrow." He held up his hand as if he were swearing an oath.

Devoted followers sign a contract and agree to work evenings and weekends for the cult for two and a half years. For that, they would get certain therapy and courses for free.

"Let it go," Peter said. "It's not going to happen. We don't play with this, I already said that." Peter raised his voice slightly.

Now Jenny started to think that this was a little strange. Peter actually had the chance to silence Pidde once and for all and even convince others who were doubting. Why didn't he just do it? Peter was ending up in a subordinate position that didn't feel good. Jenny had never seen him lose a discussion. But now? Jenny thought a few people in the room probably felt like she did. A little bit of doubt snuck in. Maybe Peter couldn't?

"You understand that this doesn't sound particularly plausible?" Pidde continued. "You claim that you've reached some sort of state, what was it you called it?"

"OT, Operating Thetan. The third level."

"Exactly. Which means you can leave your body and do things. Or is it just to observe? Can you do things, too?"

"You regain abilities that mean that you can impact what we call MEST: Matter, Energy, Space, and Time, without us being dependent on our bodies. Regaining is important, it's abilities we had once before. Even a materialist like you, Pidde." Peter looked around and smiled. The smile was reflected back at him.

Pidde gave a chuckle.

"He was smart, that Hubbard guy! What ten-year-old hasn't dreamed about having the ability to be invisible and run around causing mischief for others? Hubbard stole ideas from Buddhism and Hinduism, made his own concoction, formulated it so it would sound scientific, came up with a few exercises and said, Voilá! A new religion! With the goal of becoming an invisible superman who fights evil. And Hubbard's bank account was filled generously over time. Because that's how it was. First, he was an unsuccessful science fiction writer who wrote so terribly that he couldn't earn any money. So he decided to create a religion instead. It's the best way of getting rich. He said so himself."

Pidde clearly came prepared, Jenny thought. This stuff about Hubbard and money wasn't new to her. And she knew that Peter had good answers for it. It was like watching a boxing match.

Peter leaned towards the table, took a cigarette out of the pack, and lit it slowly. Now he was in his element, Jenny knew. She had heard this discussion before.

"L. Ron Hubbard has written forty books about Scientology. He's written seventeen seven-hundred-page volumes about therapeutic techniques and processes. He has written an additional eleven eight-hundred-page volumes that have to do with how to lead a Scientology organization. He has held over five thousand lectures and has worked around the clock for thirty years. Do you seriously think that a person who just wanted to get rich would sink so much time into a business project? He hasn't even had time to enjoy the money, for heaven's sake! It's be easier to sell some random product instead."

"Whatever," Pidde said. "You and some of the others here clearly think he's a genius. The only thing I want to see is proof. Give me proof that you can leave your body, and I'll join. Totally and completely."

"There is tons of proof," Peter answered. "The Stanford Research Institute in California has researched some of the OT's abilities to leave the body, such as a guy named Ingo Swann, who demonstrated that he could leave his body and see things, completely perplexing the scientists. It happened in experiment after experiment. The American government is putting millions of dollars into research because they think the Russians are ahead of us. They think the Russians have developed methods to allow people to affect and disrupt atomic bombs and missiles from a great distance."

"I want to see that evidence," Pidde said.

Peter leaned back in the sofa and nonchalantly exhaled smoke.

"The research is classified," he said, stubbing out his cigarette. "And do you know what? Even if I laid out the evidence for you tonight, I'm positive you still wouldn't have given in. Because you've already decided. You don't believe in it and only accept what supports your explanation of things. It's completely natural. Researchers called this 'confirmation bias'. We Scientologists have full respect for the freedom of opinion. You get to think exactly how you want to. All that's important to me is things that work, that make people feel better and can be developed so that we can become free and independently-thinking creatures that can reach our full potential."

Peter fell silent. Pidde looked at him. A small smile played at the corners of his mouth.

"So you're not going travelling tonight, then?"

Peter shook his head.

"Ok. Now I know. Thanks for the grub. It was good. That Laughing Cow stuff especially." He got up, turned on his heel, and left the apartment. The door slammed behind him.

"Pidde is a shining example of the brainwashing that we have been subjected to over the past fifty years," Peter said. "Completely locked into the body and material things. Damn unfortunate. It is our duty to try to get people to elevate their consciousness, get them to see their own greatness and get them to want to seek the freedom and free themselves from this prison. The future of the planet is at stake. So we can't go playing around with our abilities. We have more important duties than that."

Peter and Mikael spent the rest of the evening lecturing about the powers, the evil powers that were fighting to stop the movement. And about how for centuries they dedicated themselves to brainwashing humanity to make people believe they are only piles of flesh and not higher levels of creatures. Peter showed a book that came out two years previously, Operation Mind Control, which revealed how the American government transformed normal people into mercenaries and spies with the help of hypnosis and drugs.

There was talk about highly-developed cultures that existed millions of years ago. About Atlantis, von Däniken, and about Jonathan Livingston Seagull, the gull who didn't want to be like other gulls, who refused to be happy just catching fish and following the flock, who wanted to test his limits and see how high and how far he could fly. When the evening was over, Jenny had completely forgotten Pidde had been there.

She felt as if she were high. High on Scientology, on these people who wanted to do so much good and who believed that she had unharnessed abilities. It resonated with something deep inside her, a string that she didn't know about until now, which lay there slumbering for all of her seventeen years but that now began to vibrate inside her. It was as if a hidden desire had been laid bare. A longing she noticed, sensed, without being able to put it into words. For the first time in her life, she felt alive, filled with a powerful energy that made her feel invincible.

When Jenny and Stefan were about to leave, Peter came out into the hall. "What do you think about what happened earlier with Pidde?" he asked.

Jenny didn't know what she should say. Stefan answered.

"Well, he's a rabid communist, so I wasn't surprised. I didn't really understand why he was invited, to be honest. But I kind of think you could have gone along with it. Now it feels like something was left hanging, and that's too bad. I would really have liked to see you win. Even if I think I understand your position."

Peter smiled.

"I seriously considered accepting his challenge," he said. "But luckily I thought better of it. It is strictly forbidden to use the ability in that way. Even if I had done it and proved to him that it works, I don't think he would have given in. Pidde is a good guy who wants to do the right thing, but Communism is a treacherous ideology that plays on people's consideration of others but that is ultimately about slavery. We want to liberate humankind. Give humankind spiritual and physical freedom. Ensure that people have the opportunity to exploit all potential that exists in every individual and use that potential to do good for humanity."

Jenny and Stefan held hands and walked in silence the first stretch from Vallgatan where Peter's apartment was located. They turned right at Amiralitet Park up towards Stortorget and on to Kungsplan where Jenny would take a bus home to Hästö. On Södra Smedjegatan, Jenny saw a group of people of various ages spill out from a gourmet restaurant on the other side of the street. She recognized the parents of a classmate from ninth grade, Bosse, and realized it was people from a division of the Karlskrona shipyard having their staff Christmas party. Several thousand people still worked at the shipyard, despite large cutbacks over the past twenty years. Her father always joked with her that kids who didn't focus in school ended up with jobs at the shipyard washing tarps. Bosse first interned at the shipyard, then got a summer job and later a permanent job there as a welder. Everyone was jealous of him. He suddenly had a ton of money and soon was going to move into his own apartment in the middle of town.

Jenny looked at the dressed-up shipyard workers as they waved to each other and she suddenly realized what an inconsequential life they lived. Wife, children, apartment, maybe a car. Slaving away from early in the morning to late in the evening with a damn boring, monotonous job at some machine, and whose great dream was to save enough money to buy a house and maybe a sailboat. A wooden one. Fiberglass boats were the sort of thing real Karlskronites snorted at in disgust.

Jenny longed for something completely different. Something that was infinitely larger than a job, house, and boat. She stopped and looked at Stefan, who turned around to face her.

"Stefan. I want to do more. I want to try a few courses and audits. I want to be a real Scientologist."

7.

It was still as the grave and hot as an oven. The blue sky was growing lighter in the distance. The sun slid forward over the islands. Luke walked along Hogland Park on his way to the police station. He was thirsty and nauseous. The rum had filled his veins and now he was paying the price. The only comfort was that he went to bed early and slept dreamlessly.

Three Polish tourists sat in the patio seating of the kiosk that sold pork and potato dumplings called kroppkakor and tested the grey Blekinge dumpling under wild discussion. That was where Viktor convinced Luke to try them for the first time. Until then, he refused to put the grey, flaccid balls of potato into his mouth. They looked like kneidels, which his aunt would serve alongside chicken soup at home in Williamsburg on Sundays. Luke hated them as much as he hated the religious rituals his aunt and her husband practiced daily. They were good people but were completely enslaved by the Jewish rituals and laws. Kroppkakor tasted different from kneidels, and Luke learned to like them. But not today. The sight of them increased his nausea and he quickly turned his gaze away.

He passed the playground, where a dad comforted his daughter after she fell from the merry-go-round. It was the same merry-go-round he pushed Agnes on just a few weeks earlier. Agnes howled with laughter when Luke got it spinning really fast.

The police station lay in the northeastern corner of Trossö, in a large, happy, yellow building. Luke stepped in. He had been here earlier in the job, and every time he went in, up popped the memory of the first time he visited the police station in the 90th precinct on Union Avenue in Williamsburg back in 1981. He was fourteen years old, and a year had passed since his mother died. Luke was a member of the Devil's Rebels, one of many criminal street gangs in Brooklyn in the 70s and 80s. Devil's Rebels was a fusion of four gangs, all with white guys. Latin Kings, Homicide Laws, The Backstabbers, and Imperial Headhunters. Luke joined early, when he was only thirteen years old. He literally beat his way in one evening when three Rebels attacked him with the aim of robbing him. Luke fought like he was possessed and flattened all three. The rumor of the gigantic and fearless 13-year-old spread, and two days after the fight, the

Devil's Rebels' president, Apache, went to Luke and asked if he wanted to become a Rebel. He had a bed at his Jewish aunt's house, but the gang became his new family. A family that was in a constant state of war with several rival gangs in Williamsburg. This was where Luke learned to fight, both with and without weapons.

It was after a clash with the Savage Nomads that Luke was caught and dragged in handcuffs into the police station by two pigs of police officers. Into a rundown, shitty hellhole. Bullet-proof glass, sour and jaded officers. He was thrown into a tight little cell where he spent two days before the social worker came and got him.

Karlskrona's police station was open, airy, and welcoming, with a long birch reception desk with large green plants at the ends of the counter. In the booth for the passport photos, a mother sat with her son and got their passports renewed. Across from the counter were two sofa groups in red with attractive birch end tables. An older woman in plainclothes sat to the left of the passport booth. She smiled and waved him over.

"Hi! My name is Luke Bergmann, and I was called here to meet someone I've forgotten the name of," Luke said. The woman looked at her screen.

"You're going to see detective Anders Loman," she said, and typed in his number on the phone. He picked up immediately.

"It's reception. Your visitor is here now." She disconnected and turned towards Luke.

"Anders is coming down right away." Luke sat down in one of the red armchairs in the waiting room. In his drugged-like state, he missed the name of the officer who called him and asked him to come to the police station. It was four days since they found Viktor and Agnes. The image of Viktor hanging from the bathroom door and of Agnes' little dead body in Therese's arms didn't want to leave him. It was good that the police had summoned him as it meant he was forced to get out of bed, shower, and take a walk.

After a few minutes, a man came into the reception room and introduced himself as Anders Loman.

"Thank you for coming. We'll go up to my office."

Anders Loman looked to be in his mid-fifties, tall and slim, fit for his age and weathered by outdoor activities. On top was a carefully-styled, clearly dyed black hairstyle that rose over the deeply tanned forehead. Every strand of hair seemed to lie in exact parallel with each other. Luke thought he looked like a chocolate-topped copy of the Marlboro Man and followed after the detective into the bowels of the police station. They went three flights up, into a room that Luke understood was his office. Luke established that Anders Loman was a pedant. A thin stack of papers lay neatly on his desk. On the shelves, binders in different colors were carefully arranged. Erik Dahlberg's engraving of urban Karlskrona from the late 1600s was framed on the wall behind the chair. A computer with a flatscreen stood next to it. A coffee thermos with two mugs were on the other end table. A green folder lay closed in the middle of the desk in front of Anders Loman. Otherwise, it was practically sterile.

Loman invited Luke to sit in the chair in front of the desk and poured coffee into two mugs. He happened to spill a small drip on the table and immediately took a roll of paper towels out of a desk drawer and wiped it away. Luke took the mug gratefully. He felt the cold sweat starting to break out, and his hands were trembling.

"You look like you need a little coffee," Anders Loman said.

"I got drunk yesterday," Luke said. "I've had a hard time sleeping since Monday."

"I can understand that," Loman said. "This is a really tragic story." He opened the green folder.

Luke didn't say anything. Anders Loman took a document out of the folder and looked down at it.

"Luke Bergmann," he said. "Moved from New York to Agdatorp outside Karlskrona in 1997, graduated in 2004 with a Social Services degree from Jämshög Community College. Treatment assistant at Apelgården Rehabilitation Center in Listerby since 2004."

"I just started at Ekekullen in Rödeby," Luke said. "I started there last week."

Loman made a note.

"Interesting history," he said, looking up. "Can you tell me more about how you ended up in this godforsaken hellhole?"

"No," Luke said. "I don't see what that has to do with this."

"Nothing, actually. It's more that I'm just curious. I like America. I lived south of Washington DC for a few months when I went to the FBI International Academy in Quantico in the mid-90s. Best time of my life."

"How is it that a policeman in Karlskrona has such an advanced education?" Luke asked.

"I worked for the Secret Service in Stockholm at the time," Loman answered. "I applied for a fellowship, got it, and since I didn't have a family, I headed there."

Luke sat silently. Loman cleared his throat.

"Anyway, I've read through what you told Sergeant Larsson on Monday," he continued, taking another document out of the green folder. "Do you want to read through it and see if you still, now after a few days, think it's correct? If it is, I would appreciate your signature at the bottom, on the last page." He handed over the report to Luke, who took it and started reading. When he was done, he signed his name and gave it back to Anders Loman.

"It's correct."

"Okay. Thank you." Anders took the report and put it in the green folder.

Luke took a small sip of coffee.

"What have you guys come up with?"

Anders Loman leaned back in his chair and looked at Luke with his clear blue eyes that shone like two unripe blueberries in the leather-brown face.

"What do you mean?"

"Well, what have you guys come up with regarding what happened? How did they die?"

Anders Loman leaned towards Luke. He rested his elbows on the desk and brought his long fingers together. He exhaled in a long sigh.

"We haven't received the results of the autopsies yet, so we can't be completely sure. But if you want to know my hypothesis, I'll gladly tell you."

Luke nodded.

"Did you notice that there was a jar with white powder next to the computer on the table in the living room?" Anders asked.

Luke nodded again.

"Natrium phenobarbital is what that's called," Anders continued. "It's a poison that, in low doses, is used as a sleeping medicine. One gram is enough to kill a person. Today, it's used by veterinarians to put animals to sleep. A notorious suicide clinic in Switzerland uses it, too. In the glass that stood next to the jar, we found evidence of the powder mixed with water. That was probably what Agnes Spandel died from. I talked with the EMTs who came to the apartment, and they say that they saw traces of the powder in Agnes' mouth. What her dad died of, we're not sure. He probably died from hanging. We'll know for certain within a few days when the autopsy reports come in from the forensic department in Lund."

29

"Do you mean Viktor forced Agnes to drink that poison?" Luke asked.

"I don't think she drank it voluntarily," Anders answered. "The substance is said to be terribly bitter, and there was a half-eaten chocolate bar next to the glass. He probably gave her the chocolate when she drank the mixture. She either spilled or spat out quite a bit. The techs found some of the liquid on the floor."

Luke shook his head. Anders looked questioningly at him.

"You don't think that's how it happened?"

"I just don't understand it," Luke said. "I have a damn hard time believing that Viktor would do something like that. How would a person get hold of that poison? Can just anyone buy it?"

"Not in Sweden, unless you're a board-certified veterinarian," Anders answered. "My theory is that Viktor googled it and bought it via some foreign site."

Luke sat silently for a moment.

"When did they die?" he asked.

"We don't know that right now, either," Anders answered. "But our forensic expert made the preliminary estimation that Viktor died around eight o'clock on Monday evening. The daughter died later, but you were in the apartment at that point, of course."

"So a half-hour before I rang the doorbell," Luke said.

Loman nodded.

"You knew him well, I take it," Loman said. "Do you have any idea why he chose to do something so drastic?"

"It's completely incomprehensible. I saw him just on Saturday, and he was in a very good mood, like always. He was feeling good."

Loman shuffled his papers.

"From what I understand, Viktor Spandel had a few periods of depression in recent years. The last was when his wife left him..."

Loman picked up a document and read.

"...2001, three years ago." He looked up again.

"Maybe that explains all of this? Maybe he ended up in a depression again, decided to take his own life, and wanted to get revenge on his ex-wife by taking his daughter with him? It wouldn't be the first time something like that happened."

His blue eyes looked intensely at Luke. Luke leaned back in his chair and tried to digest what he just heard. Revenge on Therese? Could that be it?

Viktor was devastated after Therese left him. But that he would go so far as to take Agnes' life was impossible. Not Viktor. He wasn't a bitter, vengeful person. And above all, he would never kill his own daughter.

"It's impossible that Viktor would have subjected his daughter, his greatest love in the whole world, to this."

Anders Loman leaned back in his chair.

"We really want to believe that we know our friends," he said. "But people don't always show what they're thinking and feeling deep inside. Not even for their closest friends. Maybe Viktor didn't want to appear weak or draw you into his problems? How long had you known each other?"

"Ten years," Luke answered. "I even lived with Viktor and Agnes sometimes. Like three years ago, the last time he was in a dark stage."

"I understand how awful this thought must feel," Loman said. "Believe me. I get it."

Anders Loman leaned forward and rested his hands on the desk. Luke now saw how wrinkled they were and sensed the man was older than he looked.

"But there was a sort of suicide note in the apartment, too. It was in the bedroom. On the pillow."

Luke stared at him. The hair on his arms stood up. If Viktor had written a suicide note, it must be true.

"A sort of suicide note?" he asked quietly, as if he were scared to know more.

"Yes. It's cryptic, but it's clearly a suicide note. You knew him well; do you know if Viktor believed in reincarnation?"

"Can I see the letter?"

Anders Loman opened the green folder and began flipping through documents. He took out a piece of paper enclosed in a plastic bag and laid it in front of Luke, who took it carefully. On it was written a single sentence:

From body's birth to / Body's grave and then / To Birth again

The text was printed out from a computer. Luke read the sentence several times. He had to concentrate in order to take in the words. The meaning. It clearly had to do with rebirth, and was written like a poem.

Viktor didn't write anything, and definitely not poetry. The only writing he did was emails that had to do with his business.

"This is absurd," he said finally. "We had a lot of discussions about religion and Viktor was agnostic, just like me, even though I was born Jewish. He told me that he was pulled into a cult when he was young, was able to get out, and for many years was a strong opponent to all forms of religion. After the divorce, he calmed down a bit and thought he just didn't care whether there was a god or whether there was life after death. That would become apparent in time, he said."

Luke looked down at the sentence again.

"Besides, this is written like a poem. Viktor didn't write poetry. He didn't read poetry either, for that matter. Only crime novels and nonfiction books about psychology."

Anders Loman stretched out his hands.

"It sounds a little strange, that's undeniable," he said. "But the letter was there, and it was printed from his printer. How can we explain that?"

"I don't know," Luke said. "I just know that Viktor never could have done anything bad to his daughter."

"So you think that someone murdered Viktor and his daughter?" Loman asked. "If that's the case, what's the motive? Nothing was stolen from the apartment, as far as we know. There's no sign of forced entry. No one broke in. We've also checked Viktor's bank account and assets. They're completely intact."

Luke put his hands over his face, leaned forward, and rested his elbows on his knees. He didn't understand any of it. Could he have been so wrong about Viktor? Obviously, people have their secrets. But why would Viktor lie about being an agnostic? He didn't understand that.

He looked up. Anders Loman sat there silently, looking at him. Luke realized he wouldn't get anywhere by continuing to claim he knew Viktor hadn't done it.

"Why didn't Viktor take that powder then, too?" Luke said instead. "Why force Agnes to and then hang yourself?" Anders got up and signaled that the conversation was over.

"Yes, good question. How can I know? Maybe he thought it was a quicker way to a new life. This stuff can take a few hours before it affects the nervous system and respiration."

Luke got up, shook Anders Loman's hand, and asked if it was okay to go into Viktor's apartment now. He needed to get a few books and CDs he loaned to Viktor, he said.

"It would be nice if you could wait a few days," Loman said. "The apartment is closed until we get the results of the autopsies. We've changed the locks and no one is allowed to go in. But as soon as we lift the ban, I'll be in touch with you so you can get your things."

Luke nodded and left the room. When he came out of the police station, he looked at the clock and was blinded by the bright sunlight. He had a half-hour left before he was supposed to meet Karin Hartman, Viktor's therapist, who had immediately agreed to see him. She knew what had happened.

He stood on the sidewalk for a few minutes. The queasiness had left him, but the heat made him dizzy. He had to sit down and think. He saw a bench on the other side of the street, crossed, and sat down. It felt like he was inside an aquarium, looking at what was outside. His image of Viktor had suffered a real blow. He thought that he knew him well, but clearly, he was wrong. Viktor had thoughts, desperate thoughts, that he didn't share with Luke.

He cast a glance up towards the police station and caught sight of Anders Loman standing in his window, looking at him. His few months' training with the FBI impressed Luke. He felt competent and pleasant, besides. Luke wasn't used to that when it came to the police. Loman waved. Luke raised his hand in response, got up from the bench, and began slowly walking downtown.

Luke met Karin Hartman a few times before. The first time was two years ago, when she took Viktor to her private clinic on Ronnebygatan after Viktor had a more minor depressive episode. She radiated intelligence and competence, and Viktor liked her a lot. Luke knew that Viktor still saw her, not as often as when things were really bad. Karin was a doctor, a specialist in depression and author of a book on the subject.

Luke took the elevator up to the fifth floor and stepped in through a door that read "Health Level 5." Karin shared a reception area and space with a few freelance entrepreneurs in the healthcare industry–a massage therapist, a naprapath, and a mindfulness consultant. It felt like entering a spa. Muted lighting, subdued furniture, scented candles in the windows, a gurgling tabletop fountain intended to induce calm and harmony.

He checked in at the reception desk and was just about to sit in one of the visitors' chairs when Karin came out from her room. She was in her sixties, her blonde hair cut in a pageboy, small, round, black glasses, and a colorful dress. And a sharp but calm gaze. She walked up to Luke and hugged him.

"I'm so terribly sorry about what happened, Luke," she said. "Come with me; we'll go into my office."

Aside from the desk, they could have been in someone's living room. A seating group near the striking turn-of-the-century window with two black armchairs in a sleek, stylish design and a round coffee table topped with glass. A booksheö filled with medical and psychology books covered one wall. Beautiful lithographies on the wall. And then a sofa, of course, a comfortable, homey piece of furniture, not the austere, geometric type you often saw in intellectual American films.

At Karin's encouragement, Luke sat on the sofa.

"Would you like anything? Coffee, tea?"

He declined.

"I'm thankful you could meet me on such short notice," he said.

"It's the least I could do," Karin Hartman said. "Viktor was a very well-liked patient whom I held in very high regard."

She looked like a model from a Gudrun Sjödén catalogue. Moved gracefully. Still beautiful, Luke thought. She must have been a real beauty in her youth. She sat in one of the black armchairs.

"Normally, I only talk to family about a patient, if I have the patient's permission," she continued. "But Viktor doesn't have any family left living, of course, and because he has talked about your close relationship, I will make an exception this time."

"I can imagine you're asking yourself why you didn't see this coming," Karin continued, expressing the exact thought percolating in Luke's head.

"I've started questioning my judgment," Luke answered. "Can't understand how I could've missed it."

"You're not the only one. I've been sitting here for many months, talking with Viktor about his emotional life in detail. And I couldn't anticipate this, either."

She leaned back in the chair, rested her hands in her lap, and shook her head as she said it.

"If I had, I would naturally have made sure he came in and received care immediately."

"You were still meeting regularly, I take it?" Luke asked.

"He came to see me twice a month. He's done that for almost a year now."

"Isn't it strange that he continued coming to you, that he invested time and money on a therapist without telling about all the thoughts he was having?"

"Viktor entrusted himself to me completely," Karin answered. "He had suicidal thoughts, but that was just after he was discharged from the hospital over two years ago. That is the most critical time for people with depression. But he got over it, and over the past year, he said nothing to indicate that he had immediate plans in that direction."

"He never told me about those thoughts," Luke said.

"Most don't."

"Was he thinking about religious things?" Luke asked. "Did he tell you he was in a cult when he was young?"

"Yes, but he said that didn't affect him today. He was, at least in part, thankful for the experience of having been in it. Even if it was completely crazy. He thought of it as youthful delusions."

Karin leaned towards Luke.

"You couldn't have done anything, do you understand that? Let me assure you on that point. It is very typical that people who commit suicide without having shown any sign of such inclinations."

"I just don't understand it," Luke said. "I was at their house on Saturday evening, and Viktor was in a great mood. Two days later, he does this."

"That's not unusual either," Karin said. "For some people, the decision to commit suicide is liberating. When they've decided, they experience a feeling of having found the solution to their problems. And then they can feel happiness. Strange as it may be."

She fell silent. They both sat quietly for a moment.

"What I have a harder time understanding is why he took his daughter with him," Karin said after a moment. "It doesn't fit the image I have of Viktor. I'm no expert, but I would believe that when a parent kills their child, it is either caused by a deep psychological issue and often in combination with being under the significant influence of drugs. No matter what, this is a deeply tragic event."

She sighed and stood up, signaling that the conversation was over.

"When such things happen, you feel quite incompetent as a doctor."

Luke stood up, too, and took her hand.

"I don't think you could've done anything, either."

She thanked him, turned around, and walked towards the door.

"You should know that your friendship was precious to Viktor," Karin said. "He often talked about you during our discussions. I hope you can find some comfort in that."

Her words brought Luke to the aquarium again. He chose to walk down the five flights of stairs. He didn't notice it was a fantastically beautiful and sunny day in the capital city of the Swedish Navy, Karlskrona.

8.

It was already eleven in the morning when Thomas Svärd drove into the lawn parking area at Blekinge Summerland, which lay right along the E22 highway between Karlskrona and Nättraby. Summerland was a popular playground with a pool and splash pad, go-kart track, and bouncy houses.

There were at least a hundred cars in the parking lot already, Svärd estimated as he opened the trunk, took the car seat out, and put it in the passenger seat.

He got up early that morning and dyed his blonde mane jet black. His beard had also received a once-over. He was really pleased when he looked in the mirror; he knew he looked good. Careful to stay in good shape, he ran a long loop out on the island every other day. On his off days, he did push-ups, sit-ups, and pull-ups. He could tell women checked him out. With his raven-black hair and dark stubble, he knew he bore some resemblance to George Clooney.

At exactly ten o'clock, he entered the Intersports shop in the Amiralen shopping center in Karlskrona. He bought a sun hat, bathing shorts, swim bag, blanket, two colorful swimming rings, a large bath towel, and two smaller bath towels. He chose one with a Pippi Longstocking motif and another with Cars. At Statoil, he bought a folding lawn chair, sunglasses, candy, and Jens Lapidus' latest crime novel.

His hands were full with all this gear when he, in his white linen shirt and navy shorts, walked through the entrance to Blekinge Summerland. It wasn't the same girl at the register as last time he was there. Then, he'd only gone in to eat lunch and look at the children. The staff were on guard. He felt their gazes linger on him, and when he took a walk through the place, he saw a woman instruct one of the girls to follow him. This time, he would be more careful.

The girl at the register lifted herself up on the desk and looked down behind him.

"Are you alone?" she asked. Svärd smiled.

"No. My ex is coming with the kids in a bit. She's just a little late. I'll pay now for one adult and two children. I'll fetch them from here when they come."

"Are they over three feet tall?"

Svärd gave a questioning look.

"Children under three feet tall get in free," the girl explained.

"Oh. One is under and one is over," Svärd said. He paid, took his things, and walked directly to the bathing area. It was full of people. Almost all the lawn chairs around the pool were taken, and families spread out their blankets around on the lawn. It was hot. The digital sign above the kiosk said 85 degrees. Svärd stood still, trying to find the best spot to sit. If he spread out his blanket on the lawn, there was a greater risk that someone would see that he was alone compared to if he placed himself in a lawn chair near a single mom. Then it might look like he belonged with her.

He walked down the stairs past the kiddie pool and slowly past the lawn chairs. He caught sight of a woman who was sitting alone, having a snack with two children. Next to her was an empty chair. Walking over, he asked if it was available and received an affirmative answer. He saw the woman looking around for his family.

"My ex is coming with the kids," Thomas explained with a smile. "She's just a little late."

The woman smiled and wiped ice cream from the face of a girl who was hopping around in anticipation of being allowed to go and swim again. She was eight, nine years old, Thomas guessed. A little too old. And too ugly.

Thomas placed his things out and turned the chair so it was at the right angle to see the kiddie pool and the entrance. He took off his white linen shirt, pulled the towel around himself, and put on his bathing shorts underneath. He noticed how the woman glanced sideways at him. She was fat and unattractive. Probably single. He sat on the chair, picked up his book, and pretended to be absorbed in it. In reality, behind his sunglasses, his eyes were searching for suitable girls. After fifteen minutes, he found her. She was around five years old with blonde, curly hair, enormously cute in a little red bikini. She came running and sat on a blanket twenty yards from Thomas. There were two other children, probably her siblings, and a mom, alone.

The children were having a snack as the mom talked on the phone. When she wasn't talking on the phone, she was looking at it. Perfect. Self-absorbed and inattentive. When the children were done with their snack, they ran off to the kiddie pool. The mom looked up and called something out to them. They didn't react. It was probably something about her wanting the older kids to take care of the little sister. Thomas got up, took his camera, and went to the pool. He stood at its edge and looked at the children as they played. There were several parents around the pool, keeping an eye on their little ones. Thomas held up his camera. The girl was kneeling on the edge and leaning in towards the water in an attempt to grab hold of a floating toy. Her bikini bottoms had crept up and revealed small, beautiful buttocks.

Thomas pretended to take pictures next to the girl, but deftly aimed the lens towards the girl for a second and took three pictures. Then he swung the camera quickly away from her again and pretended to take pictures straight into the pool. He lowered his camera and glanced around. None of the parents were looking at him. Then he realized the girl was leaning too far out, and she fell down into the pool. It wasn't deep, but she got scared and flailed her arms, splashing wildly. Her siblings were on the little water slide and didn't see what happened. Thomas quickly set down his camera on the concrete tiles, hopped down into the pool, and lifted the girl out of the water. She sniffled and wrapped her arms around him. He comforted her and sat her on the edge of the pool.

"Were you scared?" he asked.

The girl nodded.

"There's no danger anymore," he said. "What's your name?"

"Anna."

"What a beautiful name. Can I walk you to your mom?"

She nodded again, and Thomas stepped out of the pool, picked up his camera, took Anna's hand, and walked with her to her mom. He told her what happened, and she thanked him.

"I'm going to have a serious talk with her older siblings," the mom said to Thomas. "They promised to keep an eye on her. Anna, have you thanked the nice man?" she asked her daughter.

Anna shook her head.

"Do it then," her mom said.

"Thank you," the daughter said, looking at Thomas, who smiled his most charming smile.

"You're welcome, Anna. Promise me you'll be careful next time you're near the pool."

Anna smiled shyly and clung to her mother. Thomas said goodbye, walked back to his chair, and sat down.

"I saw what happened," said the woman in the chair next to him. "Well done."

"Thanks," Thomas said. "She probably would've been fine anyway; it's not that deep where she fell in."

"You never know what could have happened," the woman said. "I don't get what that woman is thinking. Sitting there with her cell phone, leaving the responsibility to the older children. Incomprehensible."

Thomas picked up his book and continued to pretend to read. He could sense that the woman in the next chair was interested in him, and he wanted to distance himself from her. He didn't have time for a fat, clingy nag. He looked towards the blanket where the mother was now scolding Anna's older siblings. After a few minutes, he saw that Anna wanted to go towards the other activities in the area. On his mother's orders, her big brother took her by the hand, and together they walked up towards the playground near the entrance and restaurant. Thomas pretended to look at his phone, stood up, packed up his things, and said goodbye to the woman sitting next to him.

"Just got a text from my ex. No swimming for the kids today, unfortunately," he said to her before heading off for the exit. He set his things down near the door and walked back out on the wooden deck that faced the playground. He saw how Anna and her big brother went down the big slide time and again. Suddenly, the brother caught sight of the go-kart track that had just opened. He gave a holler and ran to it. Anna was on her way down and didn't see him run off. She looked around for him and then caught sight of Thomas, who waved to her. She smiled and waved back. Thomas gestured for her to come over. His pulse quickened when he saw her immediately come running towards him. He looked at the pool area. He couldn't see the mother from where he was standing. The brother stood in line for the go-karts and didn't notice anything.

Thomas crouched down near the steps when Anna came up.

"Anna, do you like candy?" he asked.

She nodded.

"I have a bag of candy out in my car," he said. "If you come with me, you can have it. Would you like that?"

Anna nodded again. Thomas stood up and reached his hand out to her. She took it, and together they went through the exit.

9.

Exactly seven-thirty on Friday evening, the fourth day after Viktor's and Anna's deaths, Luke came walking down the hallway in the Ekekullen Group Home in Rödeby. He was on the night shift and just arrived at work. The first day after his involuntary time off.

His visit to Karin Hartman was depressing. Most of all, it was finding out that Viktor had suicidal thoughts before. Luke felt disappointed that Viktor never told him about it. He thought Viktor trusted him completely. It certainly felt that way. It would take time to accept that he was wrong.

Now he decided to let it go and instead concentrate on his job and his own life. He would talk to Åsa Nordin today and tell her he'd like to take more shifts. Åsa was Ekekullen's director, and she hired him. Working as much as possible would make it easier for him to manage.

Further down the hallway, he saw three people in night shift uniforms dragging a screaming, wildly-protesting Gabriel into his room. Gabriel was sixteen years old and one of ten teenagers placed at Ekekullen right now. Luke only worked two days at Ekekullen before he asked to have four days off, but that was enough time for him to learn the names of the six boys and four girls who lived at the home. Gabriel was the one the staff had the biggest problems with. Luke tried to get closer to him on his first day on the job. He recognized a lot of himself as a sixteen-year-old in Gabriel. The same obstinate, frustrated behavior towards adults and towards the establishment. It hadn't gone as far for Gabriel as it did for Luke. Not yet.

Luke approached the three who now stood outside Gabriel's door, listening.

"I'm going to fucking kill you! All of you!" Gabriel screamed from his room. There were crashing sounds as he began throwing things against the door.

Luke recognized two of the people standing outside. They were Åsa Nordin and Olle Nordlund, a psychologist. The third man was someone Luke hadn't yet met. They didn't hear Luke come up behind them, probably because of all the noise Gabriel was making from inside his room.

"Maybe we should take all the loose objects out of his room," the third man said. "He's spinning out of control."

"What's going on?" Luke asked.

The three turned around and saw Luke.

"I didn't see you coming, Luke," Åsa said. "Gabriel's flown into a rage. He was harassing a girl in the line for dinner and wouldn't stop, so we've locked him in until he can calm down."

"It doesn't seem to be going very well," Luke said with a lopsided grin. "Hi, by the way." He turned to the man, who looked like he might come from somewhere in the Middle East. He introduced himself as Hamid Dabashi, rehab assistant.

Luke turned to Åsa.

"Is it okay if I go in there with him?"

The other three looked at him. They looked up because he stood a head taller than Hamid, who was already taller than all of them at six feet.

Åsa looked at Olle, who nodded.

"Of course," she said. "Be our guest." She walked to the door and unlocked it just as there was the loud crash of an object hitting the door. Luke took hold of the handle, pushed down, and walked in.

The screaming and throwing inside the room stopped. Åsa, Olle, and Hamid stood still, listening for a moment. It continued to be quiet inside the room, and they went back to the dining room.

Twenty minutes later, Luke came into the dining room, walked to the long table, and began arranging some sandwiches on a plate.

"What's going on, Luke?" Åsa asked.

"He's hungry," Luke answered. "I'm just getting a few sandwiches for him."

"Has he calmed down?"

"Yep."

"How did you fix things?" Hamid asked.

"Didn't need to do much," Luke answered. "He calmed down immediately when he saw me. Then I showed him some of my tattoos. And he showed me his. Tends to work."

Luke took the plate and a glass of juice and went back to Gabriel's room. When he re-entered the room, he saw that Gabriel had crawled down in bed and fallen asleep. Luke walked quietly to the desk next to the bed and set down the tray with the food. He pulled down the shades and turned off the light.

He stopped. Turned the light on again. Looked at the clock. Eight o'clock, the same time Loman said Viktor died. He walked to the window, pushed the shade to the side, and looked out. It was still light out, as it was at this same time four days ago. It struck Luke that it was completely dark in Viktor's apartment when he and Therese finally made it inside. Pitch black. He was almost completely sure of it. His senses had been tuned in to Viktor and Agnes when he and Therese rushed in and realized he could be wrong. But hadn't it been dark? Yes, it was.

A question followed. Would Viktor have taken Agnes' life and his own in complete darkness? Luke closed his eyes to go through the course of events in detail. Yes, it was definitely dark throughout the apartment. The shades were drawn. That's how it was, for sure. He was so focused on Viktor and Agnes that he hadn't thought of it before now.

Why in the hell would he want it dark in the apartment when he was going to kill himself? Was it even possible to do that without being able to see?

Gabriel snored loudly. Luke walked to the lightswitch near the door and turned it off. He stood still for a few seconds, listening to Gabriel's breathing and waiting until his eyes were used to the darkness. He could sense the silhouette of the bed. He walked forward and sat at its foot. He imagined the events. Saw in his mind's eye how Viktor planned everything. The message, the rope, the poison, the chocolate. Pulled down the shades, turned on the music, given Agnes the poison. When did he turn off the lights? He must have done it just before he hung himself. But why did he want to do that in the dark? And if he took the poison himself, he must have been dizzy from it. Why make it so difficult for yourself?

Luke stood up. Gabriel was sleeping deeply. Luke went out of the room, closed the door and didn't bother to lock it. He decided to go to Viktor's apartment the next evening and try to reconstruct things. Pull down the shades and see just how dark it got.

10.

Despite it only being February, Jenny could smell the earth as she walked along Östra Vittusgatan on the way towards the Church of Scientology on Möllebacken in central Karlskrona. Three hundred and twenty years earlier, farmer Vittus Andersson's herd strolled around the same area, grazing. Now, the street that received the farmer's name was edged with yellow and red brick apartment buildings built in the 1960s. Jenny shivered. She thought the buildings were some of the ugliest in Karlskrona.

Who knows, maybe I was a farmgirl at Trossö in the 1600s. Who a hundred years later headed to Paris and danced in the finest salons. The thought was titillating, and she let out a laugh.

It was an unusually mild winter, and the spring usually took a little longer to get to Karlskrona because it literally lay out in the archipelago. The cold sea always holds spring at bay and makes sure Karlskronites keep their winter jackets on a few weeks longer than the inlanders.

It maybe wasn't the premonition of the arrival of spring or the thought that she might have lived a previous life in Paris that made Jenny feel so exhilarated. Today, she would have her first therapy session, or auditing session as it was called within Scientology. And it wasn't just any old auditor. It was Peter, and he was one of the best. Peter said it was permitted to give beginners a sort of trial therapy after careful review of the person's psychological state. It was more like a sample, with the idea that you could get a sense of it in order to later, if you liked it, either pay or begin working for the Church of Scientology. The Center, as the members in Karlskrona liked to call it. The word *church* wasn't cool among kids. Jenny received an explanation for why it was a church and a religion. It was to do with the word *religion* and its original meaning. "Re," which means back, and "ligare," which means origin; back to the origin, to what once was. People will develop and regain their original abilities, the ones they once had. Jenny thought it was beautiful and after that had no problem saying she was a member of the Church of Scientology.

The Center was located in an old furniture store on Bryggaregatan, with picture windows facing the street. It contained a few rooms on the ground floor, and a large basement where the furniture store kept its stock.

A lot had happened in Jenny's life over the past year, her nineteenth on earth. Besides graduating, her entire life had taken on a clear purpose, a meaning. She was pulled more and more deeply into the group and the movement and was now completely occupied by these people and by Scientology. Stefan wasn't as charmed by it as she was. Besides, he had his orienteering and spent all his time running around in forests, looking for markers. And so they drifted apart. When she took the communication course two months earlier, she did some exercises with a guy who was just as green as she was. His name was Daniel and he was a year older. He was tall and shy but had a charming smile.

The course went on for a week, and began with them sitting on chairs facing each other. Hands on their thighs, and their eyes closed at first. After a few hours, they could open their eyes. The exercises were intended to increase their ability to encounter another person, their ability to just be there in the situation and be content. It was very important not to think anything, but just to be present. The next step was that to try to provoke each other in different ways, try to make the other person drop their mask. Daniel and Jenny laughed a lot during these exercises. They talked a lot with each other during breaks and also met at the shared evening gatherings. After just a week, she felt like she was falling in love with him, and she could tell that Daniel felt the same way. Two weeks later, Jenny broke up with Stefan and started dating Daniel. One month later, they moved in together.

Daniel had his first therapy session two days earlier, and he was bursting with happiness when he came home. But he couldn't tell her anything about it. That wasn't allowed. The only thing he said was that he had his first previous-life-experience. Now Jenny would get to do the same thing.

A whole lot of people are here today, Jenny thought as she hung up her jacket and walked into the small reception area. On the walls were several framed prints, some with quotes from the founder, L Ron Hubbard, or Ron, as the confirmed Scientologists said. Jenny liked one quote in particular, "A man is as dead as he can't communicate. A man is as alive as he can communicate."

On the wall behind the reception desk hung a framed picture depicting a bridge whose one end ran straight into a large sun. Under the image, it said, "The bridge to total freedom." In the large room, the one with a drab brown wall-to-wall carpet, the one that was previously the furniture store's sales floor, sat five pairs of people doing communication exercises. The picture windows were covered with large posters advertising the movement. Previously, there was nothing on the windows, but too frequently, children and teenagers stood with their noses pressed against the window-panes, eventually starting to throw things and spit at the windows.

At the far back sat Maria, Camilla, and Mikael, their noses buried in different books Ron had written. All three were dedicated Scientologists, working for the movement in their spare time. Daniel's sister, Åsa, had just begun, and she was practicing the exercises with another new member. Peter was standing at the reception desk with a cup of coffee in his hand and talking with George, the mythical, mystical Englishman who started the movement in Karlskrona. Jenny had only seen him there briefly once before. But she'd heard a lot about him. He even worked with Ron in the late 60s, which she understood was a big deal. He was one of the ones on the Apollo ship that Hubbard used for traveling around Europe and Africa in the beginning, when he was spreading his message. The others talked about George with reverence. How smart he was, and that he was one of the first in the world who reached the state of OT VI, almost as high as you could get on the way towards spiritual freedom. Jenny gathered up all her courage and walked up to them. Peter lit up, took a step towards her, and hugged her.

"Ready for the big day, Jenny?"

"Yes, it'll be really exciting," she said. "Daniel was practically on fire when he came home after his session."

Peter set his cup down on the reception desk and turned towards George, who stood there chewing on his pipe.

"George, this is Jenny. She just took the communication course and will be having her first auditing session today."

George took his pipe out of his mouth, smiled, reached out his hand, and gave a little bow. He was small and wiry, with a blonde goatee and curly, reddish hair, and a beige sweater over a white Oxford and beige gabardine pants.

"Welcome, Jenny. Enchanted," he said in English.

Jenny took his slim hand and didn't know quite how to act. She felt small and insecure, considering everything people said about George. So she curtsied, and regretted it as she did. She felt like a little girl.

"Thank you. I've heard a lot about you. Glad to finally meet you," she responded, also in English.

As the words left her mouth, she heard how stupid they sounded. "Heard a lot"—now he would surely ask what she'd heard, and what should she answer? Peter saved her.

"George understands Swedish, Jenny. But he likes speaking English best."

He turned to George with a big smile, continuing in Swedish.

"You can speak Swedish too, isn't that right, George?" Peter said in Swedish with a clear English accent and laughed loudly. George also laughed loudly, a strange, falsetto whinny.

"Yes, you bet I can!" George answered, still laughing. Peter took Jenny's arm and led her into the room where the therapy would take place. The room was small. In the middle stood a beautiful old oak desk. In the middle of the desk stood a small, brown wooden box with a circular red sticker in the middle. In the middle of the sticker, a large S snaked through two triangles. From one side of the wooden box, two cords wrapped around to where they were fastened via two clamps, each in an aluminum can. They looked like small beer cans without anything printed on them. Peter sat in the office chair and asked Jenny to have a seat in the armchair.

"This is an e-meter," Peter said, lifting up the wooden box. "An electrometer. One of the older models. They make new ones in plastic, but I like this old one. There's a little more feeling in it."

He opened it. Took off the lid, turned it over, and set it back on its side so that the lid formed a support for the thicker part. Now, the innards were angled diagonally towards Jenny. On a bright blue glass surface sat a display that covered more than half. A small, narrow metal arrow moved inside the display along a half-moon shaped dial with four different steps—rise, set, fall, and test. Three round black buttons sat under the glass of the face, and to the left of the glass were two larger controls. Peter asked Jenny to hold the two cans, one in each hand.

"When I turn the e-meter on, a weak electric current will pass through your body and back into the apparatus," he explained.

Jenny raised her eyebrows.

"You don't have to worry," Peter said. "The current is so weak, it can't do any damage," he said. "It's as weak as a flashlight battery. You can be completely calm." He turned on the apparatus and looked at Jenny.

"You don't feel it, right?"

Jenny shook her head.

"Now look at the arrow," he said.

Jenny leaned forward and saw that the arrow was now standing straight up, in the middle of the dial. It was hardly moving, vibrating only weakly.

"Continue to watch, and I'll tell you a funny story," he continued. "Listen to what I'm saying and watch the arrow the whole time. Two tomatoes were out walking on a street. Suddenly, one got run over by a car. Then the other tomato said, Come on now, ketchup, let's go."

Jenny laughed. The arrow had begun moving already in the first sentence. She knew the old joke well, and it was so comical that she laughed.

"What happened with the arrow?" Peter asked.

"It started moving back and forth exactly when I knew what story you were going to tell," Jenny said.

"Good," Peter said. "What happened was that the resistance in your mental energy was transformed when the positive thoughts arose in your head. The resistance lowered, and when that happens, the needle 'flows', as we say. It moves evenly and beautifully with small movements over the dial. We use this tool to find painful events in a PC, a pre-Clear. We people have a tendency to suppress difficult events, called trauma in the world of psychology. We call them *engrams*. For survival, all sensory perceptions are stored in the subconscious so that we can recognize them and would be able to avoid similar events in the future. The problem is that if you have too many engrams, you feel bad and act unreasonably. All psychological illness is caused by engrams and creates a great deal of suffering. With the help of the e-meter, I can see when your thoughts encounter an engram. The needle jerks and I can try to help you pull out the memory from the event that must be brought to the light, pull it into your consciousness, in order for you to get rid of the negative energy that resides in it. Do you follow me?"

Jenny nodded and adjusted her posture in the armchair. She had butterflies in her stomach.

"When we've washed away all of the engrams in a person, she can become Clear," Peter continued. "A Clear is no longer affected by her engrams. A smart, content, happy person who has control over her own life, quite simply."

Peter moved the e-meter and set it before him on the desk. He took out a large notebook and a pen.

"How does that sound to you?" he asked.

"Really great," Jenny said. "Exciting."

"Good. Then we'll get started. We're going to try a series of engrams on the theme of headaches."

He looked at the e-meter and made a note. Jenny felt that she was holding the cans spasmodically. She relaxed her grip. Peter looked up at her.

"It's good if you find a grip on the cans that feels comfortable and then try to keep still. When you change your grip, it has an effect on the needle." Jenny nodded.

"I'll keep still," she promised.

"Good. Let's get started. Think about a situation when you last had a headache."

"It was last Wednesday, I think," Jenny said. The answer came quick as lightning. "I came home after the three-hour communication course here. The headache snuck up on me, and I was in real pain when I went to bed. I had to take an Excedrin to get rid of it."

Peter asked Jenny to tell him all of the details surrounding the event. She had to make a real effort to remember, and not until she told the same story three times was Peter happy.

"Good! Now the needle is flowing," he said, smiling widely. Then he went on and asked if there was a previous similar event where she had a headache. Jenny didn't usually have headaches, and couldn't think of anything. What finally came up was the first time she drank alcohol. She got violently drunk and woken up with a serious hangover. They went through the event just like before. And then they continued. Down to one time when Jenny was six years old and fell from the dinner table at home, cutting a large gash in her forehead. She still had the scar. She knew it happened; her parents sometimes talked about it. She didn't think she would remember anything about it herself, but Peter was, in some strange way, able to make her remember. She thought this was her own memory, anyway. When they were done, Peter asked the same question again.

"Is there any earlier similar event where you had a headache?"

Jenny looked at him incredulously.

"Now we're down to when I was a toddler. I can't for the life of me remember if I got hurt or had a headache when I was so little."

Peter didn't say anything. He waited for her. Jenny fell silent and tried to think. She imagined herself as a little baby. Her mind was completely blank.

"No. It won't work. I can't remember anything."

"I'll ask the question again. Go into an earlier event when you had a headache."

Jenny looked at him. He doesn't give up. She tried again. It was silent for a few moments. Then she laughed.

"What's happening?" Peter asked.

"Oh, I see a little baby lying on a changing table who falls down into the bathtub. But I'm just making up to make you happy."

Peter looked at her calmly.

"Tell me what you see."

Jenny told. She came up with a ton of details. Or remembered. If it was true or not, she didn't know; but right now, she didn't care. The words just flowed out of her. She thought she should check with her mom if she remembered Jenny falling and hitting her head in the bathtub when she was little. After she told it a few times, emptying her memory of all possible details, Peter said the needle was flowing and asked the same question again.

"Go to an earlier similar event where you had a headache."

Jenny looked at him again. He was completely serious. She tried to turn her thoughts towards some period before 1972.

It was quiet for a long time. She felt sleepy, and nothing came. Peter asked the question again. She sat up in the chair.

"There," Peter said suddenly. He looked down at the e-meter. "What was that? What did you think of just then?"

Jenny smiled. She felt stupid, but she just let the words come. "I saw an office."

"Where are you?" Peter asked.

"New York." The words flowed out of her. "I think it's the 1940s. It's a bank office. I'm standing on one end of the large office and have a shooting pain in my head. I've just found out something terrible. My son-in-law, whom I hired—I'm the bank director, by the way—has been embezzling a ton of money from the bank. I'm standing there, looking at him. He's looking at me, and I see that he knows I know." She fell silent, sinking deep into her thoughts.

"What's happening?" Peter asked.

"I'm just thinking. It's strange I was a man in my past life."

Peter didn't say anything.

"I, um, I'm seeing terrible things," Jenny continued. "I think I confronted him with what I found out. He admitted it, was devastated. I fired him and he left the office. He was the father of my grandchildren."

More images, or fragments of images, came through. And Jenny just let the story spill from her mouth.

"He clearly went to a bar first and drank a ton of liquor. Then went home to his house. He put his wife, my daughter, and my two grandchildren in the car and drove off a cliff. Not surprising that I had a headache."

Jenny gave a chuckle, feeling both happy and depressed by the event she just described. She was really affected and described the story a few times, coming up with more details each time. Peter ended the session and looked pleased. They didn't decide on any next steps. Peter wanted her to come back to discuss if she wanted to work for them. Therapy comes at a cost, actually, but you can get it for free if you work, he explained.

Jenny felt giddy as she walked away. The images that appeared seemed so real. Could it really be true? She thought. Maybe she could find out a person who was married to the daughter of a bank director in New York and killed both himself and his family in the 1940s? She could hardly wait to get home to Daniel. She just had to tell him about this.

When she stepped into the apartment, lit candles were flickering everywhere. Daniel made tea. "Black Velvet" by Alannah Myles was playing on the CD player. It was really cozy. Jenny was bubbling with the anticipation of telling Daniel. Despite that they weren't supposed to. But Daniel agreed—they promised each other they wouldn't say a word to anyone else.

Jenny went first and told him the whole story. All of the details. Jenny was so involved in her story that she didn't notice Daniel's reaction. Suddenly, she stopped talking. Daniel's face was pale, and he sat with his hands behind his neck on the sofa, looking up at the ceiling.

"What is it?" Jenny asked. He took his arms down and leaned towards Jenny.

"I was the son-in-law."

11.

Anna walked in front of Thomas Svärd out through the doors of Blekinge Summerland. When they were a few yards from the building, he turned his head slightly and looked quickly behind him. No one seemed to notice anything. He continued walking straight ahead and saw that Anna was going in the wrong direction.

"This way, Anna!" he called, nodding his head to the left. Anna stopped and turned in that direction.

"It's the white car over there," he said, pointing with the arm he was holding the beach bag with. He saw Anna catch sight of something and start running.

"Daddy!" she called out, and Svärd saw how she ran straight towards a man in a suit, around thirty-five years old, who was getting out of a blue Audi fifty yards from them. Anna rushed to him, and he bent down and picked her up in his arms.

Svärd saw how they were talking and that Anna turned and pointed towards him. He walked over to them.

"Oh, how lucky that you came," he said to the man. "Are you her father?"

"Yes," Anna's father answered. "Who are you?"

"I was just going to head home when I saw her walking around out here in the parking lot, completely alone," Svärd answered. "I was going to just put my things in the car and then take her back in to see if I could find her parents."

The man looked at Svärd with suspicion.

"Anna says you were going to give her candy."

Svärd laughed.

"Yes, my own children were going to come here, but my ex-wife changed her mind and refused to drive them here. I had a little candy left in the car that was intended for them. I thought Anna could have it instead." As he said the last sentence, he saw out of the corner of his eye the girl from the reception desk leave the building with Anna's mom. She pointed towards them. Svärd realized he had to disappear—fast.

"It was lucky she found you," he said, walking to his car. He tossed his things in the back seat, got in, and drove quickly away from the parking

52

lot. He saw Anna's mother come running and waving at him. He ignored her and drove out onto the E22 highway. He was furious, slamming his hands on the steering wheel and screaming loudly.

"Damn it! What a fucking disaster! I was so close!" He turned and saw that no one was following him.

Once back in Sturkö, he parked by the tool shed that lay a stone's throw from the bunker. He grabbed his toolbox and removed the license plates from the car. He went into the shed again and pulled out two old license plates and screwed them on.

As he put the toolbox back in place, he felt his stomach growling. He walked the fifty yards to the bunker and took out a few eggs and small Vienna sausages from the little refrigerator. He prepared an omelet and fried the sausages on the little stove. As usual, he left the door wide open and opened both of the homemade mini-shutters so he wouldn't die of smoke inhalation. When he was finished, he sat down at the computer. He checked his email first.

Bingo.

He had already received answers from three preschools on Kungsholmen who were interested in him. One of them asked if he could come already on Monday for a job interview. The other two wanted to put him on a sub list, but they wanted to meet him first. Svärd answered them and suggested times on Monday. He smiled inside. So easy. Things would work out with the money. But he needed to secure a little larger fund more immediately. He couldn't be sure his Plan B would work as quickly as he thought. So Svärd sat at his computer for several hours, not noticing as it got dark out. He worked feverishly, attempting to peddle pictures, surfing around on a number of different sites, fishing for customers. By around midnight, he was able to collect enough money to spend at least three or four days in Stockholm, even if he didn't get to take any good pictures from a preschool. It had to be enough, he thought.

He ended by googling his next victim one last time, a corporate lawyer on Kungsholmen. He memorized her appearance, the path from her apartment to her office near Central Station, and went through her latest Facebook updates. He would have to map out the rest when he was there. Should be simple. A single woman was an easy hit. He shut down his computer, turned off the lights, crept into bed and fell asleep.

The dream came quickly tonight. The doorbell, two angry tones. He checked the clock. Three o'clock. The middle of the night. New angry tones. Dazed, he got up and opened the door. Two huge bikers were standing outside, and they pushed him brutally into the apartment. He fell backwards. Then he saw that they were his mom and dad. Mom took out a huge knife. Dad took hold of his arms. Mom put her knee over his legs. Pulled down his boxers.

"You disgusting pedophile. Say goodbye to it. It's gone."

It was his mom's clear voice. The typical southern Swedish farmer's dialect. He screamed that he'd stopped. That he'd never do it again. He begged his dad. Then everything went incredibly fast. Mom took hold of his cock and quickly cut it off, almost at the base. The blood spurted out and it hurt so unbelievably much. He howled, a primitive moan that must have echoed throughout the whole building. They released him and he tried with both hands to stop the flow of blood. It was pouring out. Pulsating. He couldn't stop it. He thought how the blood felt warm, then everything went black.

Svärd woke up lying on the bunker floor with both hands pressed to his crotch. His pulse was racing, sweat running off him in rivers. He was crying.

What a fate, he thought when he sat on the bed and calmed down. The same damn dream. Not every night anymore. But often. Forced to experience it again and again.

He fumbled for the bedside lamp, found the button and turned it on. He reached towards the little bedside table and took the pack of cigarettes and lighter. He lit a cig. It was hot as hell. The sun had shone down on the bunker all day.

With much effort, he took off his t-shirt and walked to the little refrigerator, took a bottle of water, and poured it down his gullet in large gulps. He purposely let it run out of the corners of his mouth. The cold water ran down onto his chest and cooled him. He turned on the little fan that sat on the table where he usually ate. It didn't help much; mostly just moved the hot air around.

He thought about Jörgen Gustafsson. The madman who cut him that winter night in the apartment in Kungsmarken. How he cursed his bad luck. How in the hell could he have known that little girl's mom was the sister of the worst crazy, criminal biker-gang psychopath in all of southern Sweden? Totally unmerciful. He would never forget Jörgen Gustafsson's gaze. His entire being as he stood in front of him in the stairwell in the middle of the night. Big. Not muscular. Just big. He immediately understood that this man could do anything. Without any hesitation.

They decided he should suffer. They mutilated him, and then let the blood slowly run out of him, from the place where his weapon used to be. He tried to get them to stop. He begged them. But they didn't say a word. He panicked and started screaming. Then they tried to cut off his tongue. They didn't have much success with that, luckily.

They tied him to his bed so that he couldn't stop the flow of blood and then they left him. He was unconscious when the door shut behind them. He knew he was going to die before everything went black.

He got up. Tossed the water bottle in the trash can in the cupboard under the little kitchenette. He took off his boxers, showered, and began preparing himself for his next assignment. He took out the forged criminal background check document for Gustav Thordén. It looked completely authentic, with a watermark and the emblem of the National Police in the right place. He sent a mental note of gratitude to his cellmate in Kalmar who helped him find the right counterfeiter. Then he went through the materials about the corporate lawyer one more time. Single, apartment on Kungsholmen. The job near Central Station. Good conditions for things to be nice and quick.

It felt good.

It wasn't his turn to suffer.

12.

Lock picks are fantastic tools. One of many testimonies to humans' capacity for innovation. When Luke first didn't find his, he went online to see if he could buy some. There were innumerable online shops offering them. He also found loads of tutorials online. Detailed films that, with the help of attractive animations, showed how a lock looks from the inside so you could understand how the pick should be moved to lift up the pins. Over twenty years had passed since Luke ended his criminal path, which among other things consisted of breaking into fashionable Manhattan apartments.

He found only one locksmith shop in Karlskrona. According to the webpage, it seemed to be fully stocked, but it was on the other side of town. He decided to look around in his apartment a bit more before heading to the shop, and he was lucky he did. The picks were in a cardboard box far back in a closet in the storage area. They were in a small leather case, where they'd rested since he left New York City nineteen years earlier. They were well-used. Hopefully they still worked just as well. He shoved the picks into the back pocket of his jeans.

It was eight o'clock when he grabbed the handle of the front door to Alamedan 30. He felt uneasy. He'd set his hand on the worn handle many times before and pushed a little extra to open the solid beautifully ornamented wooden door. It felt heavier than ever before.

Luke walked the three floors up to Viktor's apartment with reluctant steps, knowing he would relive what happened the last time he was there.

It smelled like cooking food on the second floor, and someone was singing loudly and powerfully. Luke knew it was Erik Sigvardsson. He was the director of the Sandgrenska Male Choir, a passionate group of older men who performed regularly around town. Luke greeted him sometimes when he came upon him in the stairwell, and now he stopped by the door. Maybe he saw or heard something last Monday? Luke decided to talk to him before he went up to the apartment. He knocked.

The song continued and Luke pounded on the door. It went silent, and after a few seconds, the door opened. Erik was a tall, slim man in his seventies.

"Ah, the big American," he said in a broad Karlskrona dialect when he saw it was Luke. "All of this with Viktor and little Agnes is so terrible. Come in!" He took a step to the side and let Luke enter.

He walked ahead into one of the three large rooms that lay in a line along the street. The bookshelf along one wall was filled with vinyl records from floor to ceiling. He invited Luke to sit down on the large brown leather sofa and asked if Luke would like a cup of coffee. It was freshly made. Luke accepted, and Erik filled a cup for him.

"It's so sad," Erik said, sighing. "Such young people."

Luke took a sip of the coffee and nodded.

"Was it you who found them?" Erik asked.

"Me, and Agnes' mom, Therese."

"No, no, no. That poor person. To see your little daughter like that."

"She's been admitted to the psychiatric ward in an acute condition."

Erik pointed up to the ceiling.

"The big living room, was it there you found them?"

"Yes," Luke answered.

"That's right above us," Erik said, looking up.

"Just think, I sat here watching TV, just two yards under them with only a floor between us, completely oblivious while he took both his own life and that of his little girl. Oh, so awful."

"So you were home on Monday evening?"

"Yes, most of it," Erik answered. "I had choir rehearsal between four thirty and seven. I was home again just after seven o'clock."

"Did you see Viktor or Agnes when you came home?"

Erik thought for a moment.

"No, I didn't see a soul. The stairwell was completely empty."

They could hear raucous bawling out on the street. Probably a group of guys on their way to some pub up on the square.

Erik looked up at the ceiling again as if he were trying to see through the floor up to Viktor's living room.

"I wonder if that was why he was playing music so loudly?" he said, as if he were thinking aloud to himself.

He looked at Luke and nodded towards the street, towards the rowdy guys.

"Yes, you can hear how poor the soundproofing is. Maybe he thought I would hear something. If the girl got sad or something, I'm thinking. So he turned the music up loud."

Erik looked at Luke as if to gain support for his theory, as if Luke had the answer. Luke shrugged his shoulders.

"That might have been," he said. "It was just so strange that he chose jazz. He doesn't like jazz."

"No, you know, I thought the same thing. Why is he playing that exact piece again and again, I thought? And so loudly? I've never heard him play fusion before. Only 1960s pop, mostly the Beatles and popular hit music, that's what he likes. Not Chick Corea."

"You recognized the song?" Luke asked.

"Immediately. I have several Chick Corea records. I listened to him a lot when I was a young student in music school. I saw him in 1981 at the Kristianstad Jazz Festival. He was a musical genius. The piece Viktor played is on a record with Return to Forever, a band Chick Corea formed in the early 1970s. Fantastic musicians, despite that Al Di Meola hadn't joined the band yet. The world's best bassist was a member, Stanley Clarke. The song is called 'Theme to the Mothership'. Wonderful piece. Just a little uncomfortable to listen to for several hours. It's on the album *Hymn to the Seventh Galaxy*, which came out over forty years ago. I'll admit that I had to check my records. I knew the song, but I didn't remember which album it was on. It took an hour before I found it."

"Do you have the record here?" Luke asked.

"Of course."

He stood up and walked to the shelf with the records. He bent down and flipped through them for a few seconds, then pulled out a record sleeve in a plastic cover and handed it to Luke. The cover was done in light colors. A drawing of a white gull in flight, or maybe it was a dove, dominated the image. The gull flew above fluffy clouds. In the gull's outstretched winds, the person who designed the cover placed four drawn faces. One of them was probably Chick Corea, and the three others the musicians of Return to Forever. Luke looked at the back. The same picture, but a mirror image and without the face. Texts describing the songs. "Theme to the Mothership" was eight minutes and twenty-two seconds long.

"I've never heard of Chick Corea," Luke said. "Jazz isn't for me. I mostly listen to punk," Luke stood up, handed Erik the sleeve, and thanked him.

He left the apartment, went up one story, and stopped outside Viktor's door. He looked at the lock. He was glad Viktor didn't listen to him when Luke said he should get another lock, a seven-pin tumbler lock. That would have made this all much harder. Viktor just laughed at him and said that Karlskrona was worlds away from Williamsburg.

He heard music and loud voices from the door across the landing. On Viktor's door stood a yellow police sign outlined in red that said that entry to the apartment was prohibited. Blue and white police tape was tied to the door handle and pulled across to the railing to further mark that the area was off-limits.

Luke took a deep breath. He wanted to be a law-abiding person for the rest of his life and was finding it hard to break in, to break the vow he made to himself. But he couldn't let go of the thought of how dark it was in the apartment when the shades were pulled down. Whether it was possible for Viktor to carry out the hanging in darkness. If your eyes could adjust enough in the dark. He was ready to take the risk, which he decided was small. It was a Saturday evening, and neither the police technicians nor detectives were on duty. Not to investigate the apartment of a suicide victim. He wouldn't touch anything except the shades. Wouldn't stay long.

He stood quietly for a few seconds. Heard nothing from the steps, besides what came from the party in the apartment across the landing. He quickly pulled a pair of thin gloves from the pocket of his denim jacket and took out the case of lockpicks. He selected a thumb turner and a pick he thought were the right size. He quickly inserted the turner and then the pick, hooked back and forth a few times, and felt how the pins held inside. Turned. It went quickly. The skills are still in my bones, he thought with pleasure as he carefully pulled the police tape from the handle, opened the door, and stepped inside.

13.

Jenny and Daniel looked at each other. In silence. The song by Alannah Myles just ended. The flame in the pillar candle on the coffee table flickered. The building wasn't well insulated. At first, Jenny couldn't process what Daniel said. The hair stood up on her arms.

He was her son-in-law.

Daniel shook his head.

"This is completely crazy. Did we know each other in a past life?"

He stood up, went over, and sat on the sofa with his arm around her. Jenny didn't say anything. She was almost in shock. How was this possible? They completed separate auditing sessions, didn't discuss anything to do with New York, banks, previous lives. She turned to Daniel.

"Do you think Micke might have talked to Peter after he audited you?"

"What do you mean?"

"Micke maybe told Peter about your story in New York before Peter audited me. And then Peter led me on that path. He's really darn good."

"Did Peter ask you any leading questions?" Daniel asked. "Who mentioned New York first, you or him?"

Jenny tried to recall the memory of how the conversation went. She was so focused on herself, that she didn't really remember.

"I think it was me," she said. "But I don't exactly remember. It's all blurry."

"If it were Peter, then that was a flagrant mistake," Daniel said. "An auditor is only supposed to listen and ask questions about the engram itself. That's what Micke did, anyway."

"Oh, I have to try to remember," Jenny said, closing her eyes. She started from the events she'd described, trying to remember how Peter asked the questions. Daniel sat quietly, waiting.

"I was the one who brought up New York and the whole story with the bank and son-in-law," she said after a moment. "He asked me to go to a previous event relating to a headache, and I sat silently for a long time. Then he said 'There. What thought did you have?' He must have seen some reaction in the needle or something. I saw an office, I said, and then he asked where I was. And I said New York. It just came out."

David hugged her. Hard. Then he laid down with his head on her knee. She caressed his hair.

"How was it for you?" Jenny asked.

"Completely unbelievable. Crazy."

"What sort of engram did you have?"

"Losses. I haven't had many, so I got down to this thing with the bank quickly. I saw exactly the same image you described. I'm sitting at my desk, lift my gaze, and see a bald man around fifty-five or sixty years old, who's clearly you. I see you standing far away in the space. You're standing still and looking at me, and I know immediately I've been found out."

They sat quietly for a moment, thinking about this incredible situation. Trying to take it in. Understand.

"Isn't it strange that you were a guy in your past life?" Daniel asked.

"Yes, for sure. Odd that you can jump between the sexes like that."

"It explains why you have so many manly characteristics," Daniel said, peering at her.

"Listen, now," Jenny said, pulling playfully on his ear. She reached over Daniel, took her mug of tea, and drank. It had gone cold.

"Do you remember that you drove off a cliff?" she asked.

Daniel nodded.

"I brought up clear mental images of it. Felt the fear. Heard the screams of the children. I felt physically ill when I talked about it."

"Do you remember why you did it?"

"I think it was because it was a huge scandal, what I did. I embezzled a lot of money, and realized that my whole future was destroyed. And my family's. So I drank a ton of alcohol and completely lost my judgment. Didn't want to leave the family in the shitstorm I caused."

Jenny took Daniel's hand.

"Do you remember last week, that evening when you couldn't go to the evening coffee at Max's place? Peter said maybe there was a reason that we, specifically we, are in this city, right now."

Daniel gave a coarse laugh.

"I wonder about that reason every time I walk in the bitterly cold wind over the square on the way home after a party."

Jenny ignored his joke.

"He thinks that we souls have an original group that belonged together at one point in time. Eons ago. We're that group."

She looked at him seriously.

"For some reason, the group split and since then, we've been trying to find each other. Now we have. For the first time in ages, we're together again."

She paused. Daniel looked up at her.

"I see in my mind a ton of people in Superman shirts flying around in the universe with binoculars, looking for their friends. And when they find them, they fall down and dive into a baby at some nearby labor and delivery ward."

Jenny developed an irritated wrinkle in her forehead.

"Can't you be a little bit serious? This is important to me."

She tried to pull her hands away, but Daniel held onto them tightly.

"I'm sorry."

She looked away.

"Continue," he begged. "Please."

"Only if you stop joking around."

"It wasn't actually a joke. I really wonder how it happens."

"It sounded like you were putting me on. You were being ironic."

"Sorry," Daniel said again. "I didn't mean to be ironic. I promise."

Jenny gave in and continued.

"Peter also said that we have a twin soul. A partner who we were together with from the very start. They've also split and tried to find each other. When you find your twin, you know it."

She turned towards Daniel again.

"This thing that happened to us today, that we, independently of each other, remembered the same event in a past life, maybe means we're twin souls."

He pulled her to him. Hugged her, burrowed his nose into her hair and whispered into her ear.

"We clearly want to be near each other. In our previous life, we were, and now we're sitting here together again. When I met you for the first time, I felt in my stomach that it was right. I fell head over heels. Immediately. It's never happened before. This theory of twin souls explains my feeling. You're my twin soul, Jenny. I love you."

14.

Strips of light from the streetlamps were reflected on the floor. Just enough for Luke to be able to keep the lights off as he prepared for his experiment. It smelled musty and images of the moments he and Therese found Viktor and Agnes forced their way into his mind.

The room looked the same as it did on Monday, except that the table where the computer and jar of poison stood was now completely clean. He looked towards the bathroom door where Viktor hung. The rope Luke took down was also gone.

He remained out of view of the windows and looked around the room for the remote control that controlled the shades. It lay on the bookshelf. He picked it up, walked along the shelf by the window, and stood to the side so he wouldn't be visible from the street. He leaned his head carefully forward and looked out towards the apartment buildings on the other side of the street. He quickly scanned the windows to see if anyone was standing and looking out. He couldn't see a soul. He pushed the remote control and one shade began slowly lowering. After a few pushes of the buttons, all three lowered.

When the shades in the living room were down, Luke walked quickly around the apartment, lowering the shades in all of the windows, except the one in Agnes' room because her door was closed. It was pitch black. He had to take out his cell phone and turn the flashlight on in order to get back into the living room. He stood in the middle of the room and turned off his cell phone light.

Black as the grave.

He waited for a few minutes to see if his eyes grew accustomed to the darkness. They did somewhat, but not enough. It must have been really difficult for Viktor to arrange the last part of the hanging. Viktor knew his apartment well and maybe could have felt his way forward and figured it out. But why would he make it so hard for himself? Why not have the lights on? It was enough to have the shades down.

Luke had the information he wanted. There were too many anomalies surrounding Viktor's and Agnes' deaths for him to be able to leave it alone. The darkness, the jazz music, the poison he was supposed to have given

Agnes. It didn't fit with the Viktor he knew. He had to get to the bottom of this.

He took the remote control, returned the shades to their open positions, and went out into the hallway. He stood at the front door and listened for any sounds from the stairwell. It was completely silent. He turned the lock carefully, pushed down the handle, went out, and closed the door behind him. The stairwell lights were off, but they blinked on as he turned to go. A pretty blonde woman around thirty-five years old stood on the landing below Luke, watching him.

"Stay there," she said. "Police."

She held up a badge. The distance was too great for Luke to be able to read what it said.

"A patrol is on the way here, just so you know. They'll be here within a few minutes. There's no point in trying to run away."

The woman stood there, examining him to see his reaction. Luke stood still.

"It's cool," he said. "I'm not going to do anything. Can I see your badge more closely?"

The woman took two steps up towards him and tossed her identification. It landed at Luke's feet, and he bent down and picked it up. Jonna Gustafson, Crime Scene Investigator, Blekinge Police. He threw it back to the woman, who caught it with both hands.

Jonna Gustafson was the most beautiful policewoman Luke had ever seen. And he'd seen quite a few. The blonde hair in a long ponytail, surely over five feet six inches tall, with clean, sharp features. Worn blue jeans, gym shoes, and a grey T-shirt. But what mostly caught Luke's attention was her eyes. Large, round, and beautiful. They looked at him suspiciously.

"Who are you?" she asked.

"Luke Bergmann. I was a close friend of Viktor Spandel's, who died on Monday."

"I know the case," she said. "I saw your name in the report. Did you know it's illegal to go into a cordoned-off apartment?"

"How did you know I was here?" Luke asked.

"How did you get in?"

Luke reached for his back pocket but saw Jonna stiffen.

"It's cool," he said. "I don't have a weapon. I'm just going to take out my lockpicks."

He took out the leather case with the picks and held it up to her.

"Your turn," he said. "How did you notice me?"

"I live across the street and saw that the shades were down," she answered. "They weren't yesterday when I looked. I knew that the apartment was still cordoned off. So I called the station to see if it was colleagues in there. It wasn't, so I asked them to send a car. When I saw the shades had gone up, I suspected you were about to leave the apartment and ran here."

"I was the one who found him on Monday," Luke said. "I just had to check something. I didn't touch anything. Besides the shades."

The last time Luke sat in an interrogation room was the end of January, 1996. It was a shabby, sad room that smelled like sweat in one of the police stations in Brooklyn, the 61st Precinct on Coney Island Avenue. He was taken there on the evening of January 18 after having witnessed the shooting of his boss, "The Crazy" Johnny Attias, with two bullets in the back as he leaned into his car outside the Sea Dolphin, a popular seafood restaurant in Brooklyn. The bullets hit vital organs, and Johnny Attias died a few hours later at the hospital.

Interrogation Room Three at Karlskrona bore a greater resemblance to a modern conference room. An oval table, four chairs with green fabric seats, shiny black vinyl floor, white walls. Luke sat alone in the room and thought about those days at the end of January, which ended with him deciding to testify against the other members of the Israeli mafia in exchange for witness protection and help getting away to London. He suspected that Anders Loman and Jonna Gustafson would check up on him and feared they might contact the American authorities to see if he had a criminal record. He hoped his protected identity was truly protected.

Luke sat alone in the room for an hour before the door opened and Anders Loman stepped in, accompanied by Jonna Gustafson.

"Luke Bergmann," Anders Loman said. "You're going to have to explain to me what you've got into that means my Saturday evening meal is now sitting there getting cold. I hope you have a good explanation."

He tossed a notebook on the table, took out a pen, and sat in the chair next to Jonna, who also had a notepad in front of her.

"Go ahead. Take it from the beginning. All the details."

Luke told how he realized that the apartment was completely dark when he and Therese walked into it. About Viktor's shades and that he'd wanted to see how dark it really was in the room when Viktor did the deed.

"Why?" asked Loman when Luke was finished.

Luke looked at him questioningly.

"Don't you think it's strange that Viktor hanged himself in complete darkness? With the shades down, it's pitch black in there. You can't see a thing."

"I don't know if I think it's so strange," Loman said.

Luke gave him an astonished look.

"What do you mean?"

"Exactly what I said. I'm not sure about your story. Tell me why you were really there."

Luke looked at Jonna for support. She showed no reaction, just looked at him coldly.

"It's true," Luke said. "Can you explain why someone would carry out a suicide in complete darkness?"

"There could be any number of explanations for that," Loman said. "If it really was how you said, that the lights were off when you walked in. Maybe he couldn't bear to see his daughter lying on the sofa. Or maybe he just liked the darkness. Besides, if you've lived in an apartment for three years, you can get around blindfolded."

He stopped talking. Looked at Luke, who shook his head.

"You're wrong," Luke said.

"I can't help wondering if you had another reason for breaking in," Loman said. "Did you?"

Luke didn't answer. He understood he was in a bad position.

"Where did you learn to break into apartments?" Jonna asked when Luke didn't answer. She laid Luke's lockpicks on the table.

"There are loads of tutorials online," Luke said. "It took me five minutes to learn."

"This leather case doesn't look like it was bought at Claes Ohlsson's just this week," Jonna continued.

"I got it from a friend many years ago. He didn't need it anymore. I've never used it before."

"Why didn't you contact us and tell us about all this with the darkness?" Jonna asked.

"I like when things go quickly. Viktor was my best friend. I wanted to understand."

"On Thursday, when we met, I told you about the apartment being cordoned off," Loman said. "You knew about it, and yet you broke in. Now I want you to tell me what your true goal was with going to the apartment."

"I have told you."

"Do you think it's strange that we're starting to wonder about your behavior?" Loman continued. "We're maybe even beginning to weigh whether you might not be right about your suspicions about this being a murder. And maybe you had something to do with it. Maybe you wanted to eliminate some evidence? Did you leave something in there?"

"You can't be serious," Luke said.

"Why not? On Thursday, you found out that we'd changed the locks and that the autopsy results would be done soon. Two days later, you break in. Were you in a hurry to clean up what you'd missed in the apartment?"

"Viktor was my best friend, and I loved Agnes like my own daughter," Luke said. "What would my motive be?"

Loman picked up the folder in front of him. The same folder he looked in when Luke met with him on Thursday.

"We've been able to see Viktor Spandel's will now," he said. "Interesting reading."

He looked up. Luke didn't move a muscle.

"He willed half a million of his over six million dollars to you. But that doesn't come as a surprise for you, does it?"

It took a great deal of effort for Luke not to react. He knew nothing about Viktor's will. And it was a completely surprise that he wanted Luke to have any of his money.

"Yes, it does," he answered. "Can I see it?"

"I don't have it here," Loman said. "In time, you'll get to see it. But as you can understand, it's a factor that makes you interesting to us. That, plus the fact that you broke into his apartment."

"What were you doing on Monday between five and eight o'clock in the evening?" Jonna Gustafson asked.

"I was making food and waiting for Viktor and Agnes to come."

"Were you alone the whole time?"

Luke thought about it. He'd taken the trash out at one point. He'd exchanged a few words with his neighbor, retired pool caretaker Stig Jansson.

"I talked with my neighbor out on the street outside my house around eight o'clock."

"Give Gustafson his information so she can check on that," Loman said.

Luke wrote Stig's address and phone number on a piece of paper, and Loman turned towards Luke again.

"It's a serious crime you've committed. If the autopsy shows there was anything strange about the deaths, you'll have seriously obstructed the investigation. If it's murder and you're not the one who did it, your actions might mean that we won't be able to catch the perpetrator."

"That's just it," Luke said. "I'm not sure it was suicide, as you maybe understand by now."

"What you believe or don't believe is completely uninteresting to us," Jonna Gustafson said coldly.

"I had gloves on, and I didn't move anything. The only thing I did was turn on the lights and turn them off. And I lowered the shades."

"That's what you say," Jonna said. "But we can't know for sure. We have to do a new inventory of the apartment and compare with the previous images. Only then can we determine how much damage you've done."

"We're going to leave this to the prosecutor now," Loman said. "The formal charge of what you've committed is gross unlawful entry and can result in prison for up to one year."

He stood up.

"If I'm honest, I don't believe you intended any harm," he said. "I'm convinced you're genuinely shaken by what happened to Viktor and his daughter. But unfortunately, it doesn't reduce the gravity of what you did. I hope you understand that."

Luke nodded.

Loman turned to Jonna Gustafson.

"Will you put this together? And make sure I receive a printed report?"

"Absolutely."

"Dinner is waiting," Loman said. "Luckily, I have a microwave." He said this last sentence as he winked at Luke and left the room.

Jonna Gustafson sat with her head bent down, writing in her notebook. When she was done, she looked up. Christ, she's beautiful, Luke thought, unable to stop himself from smiling at the effect her appearance had on him. He couldn't resist the signals from his libido, despite the fact that he'd just found out he was at risk of a year in prison and despite having seen the ring on her finger. Jonna Gustafson didn't look pleased.

"What's so funny?" she asked.

"Darwin," Luke said.

Jonna raised her eyebrows.

"I've just received confirmation how right he was," Luke continued.

She still looked confused.

"Despite the situation I'm in, I can't help but be fascinated," he said. "And it came completely reflexively. I couldn't guide it with the strength of my own will."

"I don't understand any of this," she said. "What is it you're fascinated by?"

"Your face. I think it's pretty."

Luke sensed a barely noticeable shift in her stony expression.

"What does Darwin have to do with that?" she asked.

"He thought that, for the purposes of survival, men have the desire to hop in bed with women as often as possible. It's in our bones."

"Oh really? What did he say about us women, then?" She looked vaguely amused.

"For you, the offspring are more important, so you are more careful when you choose your partners," Luke answered. "It's more about an investment for you."

"Interesting," Jonna said, standing up. "If it goes badly, you'll have to make sure to hop into bed with as many as possible in the coming days, before you end up behind bars."

She walked to the door, opening it and holding it for him.

"Is it that bad?" Luke asked as he stood up and walked towards the door.

"It's very unusual to receive a prison sentence for unlawful entry," Jonna said. "I'd bet on a fine."

15.

An hour remained before Svärd's interview at Beehive Preschool. He had plenty of time. The preschool was only a quarter-mile from the hotel, which was on St. Eriksgatan on Kungsholmen.

Svärd sat in front of the mirror at the small table in his hotel room. He opened the contact lens package, took out two brown colored lenses, and took a painfully long time to get the lenses in place. He wiped his watering eyes with towels and looked at himself. His hair, which he'd dyed black, had begun to grow long on his neck, and with his black beard, Bart Simpson T-shirt, and blue jeans, he looked like the exemplary male preschool teacher—gentle and playful.

He cast a glance at the TV. A woman was sucking off a man while another thrust into her from behind. The volume was on mute, but he knew how it sounded. He'd left the TV on all night. Not because he was turned on, because he wasn't at all. The actors, or whatever you'd call them, were too terrible and too boring. And above all, too old. They disgusted him. But he left the TV on to remind himself that others, too, had shameful desires.

Svärd turned around, opened his laptop, and went online. He first checked if any more orders had arrived, but his inbox was empty. Then he went to the local newspapers' webpages to see if there was anything about the event on Friday at Blekinge Summerland. There was. "*Attempted child abduction at popular Summerland,*" read one title. He swore over the fact that both newspapers' articles were only available for subscribers.

He got up and picked up his pride and joy, his camera. A Canon EOS 700D. He bought it last spring, before the attack, for seven hundred dollars at a camera shop in Karlskrona. 18 megapixels, video in full HD; it took fantastic pictures. He tucked it into his backpack but didn't bother putting in the zoom lens. He could zoom in well enough with the standard lens.

He looked at the clock. Twenty minutes left, best that he set off now. He laid down the special gloves he wore so he wouldn't leave fingerprints, checked one last time that all of his documents were in his folder, put on a ridiculous sunhat and sunglasses, and left the hotel.

He walked calmly south on St. Eriksgatan. It was clear that it was prime vacation time in Stockholm. There weren't many cars on the street or

70

people on the sidewalk. The air felt clear and pure, and the sun peeked out from behind fluffy white cumulus clouds, resulting in a pleasant temperature. After the meeting at Beehive Preschool, Svärd had two hours before his next meeting, which he hoped he would be able to cancel. The woman who called him from Beehive sounded very keen. Staff vacations and illnesses meant she was sitting in shit, as she'd expressed it.

Beehive would be perfect for him. A small preschool with just two sections, one for 1- to 3-year-olds, and one for 4- to 6-year-olds. Just five co-workers, normally, for twenty-nine kids. Now that it was summer vacation, though, only two people were working, and this week there were ten kids. There should be opportunities for a few moments completely alone with a couple of the kids.

The preschool lay in an idyllic location, a courtyard with a little yellow wooden house with a ramp for wheelchairs leading up to the door. In the yard was a playground with bright, modern equipment. There were no children in sight. All he could hear was the chirping of birds echoing between the buildings.

Svärd put on his thin, white eczema gloves, and at exactly ten o'clock, he opened the door and was immediately met by a plump blonde woman in her forties holding a little child in her arms. She introduced herself as Annika Engvall, owner and preschool director. She was the one Svärd was in contact with.

"Oh, so good you could come," she said. "Let's go into my office. I'm just going to set little Ture down. You can wait here."

She turned on her heel and walked away down the hallway. After a few minutes, she came back and showed Svärd into a small office cluttered with boxes, papers, and binders. She moved some binders from a visitor's chair and asked Svärd to sit. She took a few documents from her desk and sat down. Svärd saw it was his papers she'd printed out. She let out a long sigh.

"This summer will be the death of me," she said. "Normally, things are pretty calm here, but this year, an unusual number of parents are working right through and not taking vacations. We don't usually have more than five or six children at this point, and that you can do alone. But this year, we have twice as many. And the staff wants to take vacation, too. I'm far too nice."

"So you have some problems right now?" Svärd asked.

"You could say that, definitely," she said. "Maria, who should have been working with me, her father had to go to the emergency room on Thursday. Probably a stroke. It's not looking good. And they're very close, she and her dad."

She stopped talking, deep in thought for a few seconds. Svärd didn't say anything.

"Poor woman," she said, finally. "She won't be coming back this week, in any case."

She looked down at the papers she was holding in her hand.

"Gustav Thordén," she read. "You received your degree in early childhood education fairly late in life. Just three years ago, when you were thirty-nine years old. How did that come about?"

"Work injury," Svärd answered, holding up his hands. "Eczema. I worked as a painter for fifteen years. I got it from the preservative that's in paint. The gloves are specially treated and soothe the itching. Continuing with painting was out of the question, so I switched careers. I like children, and it was fairly easy to get into a program. So that was that."

Annika nodded empathetically. It always works, Svärd thought. It was so easy to fool people.

"I see that you live in Karlskrona," Annika continued. "How is it that you're applying for an hourly sub position in Stockholm?"

"I've had a hard time finding a permanent job in Karlskrona. I've done short-notice subbing there and therefore don't have paid time off. And now, during the summer, almost all the preschools are closed. I thought I'd combine a vacation in the capital city with a little work. Stockholm is supposed to be a great place in the summertime, I've heard."

"It truly is," she said. "Try to get out into the archipelago if you can. There are some fantastic places out there."

Svärd nodded.

"When can you start?" Annika asked.

"I'd be able to start today."

"I've solved things with another sub today. But tomorrow? And probably the rest of the week. Would that work?"

"Absolutely. It'd work great for me."

"Oh, how nice!" Svärd could hear the relief in her voice.

"Then I have just one more question," she said. "The criminal background check, do you have that document with you?"

"Of course," Svärd said. He picked up his backpack and took out the document.

Annika quickly glanced through it.

"Looks good," she said. "I'll just make a copy."

She got up and walked to the copy machine, which stood on a small table by the bookshelf.

"Do you have some references I can call?" she asked while she waited for the copy to come out.

She turned towards him, but before Svärd could answer, she continued.

"Well, you know...uh...the cases these past years with pedophiles at preschools have meant that we've been forced to sharpen our protocols when we hire. So I would need to call someone you've worked with. Just to have that done."

"That's not a problem," Svärd said. "I understand that completely. It's not easy to be a man and a preschool teacher. You're met with suspicion nearly everywhere. It's almost enough to make you think about just letting it go and changing careers again."

"No, no, no, you shouldn't think that way," Annika said quickly, sitting in her chair again. "We need men at our preschools. Absolutely."

She returned the background check document to Svärd.

"Well, I'd think it would be impossible to get hold of anyone now that everyone's on vacation. Forget about the references. You can start tomorrow."

16.

Luke lay on his back in bed and stared up at the white-painted wooden ceiling in his bedroom. A fat blowfly buzzed obstinately around the room. He tried following it with his gaze. Usually, he would have been intensely irritated by the fly, hunting it with a newspaper in his hand. Now, he didn't have the energy to care.

It was Monday morning. A week since they died. He'd worked all Sunday, gone to bed early, and slept for twelve hours. He didn't want to get up. And he didn't have to because he had the day off.

Four days until the funeral. What should he wear? He didn't have a suit. He decided to buy a new one. Was a white or black shirt more appropriate for a funeral? He would have to ask at the store. He would take care of it today.

It wouldn't be the first funeral he'd attended, but the first one in Sweden. He tried to count how many friends he'd buried, and arrived at nine or ten. They usually swiped the casket from the chapel at Evergreen Cemetery and, high on PCP, marijuana, and cocaine, carried it around their neighborhood with the dead person inside, all the while chanting the Devil's Rebels fight song. The last two they'd even buried at the cemetery by themselves. He was damn lucky not to end up buried there himself.

It was easier said than done to find a suit that fit him. All of them were too small. But the clerk at Hogland's Men's Outfitters solved this by calling their tailor, who promised he would be able to let out both the pants legs and sleeves and have it done by Wednesday. Luke chose one of the three he tried on and left the shop.

When he came out on the street, he decided to make a visit to Trossö Marine & Leisure. The owner was one of Viktor's previous partners who knew Viktor for many years. Maybe he knew something that would explain who might want to see Viktor dead. Trossö Marine & Leisure was a quarter-mile north of downtown, and it took Luke fifteen minutes to walk there. The company was located in a renovated industrial building near the train tracks. Luke opened the door to the building and went in. There were no people but many boats, mostly luxury yachts of all sizes. Luke crossed between the boats and looked around for someone who worked there. He heard music playing and recognized the song: "Take the Long Way Home" by Supertramp. He went towards the music. It came from the largest boat, which stood furthest back in the building. He stopped below it. Saw that the boat was swaying slightly.

"Hello!" Luke had to call loudly to be heard over the music.

A few seconds later, the volume decreased and a black-haired, well-groomed head stuck out over the railing. It was Björn Lööf, owner of Trossö Marine & Leisure, Viktor's previous partner.

"Luke. Come up," he said.

Luke climbed up the ladder and up over the railing. Björn had laid out a mattress and pillow on the floor. Next to them stood a bottle of whisky and a glass.

"I'm lying here, philosophizing," he said. "In the summer, when it's sunny and things are completely dead here. Everyone's out in the archipelago. Want some?"

He took the bottle and held it up to Luke, who hesitated.

"Of course you should," Björn said. "We have to have a drink to the memory of Viktor and Agnes."

He disappeared down the stairs and came back immediately with a glass. He poured and gave Luke the glass. They raised their glasses in a silent toast and Luke let the burning liquid run down his throat. Björn reached the whisky out again to Luke, who shook his head.

"Just one more of these, anyway," Björn said, filling his own glass. He looked up at Luke. "I don't do this every day, if that's what you're thinking."

Luke shrugged his shoulders.

"I hardly drink on the weekends, either," he continued. "But today, I felt like it."

Luke looked at him as he downed the half-full glass. He was around forty-five, with thick, nicely cut black hair, was short but generally attractive. He and Viktor were former partners of Twain Technology, the company that laid the foundation for both men's wealth. They worked together at Ericsson's in Karlskrona in the mid-nineties. Both quit along with a few other higher-ups at the company and started Twain just at the right time, when the IT boom was happening. The company went public quickly, and the value of shares shot up like a rocket, just like the shares of so many other companies that were really just full of hot air. It was enough that a business had "Telecom" or "IT" in its names and trumpeted world domination in its plans for investors to begin throwing money at it. The difference between Twain and the majority of other IT companies was that the owners of Twain sold off their shares at exactly the right time.

In December of 2001, Twain was bought by another, larger IT company, and the seven owners cashed out with between six and ten million each. Luke knew that Björn and Viktor stayed in touch, and that they subsequently made a number of investments together. Björn was one of the people who knew Viktor best from their time at Twain.

Björn turned around and turned up the music. Still Supertramp. "The Logical Song."

"We listened to this song until the record broke when we were in high school, Viktor and I," he said.

They sat silently and listened as the song finished.

"It's completely incomprehensible," Björn said when the music ended.

"Inconceivable," Luke said.

"Why in hell would he commit suicide?" Björn continued. "He wasn't that type. When things were tough at the company, it was always Viktor who tried to make the rest of us see the possibilities and not entrench ourselves too deeply into the problems. He never let setbacks affect him."

"Do you know if he made any enemies?" Luke asked. Björn went silent, an astonished look on his face.

"Why are you asking that?"

Luke didn't answer.

"Do you think someone killed them?" Björn asked.

"I'm just trying to get a sense of all the possibilities," Luke said. Björn took a sip of his coffee.

"No, I can't come up with anyone who thought badly of Viktor," he said.

"Things can get heated in business sometimes, right? How were things when you sold your shares in Twain? Any fights then?" Luke asked.

Björn thought for a few seconds.

"That was a turbulent time, when we were about to sell our shares," Björn answered. "One of the part-owners, Thomas Franzén, decided to quit a few months earlier and sold his shares to the rest of us. He was really bitter when we cashed out to the tune of millions of dollars, and he was standing there with pocket change. It was Viktor who had to talk to him, mostly because he was the one who was best at that sort of thing. But

Franzén's anger wasn't directed at Viktor specifically, it was towards the whole group of owners. Viktor wasn't the type of person who made enemies. He was diplomatic and responsive to other people."

"Did you do business in Russia?" Luke asked.

"Twain, you mean?"

"Yes. St. Petersburg or Kaliningrad?"

"No, we stayed away from that market very deliberately. Wouldn't want to do business there now. No ethics or morals. Why do you ask?"

"Do you know if Viktor did any business there over the past few years?" Luke asked.

Björn shook his head.

"Not from what I know. He stuck mostly to properties here in town. I don't think he had anything going on in Russia. Almost sure of it. Why are you wondering?"

"Over the past two years, he made several trips to Kaliningrad and St. Petersburg," Luke answered. He didn't want to tell me what kind of trips they were. He always used to talk about his business deals otherwise, but when I wondered what it was he was doing on these trips, he got so secretive. I'd find out in time, he said."

"If it was about business, I think he would've talked with me about it," Björn said. "He would always ask me for advice when he would get involved in something, but he hasn't said a peep about having anything going on in Russia."

They sat silently for a moment. Luke contemplated for a while. Then he decided.

"This is what's up," Luke said, leaning forward towards Björn. "I don't think Viktor committed suicide. Nor that he killed Agnes. Someone murdered them. And there must be a motive. I've decided to figure it out. If you happen to remember something that could help me, I'd be grateful if you would be in touch."

Björn leaned back on the bench and laid his arms on the railing. He looked intensely at Luke.

"That thought sounds even more messed up than suicide," he said. "And I have a very difficult time seeing a motive. If anything, it could be that someone wanted to steal his money. That's probably the only thing I could see."

"Everything is still there, according to the police," Luke said, getting up. They climbed down from the boat and walked together towards the exit.

"How long did you know each other?" Luke asked.

"Since high school. We were inseparable. Until he was pulled into Scientology."

Luke stopped.

"The cult," he said. "How long was he in that?"

Björn thought about it.

"We were eighteen or nineteen when he started. And then he stopped everything, sports, friends, partying. I don't know exactly when he quit. Four, five years later, maybe. After that, he was normal again and we started hanging out again. He never talked about what he was part of. But he was damn critical of all religion after that."

He laughed.

"He didn't talk about it much but he was public about having left the cult. A few years after leaving, he and another defector contacted the newspaper and they staged a book-burning where they burned all of their Scientology books. They ended up on the front page of the newspaper that day."

"Do you remember any of the others who were part of it?" Luke asked. "What was the name of the other defector?"

Björn scratched his head.

"Damn, my memory isn't what it used to be. I don't remember. But I remember one of the girls. Anna Adams. A real cute little thing I had a little flirtation with, before she also became a Scientologist. She lives in Copenhagen now and works in film."

"Do you have her phone number?"

"No, but I can easily find it," Björn answered. "Wait here."

He disappeared into a glass-walled office. Luke saw him sit at the computer. He typed something in, seemed to find what he was looking for, wrote something down on a yellow post-it, and returned.

"We have some Danish clients," he said, handing over the paper with a telephone number on it. "I've learned how to find people on the other side of the Öresund."

17.

Peter laid two sheets of paper on the desk in front of Jenny and Daniel. The contracts. One for each of them.

"Are you completely certain about this?"

Peter lit a cigarette, leaned back in the brown leather armchair, blew the smoke out in a long exhale, and waited for their answers.

Jenny looked at Daniel, who sat next to her in front of the stout oak desk. They were sitting in the same room they were in for their auditing sessions.

It felt ceremonious, Jenny thought. Like they were sitting before a priest, about to get married. Peter dressed up to celebrate the day. He usually wore nice clothes, but today he had gone the extra mile with a light blue silk scarf tucked into a white shirt, a navy sweater, and beige corduroys. He was diminutive overall, but he had such power, both Jenny and Daniel thought. Peter pushed up his glasses, which tended to slip down his nose, with an elegant gesture.

Daniel smiled at Jenny.

"Yes. I have no hesitations. Right, Jenny?"

Both Daniel and Peter looked at her. Honestly speaking, she wasn't completely certain that she really wanted to sign the contract. She wasn't doubting Scientology or that she wanted to be audited and take the courses. It was the thought of restricting her free time completely for two and a half years. She had a lot of other things she wanted to do with her life: horseback riding, piano playing, friends. Daniel was completely sure. And he'd convinced her. It was after the evening when they realized they were related in a previous life that Daniel became convinced. Since then, he was completely obsessed with the message, the courses, the people at the church. He wanted to become Clear. Just like Peter and some of the others. To have that power, the confidence, the strong intention in his personality.

"It's only two and a half years," Daniel said one evening when they talked about it. "Down in Copenhagen, they sign up for a billion years."

Those who signed on the dotted line received, in exchange for their work for the Church of Scientology, all the courses the movement provided in Karlskrona, completely free of charge. And the courses were expensive. Plus, they received a good deal of therapy for free. Otherwise, therapy could cost tens of thousands of dollars.

"Are you unsure, Jenny?" Peter asked.

Jenny straightened up in her chair.

"Nah. It just feels like a big step. I'm not at all hesitant about all of this," she said, gesturing towards the area where the courses were taught. "But I ride horses in my free time, and I play piano. I'll have to stop all of that now."

Peter leaned back against the chair and clasped his hands over his stomach.

"I understand your hesitation," he said. "It's quite simply a sacrifice you have to make. But we don't demand that you quit all of your leisure activities. The contract requires thirty hours work each week. In a month, that's one hundred and twenty hours. Do you know how many hours there are in a month?"

Jenny blushed. She knew where Peter was going.

"No, not off the top of my head," she said, hesitantly.

"Seven hundred and twenty," Peter replied quick as a flash. "This means you have six hundred hours left with which to sleep, ride, play piano, or anything else you might want to do."

Jenny felt stupid.

"One hundred twenty and hours of over seven hundred, to work for the future of humanity," Peter continued. "Do you think this planet is on the right path, Jenny?"

Before Jenny could say anything, he continued.

"Do you know how many wars have been started since World War Two ended almost forty-seven years ago?"

Jenny shook her head. She wanted this discussion to end. Peter answered himself.

"One hundred and sixteen."

He paused dramatically, letting the number sink in. He sat up and laid his arms on the table. He looked intensely at Jenny.

"One hundred and sixteen wars. The United Nations was established so that there would never be a war again. That's how well they've done, you see? The Iraq War is the latest, and the civil war in Yugoslavia will most likely intensify. This planet has probably never been worse off than right now, I would say."

Jenny squirmed uncomfortably.

"Now, it's not that our goal is to replace the United Nations," he continued, smiling. "But what is it that causes war?"

"It must be a lot of different things," Jenny answered, unsure.

"People, Jenny. People. And it's people we work with, right?"

Jenny nodded.

"People's minds," Peter continued. "That's where the cause lies. A person who has been subjected to engrams throughout all her lifetimes will finally become evil. It's completely natural, since engrams are there to protect us from threats to our existence. We are to subconsciously avoid situations that threaten us. The problem is that when we have too many, eventually everything and everyone around us become a threat and then we start wars. The engrams mean we can no longer see differences, and the definition of intelligence is just that–the ability to see differences."

Jenny had finally heard enough.

"Peter, you don't need to say any more," she said, smiling. "I get it."

"Good. I just want to say one more thing, and then I promise to end my lecture. If we are going to be able to stop all this craziness, we have to start with where the cause resides. We have the tools; we got them from L Ron Hubbard. Now we have to just make sure to act. To get as many as possible to achieve the potential they have within themselves and get them on board. Every person we can bring with us is incredibly important, and that's why I've dressed up a little extra today. For me, this is a big day. Today, I hope," he said, winking at both of them, "we gain two more people who have realized what is important and who are ready to push up their sleeves for the fourth dynamic, the species."

Jenny looked at Daniel, who took her hand.

"Peter, you're a really clever salesman," he said with a wide smile. "I was convinced before, but now I'm ready to sign up for all of the lifetimes, ever."

Peter laughed and stood up.

"So, what do you say? Should we take out the pen?"

He looked at Jenny when he said it. Jenny realized that all possible resistance she felt had been blown away.

"Yes, take it out. I'm sorry I hesitated, but I'm in. A hundred percent. Of course we're signing up."

Peter took out his expensive ballpoint pen, a Parker. He laid it on Daniel's contract, uncorked the wine, and poured three glasses that stood on his stout desk. Daniel took the pen and signed. He handed the pen to Jenny, who did the same.

"We don't usually drink alcohol here," Peter said, smiling. "But in such situations, we make an exception. Cheers to a wise decision. And welcome aboard. Now let's save this planet."

18.

Outside playtime would last a half-hour longer. At ten thirty, he would make sure all seven children went in. The two youngest would get fresh diapers, and at a quarter to eleven, they had circle time. Svärd hoped already today he would have the chance to be alone with the children during nap time after lunch.

Wearing shorts and a T-shirt, he stood somewhat distractedly and pushed the two and three-year-olds in their kiddie swings. He stood between the swings and pushed one with his left hand and the other with his right. The weather was fantastic, over eighty degrees despite it being only ten o'clock in the morning. The five children in the three- to six-year-old group went up and down the slide and took care of themselves in the little fenced-in playground. A half-hour earlier, Annika went in to prepare the lunch that would be served at eleven fifteen.

It was Wednesday, his second day as a sub at Beehive Preschool. He had the sense that Annika thought he did well with the children, and he really made an effort to make a good impression. He'd taken the initiative many times, played a lot with the kids, goofed around with the younger ones, and led the afternoon music time all by himself. He wanted Annika to trust him so that she would dare to leave him alone with the children at naptime on one of the next few days. He really needed some good pictures. His money wouldn't last much longer.

After the successful job interview on Monday, he spent the whole afternoon and evening tracking Maria Palm. She was a forty-five-year-old corporate lawyer, lived alone on Kungsholmsgatan 24 in a beautiful turn-of-the-century building, and worked at a law office in the World Trade Center building near Central Station. He started by calling the firm's main number and asking for her. When he was connected, he quickly hung up. She was there. Then he walked there and searched for the office, which was up on the fourth floor. It was three o'clock when he found a spot to wait inside the cool entry foyer to wait. There was only that one way down, unless she took her car to work, which he decided was improbable because she lived only six hundred yards away.

Maria Palm worked late. It was seven fifteen, after Svärd had waited a full four hours, when she came walking down the steps and went out of the building. Svärd recognized her immediately from the pictures of her he found on the law office's webpage. She looked like the typical business-woman, strictly dressed in a white blouse, black jacket, and a tight, black, knee-length skirt. She looked fit, and her brown hair was tied in a chignon at her neck. She had quite broad facial features, was soberly made-up, a stylish businesswoman. She walked with quick steps west on Kungsholms Bridge and Svärd followed her at a distance. When she was almost at her apartment, she turned off and went into Hotel Amaranten. Svärd went to the other side of the street and stood across from the entrance. He looked through the plate glass window and saw her sit at the bar and order.

At ten o'clock she left the hotel and walked the fifty remaining yards to her apartment. The next day, Svärd hurried to the World Trade Center when he finished at the preschool. The pattern repeated itself. She did exactly the same thing. Left work just after seven. Went into Amaranten and ordered food. Walked home a few hours later.

Svärd thanked his lucky stars. She seemed to eat dinner at Amaranten every evening.

His thoughts were interrupted by Annika opening the door and coming out into the entrance. She waved to him.

"Get them to come in now, Gustav," she called. "Diaper changes and circle time."

Svärd gathered the children and got them inside. They changed the diapers of the two small ones. Gustav changed diapers before when he subbed at a few preschools in Småland ten years ago. He thought it was disgusting and tried to avoid it as long as possible, but he was forced to do it a few times. Now he went very slowly so he would see how Annika did it. She chattered on about a problem the preschool had with a parent and didn't notice Gustav studying her every move.

"Say, by the way," she said when she was done with her child. "I need to run an errand downtown over lunch. Could you do lunchtime yourself, do you think? Everything is ready."

"Of course," Svärd said. "No problem. How long will you be gone?"

"I think it'll take an hour and a half, max," she said, looking at the clock. "Oh, yes. We have nap and rest time, too. That might be harder for you to do. We can just wait for that until I'm back."

"No," Svärd said. "I'll take care of it. There are only seven, and not everyone will sleep, right? You just relax and take care of your errand, and I'll handle things here."

Annika looked at him.

"Are you sure? I'll be as quick as I can."

Svärd assured her that it would be fine and that she didn't need to stress about getting back quickly.

They set the table and put out the food in the little dining room. When the children were all seated, Annika set off. Svärd asked a few of the bigger kids to help the little ones. Then he went into the nap room to prepare for a photo shoot. He went into the playroom on the way and found two doctor bags he saw in there earlier. He pulled down the shades, moved all the mattresses except for one into a corner so that he would have a clean, empty area in the middle of the room. The remaining mattress he laid in the middle of the floor. He took out his camera and got a ladder from the cleaning closet. He set the camera in the right spot on the ladder and adjusted the settings. The light from the ceiling fixture wasn't good, and he didn't want to use the flash. He went quickly to the window that faced the back of the building, pulled up the shade, went back to his camera, and looked through the viewfinder. If he moved the camera so the children were illuminated by the window, it would work. He went to the window, which now didn't have the shade pulled down. He looked out to see what was out there. A narrow gravel area that ended at an outer wall, just across from a tall hedge. Not a place anyone would pass through. Perfect.

When he was done, he went back to the dining room. He stopped by the entrance and locked it just to be safe. Most of the children were leaving the table. The bigger kids were clearing dishes. Svärd took the two toddlers and went straight into the nap room to get them to sleep quickly. The other five children came quietly in and asked why the mattresses weren't where they usually were.

"I thought we'd forget about resting today and would play instead," Svärd said.

The children cheered and immediately began suggesting what they would play.

Svärd held up the two doctor bags.

"Today it's my choice," he said. "We're going to play doctor."

The children were instantly on board, and Svärd gave them instructions.

"This isn't just any hospital," he said. "This is a hospital in Africa, where it is very, very warm. So the patients and the doctors there don't wear any clothes. They're completely naked."

He looked at the clock. Fifty minutes had passed since Annika left. Just forty minutes left.

"There you go! Hurry now. Otherwise the patients might die. Take off your clothes. Who's going to win?"

It was three girls and two boys, four and five years old. The boys were the quickest and ripped off their clothes within a few seconds. One of the girls had a problem getting her dress over her head, and Svärd helped her with it. None of them seemed to think being naked was strange. No one protested; they all seemed to think it was a fun game. Svärd quickly gathered the clothes and lay them in a pile on the mattresses in the corner. He felt his pulse quicken when he saw their beautiful little bodies. Wonderful. So soft and innocent and natural.

Quickly, he chose a boy and a girl. The most beautiful ones. The girl would be the patient and the boy the doctor. The others sat on the mattresses in the corner. He took the girl by the hand and led her to the mattress in the middle of the floor and told her to lie down on her side. He helped her lie correctly. Like a grown woman, posing with one leg over the other in a sexy pose. He ran to his camera.

"First, we have to take pictures of the patients. That's what they do in Africa so they can see how healthy the patient gets after the doctor has given them medicine."

He quickly focused the camera and took several pictures with different framings. The children were simple and obeyed him. He didn't need to raise his voice even once. He worked quickly and took pictures of all the children in a tangle, pictures of each one in different positions, and felt almost done when a couple of the children pointed to the one window whose shade wasn't pulled down.

"Annika! We're playing doctor!" called one of the girls, waving.

Svärd looked at the window and saw Annika standing with her face pressed against the pane, her hands at the sides of her face to shut out the bright sunlight.

19.

Brolæggerstræde was a little street running parallel to Strøget in the middle of central Copenhagen. Luke stood at the front door of one of the buildings and pushed the button that stood beside the nameplate that said "Anna Adams." He took a few steps out towards the street and looked up at the house. It was three stories high, red tile with green trim around the windows. He looked down. A man in a white sports coat and holding a computer case stood next to the door, waiting for someone.

The conversation with Anna Adams a few days earlier turned out to be interesting. When she first answered, she sounded bubbly and pleasant, but when Luke introduced himself and asked if she knew anyone named Viktor Spandel, the mood changed. She became guarded and curt in her tone. She asked if Luke was from the Church of Scientology and said that if he were, she intended to hang up the phone. Luke then explained that he wasn't a Scientologist but one of Viktor's best friends, that Viktor was dead, and that Luke thought the death might have something to do with Scientology.

At first, Anna Adams was completely quiet. Then she said she didn't want to talk about it on the phone but wondered if they could meet. They decided he would travel down to see her on Wednesday, the day before the funeral.

Luke went to the door again and pushed the button one more time. This time, there was a click at the door and Luke went in.

Anna lived on the top floor in a large apartment. The nameplate only had her name, so she probably lived alone. She had left the door open a crack. Luke knocked cautiously and went in.

Anna Adams was in her early forties, short, with curly brown hair, and a face that made Luke think of a deer. Graceful features, pretty eyes, a narrow, thin nose. She was wearing a green kimono, and Luke made out a nicely-formed, somewhat plump body underneath.

Luke looked around in the apartment and understood that Anna Adams lived for her work. The walls were filled with framed film posters from different film productions. Anna asked Luke to follow her to the kitchen, where she had laid out tea and open sandwiches. On one wall was a film poster that showed two hands unbuttoning the dress from a woman's body. Luke recognized it, he saw the film many years before. During the period when he'd tried to learn the language. The film was called "All Things Fair."

Luke sat down and Anna poured tea, inviting him to enjoy the sandwiches. Luke didn't feel particularly hungry. There was a smell of old foot sweat lying over the table. Anna saw his hesitation.

"It's Old Ole that stinks," she laughed. She took one of the sandwiches with cheese on it and put it under her nose. "It smells terrible, but it's the best cheese I've ever had. You have to try it." She reached out the tray with the sandwiches and Luke took one. He stopped breathing through his nose and quickly shoved the bit of bread into his mouth. It didn't taste as terrible as it smelled.

"You'll have to forgive me if I sounded a little distant on the phone," Anna said. "I left Scientology over twenty years ago, but they still sometimes contact me and try to convince me to start again. I've tried to forget those years of my life, and I never talk about them with anyone."

"How long were you in?"

"A couple years. I was only seventeen when I took my first course. Then I was slowly pulled in, got hooked, and a year or so later I started working for them."

"And Viktor was in at the same time as you?"

"Yes, he belonged to the innermost circle and had been in it a few years before I started," Anna said. "I wasn't part of it as long as Viktor. And not as dedicated."

"The innermost circle?"

"Yes, there were about twenty-five of us young people who were members, some really passionate about it while others a bit less obsessed. But a smaller group, comprised of maybe ten people, were clustered around the Englishman who had started the whole thing. He was seen as a guru, had even worked with L Ron Hubbard, the founder, in the late 1960s. He was on Hubbard's ship, which he sailed around the world on to spread the movement's message. That one of the people who were part of it from the very beginning had put down roots in Karlskrona was huge. We all wanted to get into the closest circle around him, but only a few chosen ones were invited. Those who had come sufficiently far in their spiritual awareness, as they called it. Viktor was one of them."

She spoke quickly and stopped just as fast. She took the tray and held it out to Luke. The kimono slipped open and Luke caught a glimpse of her large, naked breasts.

"Take more," Anna said, then looked down and pretended to be surprised. She stood up without pulling her kimono closed. "Oops," she said, looking at Luke. "Hope it didn't ruin your appetite," she laughed. "Maybe you'd like to have some other bread, too? A grand pair of Danish buns? At least they're more like buns than dog's ears, don't you think?"

She roared with laughter at her imagery, set the tray on the table, and pulled her kimono closed. Luke took another sandwich, this one with a thick layer of liver paste and pickles on top.

"I think I'll do just fine with liver paste and pickles," he said. "Hope you're not offended."

"Oh, no, not a problem," Anna said. "I was just having a little craving. But we can take that up another time." She laughed again and sat down. "I've probably lived in Denmark a little too long. Where were we, anyway?"

Luke swallowed a bite and rinsed it down with a gulp of tea.

"You said there was an innermost circle, and that Viktor was in it," he said. "You also said you two worked for the movement. What did you do?"

"It was primarily about trying to get more members. We went into town and tried to recruit people, conducted simple courses that were free or cost next to nothing. In communication, effectivity, personal development, things like that."

"What was Viktor's role?"

Anna stopped and closed her eyes. She seemed to be searching for the memories.

"Hmm. He had done his street service...I think he held a number of courses, too, and he was a trained auditor, which was a sort of therapist. I think he led a lot of therapy, too."

"What was the therapy about?"

"Oh, it was a mix of traditional psychology and reincarnation theories," Anna answered. "It was about how you would become superhuman and gain supernatural qualities. Tempting and cleverly packaged. It was easy to lure naïve people in." She fell silent. Luke said nothing, waiting for her to continue.

Finally, he asked, "Is there anything in all of this that you think could make someone want to kill Viktor a full twenty years later? Did he have any enemies?"

"Viktor was well-liked by everyone," Anna said. "I have a hard time believing he was on the outs with anyone. Of course, it might have something to do with the innermost circle he was part of. But that feels like a long shot. It was so many years ago."

"What was it they were doing?"

"It was all very clandestine, so I don't really know. It was a sort of project. There was talk about it among those of us who weren't part of it. Everyone wanted to be included, and many people tried to prove they were capable of being included. But only a few were invited. I only know that everyone in that group was to move out to a village outside the city. A few had already, such as the Englishman and his girlfriend. I think the group surrounding them even built a house for them out there. Not everyone had the chance to move out there before the whole thing imploded."

"Imploded?"

"Yes. I'd left both Scientology and Karlskrona by that time. I'd been accepted to film school and moved to Stockholm. But I heard that a girl who was a member died from some illness, and that led to the rumor that their clandestine project spread here to Copenhagen where the Scientologists' European center is. One day, the Scientology police conducted a raid in Karlskrona and the whole thing was exposed. It was clearly something heretical, something that went against the policies of the movement. I know that some of those who were part of it had to clean the movement's facilities as punishment. The whole thing was swept under the rug. I'm glad I got out of it in one piece."

Anna fell silent again, took a sandwich, and sat there, deep in thought. Luke was also quiet.

"Oh, right," she said after a moment. "Something terrible happened in connection with this whole dissolution, too. One of the guys in the innermost circle committed suicide."

"In connection with the raid?"

"I think so. But I'm not sure. It was approximately the same time, anyway. I think. Ugh, I don't remember. And I don't know if it had to do with the raid or what's happening now. Just that it was one of them who killed himself. It was terrible, anyway."

"Do you remember his name?"

She took a sip of tea.

"Oh, what was his name, now?" she asked herself. "No, I'm not coming up with it, unfortunately. I have no recollection."

"Do you have contact today with any of the other members?" Luke asked.

"No not any of them. I haven't seen anyone at all over all these years."

"Do you remember the names of those who were in the innermost circle?"

Anna's forehead wrinkled.

"I got burned out three years ago after a couple of really stressful films," she said. "My memory isn't what it used to be now. I remember a few of them, though."

"Can you write down the names for me?"

"Of course," Anna said, getting up and taking a pad of paper and a pen from the beautiful old sideboard. She sat down again and immediately wrote two names.

"These two, Peter and Fredrik Ek, were brothers, and it was especially the younger one, Peter, who had some sort of leadership position."

She quickly wrote three more names.

"George Knightly was the Englishman, his girlfriend was Maria Palm. I've had contact with Maria, I'm remembering now."

She shook her head at herself.

"How could I forget that? Maria moved to Stockholm, studied law, and now works as a corporate lawyer. She was hired as a copyright attorney on one of the productions I worked with a few years ago. Talked to her just a little then."

She looked down at the paper and remembered one more name.

"Max Billing!" she said, triumphantly. "That name is so special. So of course I remember it."

Then she stuck the pen in her mouth and tried to remember more.

"Oh, I see their faces before me, but I have such a hard time with names," she said. "I only remember a couple of first names, Åke and Jenny. But there were more, at least two, maybe three more."

She wrote down Åke and Jenny on the paper, tore it off, and gave it to Luke.

Luke looked at the names but didn't recognize any of them, except one, although he wasn't sure where he first saw it: Max Billing.

"This Max Billing, what can you tell me about him?" he asked Anna.

"Well, what can I say," she said, slowly. "He was a few years older than me. He and Viktor were good friends, I think. But I don't remember any more than that."

Then Luke remembered where he saw the name. On Saturday, in a flight booking at Viktor's. The booking was lying on Viktor's office desk. Max Billing was going to go on the trip to Kaliningrad that Viktor was supposed to go on in two weeks.

When Luke left Anna Adams' apartment and stood down there on Brolæggerstræde again, he took out his phone. He cast a glance up at her window and saw her standing there. When she saw that he was looking, she opened her kimono a little, held her hand to her ear as if she were holding a phone, and smiled a wide smile. Luke smiled back, waved at her, and started walking towards Hovebanegården to take the train home.

He called directory assistance and quickly received the phone number for Max Billing. There was only one person with that name in the whole country, in Olofström in Blekinge province. Max Billing had two phone numbers, one private and one for his company, a security system company. Luke called both numbers but didn't get an answer. He left a message on both and asked Max to call him back. On the train, he googled Maria Palm, lawyer, and got a hit immediately. There was only one person with that name in Sweden who worked as a lawyer. She was a corporate lawyer at a large law firm in Stockholm. When the train stopped in Karlskrona, he picked up the phone, called the law office, and asked to be connected to Maria Palm.

"I'll put you through to Maria's secretary," the receptionist said, connecting the call. She answered quickly and told Luke that Maria was visiting a client, and that after that, she would be in a partners' meeting until seven o'clock.

"Would you be able to give me her cell number?" Luke asked.

"Are you one of Maria's clients?"

"No. But it's important."

"So it's private. Well, then I unfortunately can't give her your number," the secretary said. "But what I can do is to give her your number first thing tomorrow morning when I see her. Or you can try calling tomorrow at one o'clock. At that time, she'll have fifteen minutes before she goes to a meeting. That's the only opening she has tomorrow."

Luke said he would call at one o'clock the next day and ended the call. While he walked home, he tried calling Max Billing's two numbers again. Still no answer.

20.

"We are under attack."

George had gathered the whole group before him. This Sunday, there was an unusually large number of people who came to help build what would become George and Maria's house. Fifteen hot, sweaty Karlskrona Scientologists were now taking a much-needed break and stood before the main house, which was almost ready for move-in day.

It was a bright, sunny, hot Sunday, and Jenny longed for the swim in the sea that they always ended their workdays with. They worked all summer, digging, pouring, raising walls, hammering, and painting. George was no carpenter, but there were several in the group who were really talented. He and Maria bought a piece of land from a farmer who owned almost all of Trummenäs Udde, a neighborhood in the archipelago nine miles east of Karlskrona. The site was nicely detached from the golf course and the summer cottage area, on a cul-de-sac, hidden from sight with the help of a small woods.

Jenny stood sweaty and hot, hanging on Daniel. Next to Daniel stood Åsa, Daniel's sister who was also a Scientologist. Åsa was twenty-one years old, just a year and a half older than her brother. Daniel convinced her to take a communication course two months earlier. She completed it in record time and jumped in with both feet. She bought into the whole thing immediately. She signed the contract after two weeks, began working for the center, and was already working hard on auditing. Jenny was a little worried about how quickly Åsa got in so deeply, but Daniel reassured her. Åsa meant a lot to him. They were like twins, very close to each other, and Daniel had never seen his sister so enthusiastic and happy. She felt really depressed two years earlier and had tried to commit suicide. Scientology seemed to give her enormous energy and strength, and it was easy to see the difference in her.

Jenny was glad that she and Daniel had already moved out to Trummenäs. George encouraged some chosen ones in the group to move there, for two special reasons, one of which he would reveal at a later stage. The

93

other reason was that Scientology had powerful enemies, and they would become stronger if they formed a community in one location. George called their community the Trummenäs Headquarters.

Jenny and Daniel were the third couple in the group that moved out there. It was only George and Maria and Max and Camilla who had lived there a few weeks longer than them. Jenny knew that several of the others had feverishly tried to find houses or lots, but they were hard to find. There were a hundred permanent residences in Trummenäs, but surely three times as many summer cottages. Since the golf course had been built a few years earlier, the interest in moving there had increased considerably.

The house that she and Daniel rented cheaply lay approximately a half-mile from George and Maria's house and was amazingly sweet. A little, red, newly-renovated fishing cottage built at the turn of the century. It had low ceilings and only two rooms, but it met their needs. They had only lived there for three weeks, but she already felt settled in. Sure, it was probably easy enough to live there in the summer, she knew. It would be worse when winter came. The cottage lay on the western edge of Trummenäs Udde and was fully exposed to the ice-cold southwesterly winds from the Baltic Sea. But the house was winterized, so it would probably be fine.

"As you maybe know, one of our publics is displeased with her auditing," George continued. "She's gone to a lawyer who is demanding full repayment plus damages. If we don't pay, we'll be sued."

"Publics" was a Scientology term for people who didn't work for Scientology but paid for their courses and auditing.

George described the whole story for the group. The person who was threatening to sue was named Julia. She studied at the college in Växjö and had problems with her studies. She was at home in Karlskrona one weekend and came in by way of the personality test. Peter convinced her that Dianetics and auditing would make her more intelligent and increase her ability to concentrate and sold her auditing courses for five thousand dollars. Peter then went with Julia to the bank to help her get a loan for the auditing. The money would be used for leadership training, they told the loan officer. Julia borrowed the entire amount, five thousand, thanks to Peter.

Julia initially believed the auditing helped her. But when it finished nine months later, something happened. She broke off all contact with the Center, wasn't in touch for a couple of months, and they couldn't reach her.

And now there was a demand letter from a lawyer who wrote that Julia had been cheated, that she had in fact got worse, and, further, that all the time she'd spent on Scientology meant she was even more behind in her studies. The lawyer also wrote that Julia suffered from a less serious type of bipolar disorder, that she was treated for it three years earlier, and that the therapy Julia bought from the Church of Scientology worsened her condition. This was supported by Julia's psychiatrist, who performed an evaluation and attested that she'd become worse as a result of Scientology. A copy of the attestation was included in the letter. The lawyer demanded that the Church of Scientology pay back the money and also pay damages of ten thousand dollars to Julia. If that didn't happen, the lawyer would submit a formal suit.

George fell silent and looked out over the group, letting it all sink in. It was the first time Jenny heard George talk for so long and so seriously. She already knew most of what George said, but not the last bit with the lawyer. Julia and Jenny talked at length on a few occasions during the time when she was at the Center. She was incredibly positive in the beginning, but towards the end, she said to Jenny a few times that she didn't think anything was happening. But Jenny had no idea that it was this serious.

No one said anything. Everyone looked at George, who calmly picked up his pipe, stuffed it, and lit it.

"We've begun an internal investigation about what went wrong," he said. "Camilla, who was the one who audited Julia, is now declared to be a Liability. During the security check, she missed the fact that Julia had a history of psychological illness. And besides, her stats have been down for a long time, and as you see, she's not here today. She's been put into an ethics program in order to get out of her condition and in order to request entry back into the group. For three months, she will study three hours every evening and clean our facilities for two hours. She is not allowed to do anything but this."

Liability, Jenny thought. In the whole time she'd worked at the center, none of her coworkers had been placed so low on the twelve-stage ethics scale. She was placed in Emergency a few times after she ended up with poor sales statistics on the books. For a couple of weeks, she was at the top, in Power.

Now Peter spoke up.

"I've gone through the notes from the auditing. Julia is, quite obviously,

PTS. Her father lies behind all of this; he's clearly an SP, and I suggest that I go and see her to try to get her to understand this. I'd really like to take Jenny with me, because she and Julia were friends."

Jenny recently took a course that L Ron Hubbard put together about ethics questions and knew very well what this was about. A PTS, Potential Trouble Source, is a person who could be a problem for Scientology or for themselves because the person is under the influence of an SP, Suppressive Person, a psychopath. Jenny learned that 17.5 percent of humans were PTSs and 2.5 percent were SPs. Those people unlucky enough to have an SP near them grew stressed, make mistakes, became sick, or were vulnerable to injuries. If you had strong mood swings, it was a sure sign that you were a PTS. Such people could be lyrical over their auditing experience only to be totally down on it the next day, thinking they should demand their money back.

"That sounds like a good idea," George said. "What do you say to that, Jenny?"

Jenny wasn't at all happy about needing to do it. She didn't feel comfortable in such situations, and actually wanted someone more experienced to go with Peter. But there was no such thing as refusing orders, as the unwritten rules said, if you didn't have an exceptionally good reason.

"Not a problem," she said as a result. "Of course I'll come with."

They traveled to Växjö already the next day. Peter asked Jenny to call Julia and try to arrange a meeting without saying that Peter would also be there. It didn't feel good to lie, but Jenny couldn't resist Peter's argument.

"I know it feels wrong," he said. "But you have to think about why we're doing this. We're working to save humanity. She's under the influence of an SP, and as you know, they will stop at nothing to stop the good forces in the world. She can't see it herself, so it's up to us to help her."

After much hesitation, Julia said she would meet Jenny, and they agreed on a time on Monday evening, the day after the gathering at Trummenäs.

Julia was twenty-three years old, stocky, with thin, pale, mid-length hair. She was aghast when she opened the door of her student apartment in the Teleborg area of Växjö and saw Peter standing next to Jenny. She tried to close the door, but Peter stuck his foot in the way.

"Julia, we just want to talk to you," Peter said. "Communication is the solution to all problems. You know that."

Julia looked angrily at Jenny.

"You tricked me," she said, opening her door and going back into her apartment.

Jenny tucked her tail between her legs and padded in after Peter. Julia sat down on the sofa in the TV room and looked down at the glass table. Peter and Jenny each sat in an armchair.

They sat for two hours and talked. Or more accurately, Peter talked for two hours. Julia sat listlessly and barely answered his questions. Jenny didn't say anything, either. She was ashamed even though she knew that Peter was right.

Peter was able to tease out of Julia that it was indeed her father who stood behind the lawyer's demand letter and he helped Julia understand that she was fully capable in the eyes of the law and could make her own decisions about her life. She received a long lecture on SPs and PTSs and, when they left the apartment around eight o'clock, Peter had a letter stuffed in the inside pocket of his blazer. A letter signed by Julia, addressed to the lawyer, in which she asked him to rescind his demands. Peter sat next to Julia and dictated what she should write.

21.

Two seconds. That was all the time it took for Svärd to make his decision.
He realized that Annika's first reaction would be to run in to them to save
the children from him. It was possible that, on the way, she could call the
police, but he didn't think that she was that smart. He wanted to get her
into the building, and he had to unlock the front door before she got there.
He ran the ten yards to the door and looked out the glass window at the
same time as he unlocked the door. He couldn't see Annika yet. She was
probably on her way around the corner. He went quickly back to the nap
room, closed the door, and told the children to start putting on their clothes
and sit on the mattresses in the corner. Then he stood along the wall by
the door and waited. After ten seconds, he heard the front door open. He
got ready. The door to the nap room was thrown open and Annika stormed
in.

"What is it you're doing..."

She didn't have the chance to finish her sentence because Svärd hit her
from the side with a clenched fist straight to the temple. He hit hard and
the pain in his knuckles was immense when they met her temporal bone.
It felt like he broke something. She went unconscious immediately and fell
heavily onto the thick wall-to-wall carpet with a dull thud. The children
screamed and two girls started crying.

"You aren't nice," one of the boys said. "Why did you hit her?" Svärd
didn't answer. He positioned himself in front of Annika, took hold of her
arms at her armpits, and began pulling her towards the door.

"Now put on your clothes, sit on the mattress, and stay there until I come
back," Svärd said to the children.

He pulled Annika out of the room, closed the door with his foot, and continued dragging her through the corridor. When he arrived at the office,
she moaned. Svärd realized she was about to wake up and hurried to get
her into the room. He laid her on her back on the floor and closed the door.
When he turned around, he saw that she was awake, holding her right hand
to the place where he hit her. She looked at him with scared, confused eyes.
Svärd realized she didn't understand what was going on.

Before she could say anything, he straddled her, leaned forward, and took a tight hold on her neck with both hands, pressing with both thumbs on her windpipe as hard as he could. Annika panicked when she realized what he was doing. She tried to scream, but only a cawing sound came from her throat. She took hold of his gloved hands and tried to rip them away, but Svärd was too strong. She started to writhe and tried to kick him. She hit at his face, but Svärd moved his upper body and kept his grip around her neck with straight arms. Her eyes grew bloodshot, and after thirty seconds, Svärd felt her strength drain away. She stopped resisting. Svärd looked right into her eyes and watched as the life ran out of her. Her eyes became stiff and empty. He held his grip for a long time after he thought it was over.

Svärd stood up and went quickly out of the office. He took the key from the inside of the door and locked it because he didn't want the children to see Annika lying dead on the floor. He set the key on the hat shelf and went back into the nap room. The children were now sitting dressed and silent on the mattresses, just as he commanded. He took his camera and put it into his backpack.

"Now, children. Our little game is over," he said. "You can play by yourselves in the playroom until a grown-up comes."

It was twelve thirty when he left the preschool and started walking back to the hotel. Then came the reaction. His legs felt like jelly, and he caught himself breathing with short, tense breaths. Christ, how that all went to hell, he thought. I didn't need to kill her. I could have just run away from there. There were no traces of me left behind. Fuck, fuck, fuck. He swore silently to himself the whole way.

He regained some control of his knees when he arrived at the hotel. He put on his sunhat and sunglasses and went directly up to his room without looking towards the reception.

In the hotel room, he washed away the black dye in his hair and shaved off the beard. He took out the colored lenses, showered, and changed clothes. He put on his dress pants and a white Oxford. When he was done, he took out his camera and transferred the pictures to his laptop. He was very pleased with the results. The light from the one window in the nap room created a special mood in the images, a soft film that heightened the sensuality. He would probably be able to raise the price of them up to a hundred dollars each. If he were lucky, he could pile up fifteen hundred dollars or more already on his first round of sales.

He sat for two hours, chose pictures, cropped, fine-tuned colors, and made copies in black and white. Some buyers preferred black-and-white photos, and these photos turned out extra nicely without color. He put the pictures up in his gallery, sent an email to some of his most dedicated customers, and told them that there were high-quality items for sale. Then he took out his little medical bag, found the pipette, and filled it with a decent amount of Theralene. He placed the pipette in a glass pipe and stuck it into the inner pocket of his sports coat. He checked that his black computer bag contained all of the necessary items, put on his sportscoat, and walked to Hotel Amaranten. He had plenty of time, so he didn't sit in the bar immediately. He took a few magazines and settled into one of the armchairs in the lobby. He decided to sit in the bar at six thirty. If he was correct in his estimations, Maria Palm would come through the doors just after seven. He would make sure she ended up next to him.

She was like a clock. Seventeen minutes after seven, Maria Palm sat on one of the open stools along the bar. Svärd sat on the stool next to her and laid one of his newspapers on the stool she eventually occupied to indicate the spot was taken. He sat there watching the entrance, and when Maria Palm came walking towards the bar and saw that all of the places were taken, he quickly took the newspaper away and gave her a wide smile.

Svärd knew that she would order something to eat, so he made sure to, with a loud voice and a broad Småland dialect, order a Toast Skagen and a beer. He knew the dialect where he came from, Southern Småland, was quite similar to that of Blekinge and he took the chance that this would capture her interest. She ordered a Caesar salad and a glass of white wine. Then she turned towards him.

"That dialect sounds familiar."

She was taking the bait.

"The border between Småland and Blekinge," he said. "Are you from around there?"

"Karlskrona," she said.

"How fun," Svärd said. "That's where I live now."

He reached out his hand.

"Tord Gustafsson."

Maria took his hand and introduced herself.

"Where in Karlskrona do you live?" she asked.

"On Sturkö right now. I live alone in a small, renovated fortification."

Maria laughed.

"That sounds cool. What sort of fortification?"

"It sounds cooler than it is," Svärd answered. "It's an old military barracks that I rebuilt into a villa. It's a really great setting. Sixty yards from the sea."

"Oh, the sea," Maria said. "I miss that up here. There's the sea here, too, of course, but it's so much trickier to get to the hidden gems."

The female bartender served them the wine glass and beer.

"Cheers to Karlskrona," Svärd said, raising his glass and taking a large gulp.

"What are you doing up here in the big city in the middle of summer?" Maria asked.

"Work. I run an IT consulting business."

"Are there customers who want work done right in the middle of summer vacation?"

"Telecom operations run all day long, year round," Svärd said. "I tinker with security systems, and now one of our clients has run into some problems, so I have to jump in."

The food was set before them. Svärd ordered more beer, but he held back on the actual drinking. He needed a clear head. He asked Maria if she would like another glass of wine.

"No thank you, I have some left," she said. "I have to get up early for work tomorrow, so I have to be careful."

It'll have to be the drops, then, Svärd thought. He'd hoped to be able to get her good and drunk so he wouldn't have to wait for her to wake up from the drug but at this rate that could take several hours.

Svärd concentrated on keeping the conversation going. On getting her to relax, to trust him, so that she would stay until the bar filled with people. He wanted to get her to drink more so that he could find the opportunity to put the drops in. The risk was that she would suddenly get up to go home. He could probably work it all out then, too, but it would be much messier.

It turned out to be simple. Most people love talking about themselves. So too did Maria Palm. He only needed to pretend he was interested and ask questions. She told him about her childhood in Karlskrona, about how she hated the city for many years, but later changed her opinion of it. She had lived alone for many years, had a few short relationships, but was happiest alone. She had a summer house on one of the Greek islands. She would move there in a few years when she'd saved enough money that she wouldn't have to work any more. She had a grown daughter she was working on to get her to come with.

Svärd was able to get her to accept him ordering more wine for her. But after two hours, she'd only drunk three glasses. She began to get a little tipsy, but it wasn't enough.

"Now it's time for a really good drink," Svärd said, waving to the bartender before Maria could protest. He wanted to have a fruity drink to conceal any possible bitterness. Before she arrived, he studied the drink menu and found one that contained both melon and passionfruit juice, 7 Up and Bacardi Lemon. He ordered two of the drink, called the "Nemo."

"No, no," Maria said. "I can't drink any more now. I have an important client meeting tomorrow."

Svärd leaned forward towards her and tilted his head.

"Just one last drink, Maria," he said, pleadingly. "The Nemo is amazingly good. And it has almost no alcohol. I promise."

She sat still and looked at him. Svärd saw that she was more drunk than he'd thought at first.

"You're damn persuasive, Tord," she said, laying her hand on his arm. "It must be going well for your firm if you're the one in charge of sales. I'll have one just for a little taste."

Svärd realized that he needed to be careful with the solution now that she was a little drunk. She couldn't get too groggy or, worst case scenario, go unconscious. Then the bartender would probably react and maybe even call an ambulance. He excused himself and went to the bathroom, where he squeezed a few drops from the pipette and went back.

The drinks were now standing on the counter before them. Maria was sitting and talking to a man who'd come up to her. She was turned away from the counter. Perfect timing, Svärd thought. The bar was half-full of people who were talking, laughing and drinking. Completely occupied with each other. He sat on the bar stool, took out the pipette, and held it hidden in the palm of his hand. Maria was still turned away, talking with the man. He took one of the drinks as if he were going to drink from it. He relaxed it down towards his knee and emptied the drug into the drink. He quickly stirred the contents with the pipette and set the glass back on the bar. Maria turned around and was about to fall off the stool. Svärd caught her by the arm. She laughed, took his hand, and sat on the stool again.

"Oooops! Thank you, my knight in shining armor. I wondered where you'd gone off to." Svärd raised his drink.

"Cheers to a fantastically interesting evening, Maria!"

"It isn't that you're trying to get me really drunk in hopes that I'll ask you to come home with me, is it?" she asked with a little smile playing at the corners of her mouth. She took the other glass and let it meet Svärd's glass with a little clink.

If you only knew, Svärd thought. I'm going to drag you home, and after you've drunk the last of this, you'll never drink anything again.

22.

The mirror in the hall hung low. Luke couldn't see his whole body in it. He got a hammer from the kitchen closet, took down the mirror, and put the nail in eight inches higher. He stood there with the hammer in his hand and looked at himself in the new suit. It was like meeting someone he'd never seen before. The only thing he recognized was his face. The face he had now. There was a big difference from his previous faces, which he'd worked so hard to get as far away from as possible in the eighteen years that had passed since he left New York. Now they were closer than they'd been in a long time.

He was nervous, and he got ready far ahead of time, starting at eight o'clock in the morning, three hours before the funeral began at eleven. He'd picked up the suit at Hogland's Men's Outfitters when he came back from Copenhagen.

Luke brushed away a thread stuck to one knee. He felt uneasy. He took the two red roses he bought on the square out of the vase on the sink. He couldn't find anything to wrap them in, so he decided to hold them in his hand just as they were. He walked straight down the hall by the athletic arena, walking slowly so he wouldn't get sweaty. A few young boys around ten years old, wearing shorts and team jerseys, jumped out of a Chrysler Voyager behind the arena and ran happily towards the entrance, their floorball clubs in their hands. The sun blazed mercilessly, and the seagull cries mixed with the sound of the few cars that passed by the Scandic hotel. He turned off towards the old stone shipyard wall and followed it.

The closer he came to Admiralty Church, the slower he walked. He knew that the next two hours would be tough. He had a hard time with grief. A hard time with crying in general. Amanda often complained about that, saying he was emotionless and lacked empathy. This time Luke thought it would be different.

When he turned off towards the church from Vallgatan, he saw there were already cars parked outside. Some people in dress clothes were on their way up the stairs towards the entrance. He knew that Viktor had many acquaintances in town and that Therese had a large family. At the entrance to the church stood Andreas, the young priest of the Admiralty congregation. Luke had had a conversation with him the previous day. He seemed good. Not overly ceremonious. Andreas greeted Luke and went into the church ahead of him to show him where to sit. Luke picked up a psalm book, walked the fifty steps to the aisle, and turned off a few steps to the left. He stopped when he saw the white caskets. One big and one small, next to each other. A large flower arrangement lay on the big casket, a small one on the little casket. Around the caskets lay piles of wreaths and flowers and lit candles. The scene hit him full force. In those coffins lay Viktor and, next to him, sweet little Agnes. Luke clenched his jaw so hard it hurt. He kept his gaze on the caskets and took the last steps to the spot Andreas showed him, in the very front.

He sat down and after a moment, he heard a woman's screams. He turned around and saw Therese, in a black dress and sunglasses, being led in by her brother and her father. She'd seen the caskets and was whimpering and screaming in turns. Luke stood up. Therese needed to be almost carried to the pew where Luke was standing. When she saw Luke, she threw herself into his arms.

"Oh, Luke, how can I go on living?"

Luke didn't say anything; he just held her. Her brother and father took Therese and sat her down on the pew next to Luke. The church filled with more and more people. Luke was surprised at how many there were. He knew many of Viktor's friends from his childhood were there. He didn't recognize a lot of them.

The ceremony was beautiful. Luke and Therese's father decided that it would begin with Eric Clapton's "Tears in Heaven." Many eyes filled with tears when Clapton came to the refrain. Then, one of Viktor's favorite songs was played: "The Sky is an Innocent Blue" with Ted Gärdestad; and for Agnes, there was a song from the Brothers Lionheart.

The ceremony took an hour, and afterwards, Therese was to be the first to go up and say goodbye. She was supposed to go alone but asked Luke to go with her because she knew she wouldn't be able to manage by herself. Therese laid her flowers on the caskets, sobbed, and hung onto Luke, who lay down his roses. One for Agnes, and one for Viktor. Then Luke led Therese behind the caskets so they could greet everyone who came forward to say a last farewell to Viktor and Agnes. Therese was calm throughout the ceremony, but now she couldn't keep it together. She cried and screamed in turns, and Luke held her so she would stay upright.

When the funeral was over, Luke left the church quickly and walked down the steps to the Rosenbom Statue, which stood there with its outstretched hand. He waited while the church emptied of funeral guests. They began walking towards the parish hall at Stortorget, where lunch would be served. When the last guests left the church, Luke was still standing there, alone. He took out his phone and called Max Billing. No answer now, either. He found the home phone number. A woman answered on the first ring. Max' wife. She sounded a little upset. Luke introduced himself and wondered if Max were home.

"I'm also wondering where he is," Hanna Billing said. "He didn't come home yesterday after work, and he's not answering his telephone. I'm beginning to get really worried. It's not at all like him."

"Are you one of his clients?" she asked before Luke had the chance to say anything.

"Maybe," Luke said. "I'd like to get some prices from him."

"I don't understand what's happened," Hanna Billing continued. "I talked with him yesterday afternoon, and he was on his way to his last client of the day. Then he was going to come home."

"Has it ever happened before that he disappeared without being in touch?" Luke asked.

"No," she answered. "Never."

"Have you contacted the police?" Luke asked.

"No. Not yet."

"I think it would be a good idea for you to call them."

"What do you think could have happened?" she asked.

Luke heard how her voice trembled slightly. He hesitated for a few seconds, fearing the worst. But he didn't want to scare her. Besides, it was too early to draw any such conclusions.

"I have no idea, and there's no guarantee anything at all has happened. Not even a full day has passed, and he could turn up at any moment. But just to be sure, I think it's a good idea to make the police aware."

"I'll call them immediately after we hang up," she said.

Luke sat still with his phone in his hand after he hung up. If it happened that Viktor's and Agnes' death had anything to do with what Viktor and Max were up to, Max Billing might be in grave danger. Maybe it was already too late. He wondered if he should head off to Olofström, but he quickly crossed that option out. Hanna Billing would call the police, and they should have a much larger chance of finding Max than he would. Instead, he decided to focus on the lawyer in Stockholm.

Luke dropped his phone into the inner pocket of his sportscoat and began following the other funeral guests. When he passed Admiralty Park, he cast a glance up at the clocktower. There was an hour left before he was to call Maria Palm.

The lunch was, in some strange way, pleasant and warm. It was as if the heavy blanket of grief that hung over the funeral ceremony was left behind in the church. Many of Viktor's childhood friends sat and reminisced. Some stood spontaneously and told hilarious stories from Viktor's life. Luke made sure to talk with a few who seemed to have been close friends in an attempt to find out more about Viktor and Scientology. But none of those who were there had been members, even if they knew that Viktor was in the cult.

When it was five minutes to one, Luke got up and went down to the first floor, taking a seat in one of the armchairs. At exactly one o'clock, he called.

"Maria never came to the office today," Maria Palm's secretary said. "As I said to you yesterday, she was fully booked today with both client meetings and internal meetings. Never, in my ten years as her secretary, has she missed a single meeting. And I can't contact her. She always answers. Even if she's sitting in a meeting, she answers with a text."

"She doesn't have any family who might know where she is?"

"Maria lives alone. She has a daughter who's just over twenty years old, Diana, but she doesn't live at home."

"Where does Maria live?"

"I don't have permission to give out the home addresses of our lawyers, unfortunately," the secretary said.

"Can you make an exception this time? I believe that Maria could be in grave danger. I can't get into why, but I really need to know where she lives."

"In danger? In what way?" the secretary asked.

"Can you at least tell me what part of the city she lives in?" Luke asked. He knew there were twenty-five Maria Palms in Stockholm.

"Kungsholmen," the receptionist said. "But shouldn't we call the police? If she's in serious danger?"

Luke said she could do what she wanted, but that the police probably wouldn't do anything because Maria had only been missing for a day. He thanked her for the conversation and quickly searched for the home address on the Eniro website. There was only one person named Maria Palm in Kungsholmen.

Two of the nine people on the list he got from Anna Adams were missing. He hoped it was a coincidence, but his gut instincts told him something different. He decided to book a refundable ticket to Stockholm on the evening flight, and if he didn't get hold of Maria Palm within the next few hours, he would go there in person.

23.

"How do your bank accounts look? Do you have fifteen thousand in them?"

The questions came in English, and Jenny looked in astonishment at the woman who asked them. Her name was Jane. She was an American and returned the look with expressionless eyes. She couldn't have been more than thirty years old, with mid-length black hair, heavy makeup, and an attractive, sharp gaze. She was serious. It felt unpleasant. She shifted her gaze to the woman's colleague, an Italian named Pier. A mustachioed, thin-haired man around thirty-five who sat next to her behind the small desk that stood in a gloomy room somewhere in the AOSH EU's large facility in central Copenhagen. Jenny was there to attend her first auditors' training session. AOSH stood for Advanced Organization & Saint Hill Europe, and was the European center for advanced training within Scientology.

Pier spoke terrible English. That's why Jane was the one driving the sales pitch. Both of them took off their uniform jackets and hung them on the backs of the chairs. Now they sat across from Jenny in their white shirts and black ties, bands on their shoulders with three yellow stripes and one star. On their chests was a fabric emblem with two golden branches, crossed at the bottom, and a star between them. They were from the legendary Sea Org. L Ron Hubbard was a naval officer during the Second World War, and he created Sea Org in the late 1960s. It was an elite organization, a sort of paramilitary force within the movement. Members signed contracts for a billion years and had to work 24-7.

One hour earlier, her course leader of the auditors' training told her Sea Org wanted to talk to her and asked her to come to the front desk. From there, she was brought to this room. Jane and Pier wanted to sell her OT I, OT II, and OT III, and they were offering her the whole package for fifteen thousand dollars. It actually cost twenty thousand, she was told.

"What bank do you use?" Jane asked.

"Um, Associated Bank," Jenny answered, after some hesitation.

"How many accounts do you have there?"

Jenny cleared her throat.

"I don't know if I want to say. Why do you want to know that?"

"Jenny, Jenny, Jenny. We know you know what Scientology is about. You know the game. We don't need to sketch out the whole story for you. You know."

Jane talked quickly and enthusiastically. She gesticulated with both arms when she spoke, and she leaned forward towards Jenny, rising out of her chair. The tone was almost patronizing, accusatory, and every time she said "you," she pointed at Jenny with her whole hand. Jenny felt as if she were pointing a pistol at her and got tongue-tied. Pier interrupted. He looked down at a paper lying in front of him.

"You've been a Scientologist for nine months, Jenny. And quickly took a big step on the bridge. You became Clear a month ago?"

He looked up at Jenny, who nodded, glad to have a break from Jane's attack.

"Do you want more people to become Clear?" Pier continued.

"Of course."

"Why?"

"Because engrams and the reactive mind in people is the cause of all misery, war, and disease," Jenny answered.

She knew where Pier was going with his questions. She'd sat in Pier's chair herself and sold Scientology to "wogs" at home in Karlskrona using the same technique. "Wog" was a British acronym for "well and orderly gentleman" and was an expression L Ron Hubbard began using when he was active in England in the 1960s, and that had been used since then within Scientology as a degrading term for people outside the movement.

"Good," Pier said, smiling widely. "Is there anything that is more important than getting more people up on the bridge?"

Jenny knew she was doomed to lose this discussion.

"Of course not," she said, looking at the clock. "It was really nice to meet you, but I should probably go back to class now. I only have limited time to be down here in Copenhagen, and I have to make the most of it." She stood up from the chair to leave the room. Jane leaned forward and put her hand on Jenny's shoulder, pushing her back down into the chair again.

"It's okay, Jenny," she said with a smile. "We've talked with your course leader and we're allowed to borrow you for a few hours. You'll get the time you need to complete the course."

Jenny sank down into the chair again. She felt like a prisoner. Like a guilty criminal in an interrogation with two police officers.

"We need people like you, Jenny," Jane continued. "This planet needs people like you. Scientology is no game. It's damn serious. This is about your children. About their survival. Do you want to leave them a world that's full of wars and a bunch of reactive people? Don't you want to be able to look them in the eyes and say that you were there and did everything you could? Don't you want that, Jenny?"

"Yes, of course," she said, sitting up in the chair. She plucked up her courage. Felt indignant. "I do a whole lot. I've signed a two-and-a-half-year contract to the Karlskrona Church, and I work evenings and weekends. I study during the hours I'm allowed to study, and I've got the hang of auditing already. I became Clear quicker than many others. It doesn't feel right to be accused of not doing anything."

Pier smiled.

"We haven't said you're not doing anything, Jenny. What you've achieved thus far is really good. But don't you think it's possible to do even more?"

"Of course."

"And if it's possible to do more, why not do it?" Pier asked. "What's the problem?"

"It's a lot of money," Jenny said.

Now Jane broke in.

"Money is only matter. And everything that's matter, we can affect. Especially if you're OT. Then you'll be able to make sure you have lots of money. Your abilities will increase manifold. You know that, right?"

Jenny was forced to nod.

"Good," Jane said. "If we're going to make the planet Clear, as many of us as possible have to become OTs. We have to increase our tempo, Jenny. The world is threatened. Scientology is threatened. We have many powerful enemies. Evil forces want to destroy us. And we need to have people with OT abilities in order to be able to conquer our enemies and make people free from their reactive minds. We need you, Jenny. And we need you as an OT. Do you want to become OT, Jenny?"

Jenny nodded again. It was no lie. She and Daniel talked about it, that they both wanted to go up the bridge as quickly as possible and become OTs. But they decided that they would wait until they saved all the money. They wanted to do the levels together, but Daniel wasn't Clear yet.

"So, Jenny," Jane continued, in a softer tone. "How are your bank accounts? Could you get together the fifteen thousand? Do you have that kind of money?"

"I have half in a savings account," Jenny answered. "Money that my parents saved for me."

"Good," Jane said, sitting down on the chair. "We're halfway there. Who could you borrow the rest from? Do you have anyone close to you that you think you could borrow the money from?"

Jenny sat quietly, thinking. She knew that her grandma said several times that if she ended up in a tight spot and needed to borrow money, she should come to her. She had plenty of money left since grandpa died. His life insurance policy left her with tens of thousands.

"Maybe my grandmother would be willing to consider lending it to me," Jenny finally said.

Jane immediately picked up the phone on the desk and pushed the country code for Sweden. She handed Jenny the receiver.

"Call her."

"Now?"

"Yes. Why not?"

Jenny couldn't help but be impressed by their sales technique. She didn't have any chance to avoid it. The deal would be sealed here and now. If they waited, their target could change her mind.

Jane stretched the receiver out even closer to Jenny.

"Jenny. It's a tough world we live in, and only the tigers will survive. And even they will have a hard time of it. A tiger doesn't just sit there waiting for food to come to it. Call now."

Jenny took the phone and punched in her grandmother's phone number. She was home, and she was happy to hear that it was her granddaughter. Jenny asked her grandma if she could loan her seventy-five hundred. She needed it for a course she really wanted to take, she said. Her grandmother said yes immediately. Jenny looked at Jane and nodded. Jane wrote something quickly on a piece of paper and slid the paper over. Jenny read, "Ask her to call the bank immediately so they can transfer the money to your account."

Jenny did as Jane said, and the kind grandmother came through. Jenny called her after ten minutes and was told that everything went well and the money was now in her account. Jenny transferred over fifteen thousand dollars to AOSH EU and twenty minutes later, Jane and Pier gave her a receipt as proof that she'd purchased the OT auditing up to Level III and released her.

Jenny felt like she'd been hit by a bus when she closed the door and went down the long hallway to the course classroom. She hoped Grandma wouldn't say anything to her father about all of this. If he found out, it would all go to Hell in a handbasket.

24.

The plane to Stockholm would leave at a quarter to seven. Luke was still sitting in the parish hall, in an armchair in the hall. The guests had left. There was clattering from the kitchen on the second floor where the staff was cleaning up after lunch.

He tried to reach Maria Palm a few times, to no avail. Now he was sitting with his phone in his hand, wondering if he should call Anders Loman and tell him about the list of names and that two of the people on the list were now missing. He hesitated. Loman wouldn't be happy to hear that Luke had continued to root around in things having to do with Viktor's death. Luke decided he needed to have more of substance before bringing it to him. Besides, there could be a natural explanation to why both Max Billing and Maria Palm were missing. Maria had, furthermore, only been gone from work for just over a morning.

When he got up to head home and change clothes before his trip to Stockholm, his phone rang. It was Jonna Gustafson from the police. She just wanted to tell him that she talked to his alibi and the information checked out. Luke thanked her and asked, "Where are you right now?" He thought he should probably talk to her about the list and about the two missing persons.

"At the station," Jonna answered. "But I'm on my way to Viktor Spandel's apartment with the technicians' photos to see just how nosy you were the other evening."

"Would we be able to meet there in ten minutes? I have some information relating to Viktor that I think you might find interesting."

"You have no lack of nerve," Jonna answered. "How would it look if I let a person who's suspected of having broken into a prohibited apartment come into that same prohibited apartment again?"

"We don't have to see each other there."

Jonna was silent for two seconds.

"Why the hurry? Can't we talk about it later?"

"I'm heading to Stockholm this afternoon," Luke said. "I promise you want to hear what I have to say."

"Okay. I'll see you at the apartment," she said. "But only if you also promise to keep your fingers away from the gadgets in the apartment. I'll wait for you outside."

It only took Luke five minutes to get from the parish hall to Viktor's apartment. A few minutes later, Jonna arrived in an unmarked police car and parked outside.

"You didn't need to get so gussied up just to see me," Jonna said as she approached Luke.

"I just came from the funeral," Luke said.

"Of course. That was today. Sorry. Stupid of me to joke around."

"It's okay."

They went together up to the apartment, which looked exactly the same as when Luke was there on Saturday evening. They went into the living room and sat in armchairs. Luke told her about Björn Lööf, Anna Adams, about the list of Scientologists and that both Max Billing and Maria Palm were missing—Max for 24 hours and Maria since that morning.

"How are things with the other seven?" Jonna asked.

"I haven't had the chance to check up on them yet. It's going to take a little more time because they have fairly normal names. I was hoping you could put some resources on it and check it out."

"Honestly, it feels like a long shot," Jonna said. "There could be a completely natural explanation that those two are gone. One of them only for a morning, besides. We'll probably have to wait before we do anything. I can't put an investigation in motion on such unstable grounds."

Luke stood up from the armchair and walked to the bookshelf. Jonna turned around and followed him with her gaze.

"I hope you're not thinking of touching anything," she said.

"Come and look," he said.

Jonna got up and went over to him. He stood leaning over, pointing at some books.

"Three Scientology books," he said. "*Dianetics, The Fundamentals of Thought*, and *A New Slant on Life*. It says 'Church of Scientology' under the titles of the spines of all three."

"And?"

Luke stood up straight and looked at her.

"Björn told me that Viktor burned all of his Scientology books in a bonfire a year or so after he quit. The local newspaper wrote about it and it ended up on the front page the next day."

"How can you be sure that he burned every last one? Or that he didn't buy new ones at some later point?"

"I can't," Luke answered. "But I've gone through his bookshelf tons of times. Books were an interest we had in common, and I've never seen these before."

"So you mean that someone else put them there? Why would they do that?"

"Someone who wanted Viktor's death to look like a suicide," Luke answered. "To make it look as if he still believed in Scientology, and explaining that quote about reincarnation."

He turned around and looked at Jonna. She held a folder and dug around in a pile of photos. She picked one of them out and studied it carefully. She handed it to Luke.

"Check it out. This is a picture of the bookshelf that one of the technicians took the same evening when Viktor and Agnes were found. It was taken a little too far away for you to be able to see properly. But the yellow book is definitely there."

Luke took the photo and looked. He shifted his gaze to the bookshelf to see where the three books were placed. Looked down again. It was clear that the book called *Dianetics* was on the bookshelf the previous Monday.

"That doesn't really prove anything," he said, handing back the picture. "The person who murdered them obviously put the books there the same evening. They weren't there before."

Jonna shook her head.

"You are one of the most stubborn people I've ever met," she said. "I think you're going to have to accept what happened and move on with your life."

Luke looked at the clock. Three hours left until the flight to Stockholm would depart. He thanked Jonna and went home to Björkholmen. On the way home, he tried calling Maria Palm again. Still no answer. He also called her secretary, who also still hadn't heard anything from her. Once home, he changed clothes and packed a quick overnight bag. By five-thirty, he was sitting on the airport bus heading towards the airport in Ronneby.

25.

The hallway smelled heavily of mildew and dust. It was on the third of five floors in the AOSH EU building at Jernbanegade 6 in central Copenhagen. On the dark green wall-to-wall carpet that covered the floor in the hallway, twelve people walked silently. Jenny was one of them. Ten of them were course participants, just like Jenny. At the front walked an Italian woman who gathered them from the front desk.

The atmosphere was tense and anticipatory. It felt ceremonious. Jenny talked for a moment with a man from Holland as they stood waiting for someone to come and get them. His name was Frank; he was thirty-four years old, self-employed, and had been a Scientologist for almost fifteen years. Frank said it was his first time at AOSH EU and also his first time in Copenhagen.

It was a broad mixture of people who were to begin OT III today. The youngest looked around twenty years old, and the oldest was a woman around seventy-five from Germany. Frank nodded towards a man well into his forties who was standing and talking to one of the women; he told Jenny the man was a Sociology professor from the Sapenzia University of Rome. The woman with whom the professor was talking was a dentist in Berlin. A fat, middle-aged man who was standing by himself owned a large grocery store chain in Belgium.

The last eight months had been turbulent and eventful for Jenny and Daniel. They'd completely abandoned their favorite activity, watching movies. Instead, they spent evenings and weekend either at the Scientology Center, on the streets of downtown Karlskrona trying to get Karlskronites to take personality tests, or in residential areas of single-family homes or apartment buildings, knocking on doors and selling Scientology books. They and several others in the group moved to a pretty little town called Trummenäs out by the coast, where they rented a winterized summer cottage. George and Maria bought a property there and were happy to see others move close by.

Jenny was in Copenhagen a lot in recent months. She took several courses and lived there for both longer and shorter periods. Like the other Karlskrona Scientologists who took higher-level courses there, she stayed with a Scientologist friend of George's, Ditte Nielsen. She owned a large house in Herlev, a suburb of Copenhagen. There were always two rooms available for everyone from Karlskrona who came down for auditing or courses. You came and went as you wanted, and you could also help yourself to food from Ditte's fridge when you were hungry. George gave Ditte auditing as payment. Most other Scientologists who were in Copenhagen to participate in the services of AOSH EU had to rent rooms at the shabby Hotel Nordland, a hotel owned by the Church of Scientology, also known as the "German hotel" because the Nazis used it during the occupation in the Second World War.

Jenny first went through security checks to ensure she was ready to go through OT III. The checks consisted of a ton of questions on a list that Jenny had to answer while connected to an e-meter. It was a standard protocol that all pre-OTs had to go through. She was approved quickly, and now she was ready for one of the most important steps in her life. The excitement coursed through her body as she walked through the hallway. She knew that George, Peter, and the other leaders at the Center at home believed in both her and Daniel. They pushed them to go through the courses and auditing quickly, and she was more energetic than Daniel, advancing in record time. Daniel was still struggling with his auditing to Clear, but even he was moving forward quickly.

The Italian woman stood before one of the doors in the hallway and knocked loudly. A short older man unlocked the door and welcomed them into the heavily-guarded classroom. There were alarms and security cameras in the ceiling. An iron bar was used to barricade the door to the room. All of the course materials were locked in a steel cabinet to which only course leaders had the key. Participants were led to their places. There was a copy of Webster's Dictionary, a notebook, and pens at every spot. L Ron Hubbard emphasized the importance of understanding the words that describe a subject, and everyone who took courses was forced to learn his study methods, which Jenny found great use for and pleasure in. Now she thought it was fun to study, in contrast to when she was in regular school. There, she made it through by pure force of will.

It was so quiet in the room, you could hear a pin drop as the older man passed out the course materials. Jenny was moved. Finally, she would become what all Scientologists wanted to become—an Operating Thetan. Gain almost supernatural abilities, able to control her surroundings one hundred percent, and become a person who gained maximum success in life. She went through OT I and OT II quickly and painlessly even though she was disappointed in the course content. OT I consisted of thirteen exercises that were all based on going around town, observing people and things from various perspectives. You decided for yourself when you were done with the exercises. It was fun to do, she thought, but it didn't seem to really give any results. It felt good to be completely present, but that was it. OT II was more comprehensive and consisted of both studies and auditing, self-auditing. Jenny sat alone in a private room with her e-meter and went through the commands, asked herself questions, looked at the needle, and when it no longer gave a result, she checked off the point.

She kept at this auditing process for two months before she finished and was approved. She didn't think she felt anything special, no great change during these first two levels. But she thought maybe it was a slow transformation she was going through and that maybe that's why her progress wasn't so obvious.

The big thing, though, was OT III, which was also called the Wall of Fire. It was the most talked-about level of all and was, if possible, even more top-secret than the others. Not many Scientology members reached it. In Karlskrona, it was only George, Peter, Fredrik, and Maria so far. George made it furthest of all, he was at OT VI. Jenny felt privileged and proud that she was sitting there now, ready to sink her teeth into the most secret information there was within the church.

The older man went through roll call, and then Jenny reverently opened her course binder and began reading. The binder was luxurious. OT III was engraved in gold on the front. It turned out to contain photocopies of Hubbard's handwritten documents. It felt unbelievably big. She sat there looking at words Ron sat down, pen in hand, and wrote himself.

Jenny read the first document, which explained what everything was about. After that, time just disappeared. Only after three hours did she look up. She was completely enthralled by what she read. Hubbard told an extraordinary story. It played out seventy-five million years ago. The main character was an evil ruler named Xenu, who ruled over seventy-six planets. These planets were overpopulated, and Xenu solved that problem by freezing billions of people, putting them in large airplanes and flying them to a planet on the outer edge of the Universe – Earth. There, people were left in volcanoes into which hydrogen bombs were then dropped. When the bombs exploded, the thetans left their bodies and were clumped together in clusters of up to a dozen. This was followed by what Hubbard described as the mass implantation of thetans. An implantation was a sort of image or idea that was planted in the thetans' minds, and Jenny laughed at one point while she was reading this stuff. L Ron Hubbard claimed that Jesus hadn't existed. He was just the result of one such implantation that was placed in our minds here on Earth.

These clusters of thetans, with their minds scrambled by implantations, were then placed in human bodies and have, ever since, created huge problems for people. All of mankind's ills, in fact, were caused by these implantations, Hubbard said. But he had the solution: at OT III, they would be driven out.

Jenny sat up in the chair and leaned against the backrest. She looked around the classroom. The other participants sat deeply engrossed in the same document that she just read through. Frank, the Scientologist from Holland, looked up and met Jenny's gaze. He smiled and gave her a thumbs up. Jenny smiled back and bent over the document again. She thought about what she just read. It sounded unbelievable. Seventy-five million years ago. Seventy-six planets. Xenu. Like something taken from a bad science fiction novel, a genre Jenny wasn't such a huge fan of. And all of this about implanting. She remembered a discussion with Peter about different sorts of phobias people can have. Fear of snakes was one. With a grin, Peter said there might be an explanation in the Scientology timeline about why many people have an inexplicable feeling of discomfort when they see a snake. This explanation was that it was implanted by Xenu. Interesting thought.

She looked around the room again. Everyone studying with great devotion. No one seemed to be questioning anything at all. Every one of them sat deeply immersed, concentrating with their noses in the binders. Everyone here is buying it, Jenny thought. Even the sociology professor.

After the theoretical class, it was time for an auditing session that was supposed to be conducted alone with an e-meter in a room, just like at the OT II level. Now the body thetans would be driven out. The first session was a catastrophe. She had a splitting headache that was concentrated in her temples. Clearly, the questions she asked herself brought forces within her back to life. She tried to manage it herself with renewed questions, but she couldn't get the pain to subside. Finally, she was forced to pull the plug and contact the course leader, who immediately fetched a highly trained auditor to take care of it.

The auditor was an Australian named Mark who said that Jenny had awoken the demons, that the headaches were because of that, and he immediately began the reparations auditing. Mark was deft, and after only a couple of hours, the headache subsided. In six more hours, he audited all of them, one after one, and Jenny felt like she was forty pounds lighter. When she left the auditing room that evening, it felt like she was walking on a cloud. Completely present in the moment, her sensations were ten times stronger, her vision, her hearing, her sense of smell. She felt strong and happy, and now she was ready to get back to the solo auditing again.

26.

The door was locked. Luke swore silently. He took a step back and looked up at the façade of the beautiful old turn-of-the-century building on Kungsholmsgatan 24 in Stockholm. It was eight thirty in the evening. Seven and a half hours after he decided to try to get hold of Maria Palm, he was standing outside her home.

Luke looked to the left down the sidewalk in the quiet hope that someone who lived there would come back after having been out on some errand. A stream of people passed him, and he thought appreciatively of the calm tempo in Karlskrona. Despite that it was evening and darkness began to fall, it was warm out.

He stepped forward and stood by the door. He leaned against the wall and waited. After a few minutes, an older couple came from inside the building. They were both very frail and shuffled forward. The man held the door open for his wife. Luke took hold of it and held it so they could both come out. The man thanked him and the pair turned off to the left towards the hotel. Luke slipped in quickly and looked at the name plates that sat right inside the door. He found Maria immediately. She lived on the top floor, the fourth. He decided to take the stairs.

The stairwell was the most luxurious he had ever seen. The marble images on the walls and on the floor, a gigantic crystal chandelier in the ceiling, two large stone vases that stood on pillars on either side of the beautiful stone steps, green plants in the window niches. He had a flash-back to the last time he went up the stairs of an apartment building looking for someone who was missing. His pulse increased as he went up the stairs with quick steps. The rising heart rate wasn't only from the physical effort.

He reached the top landing and stopped with one foot on the top step. The marble floor looked like a chess board with black and white painted squared. There were two apartments off of the landing. Two large, beautiful, grey wooden doors next to each other.

Luke stood still for a moment to catch his breath. The elevator started moving with a low screech. He was struck by how quiet it was. Must be a well-insulated building, he thought, walking to the door that said "Maria

Palm." He pressed the doorbell but didn't hear anything. He pressed his ear to the door. The hairs on his arm stood on end. He heard music.

Jazz.

He knew the song.

27.

Jenny put her finger on the dirty yellow doorbell and pressed twice, quickly. The light in the stairwell turned off again and she took two quick steps to the red button and turned it on. She heard how someone rattled a security chain behind the door and simultaneously mumbled something. Then the door opened, but only an inch. It looked like an older man in pajamas. Hair streaked with grey, large, bushy eyebrows over a pair of large-rimmed black glasses. Jenny leaned forward and a stale, sour smell reached her nostrils; she carefully pulled her head back. She held up the book and smiled. She knew the man wouldn't be buying any books and decided to forget her whole sales pitch and just get straight to the point.

"Hi! I'm from the Church of Scientology, and I'm wondering if you might like to buy this book? It's about what you can do to feel a little better, stuff like that."

The man mumbled something unintelligible and closed the door. Jenny stuffed the book into her bag, went down the last flight of stairs to the front door and went out into the large yard, which was enclosed by a dozen yellow apartment buildings. It was Monday evening, the first evening of the new sales week, and she had sold three books. It took three hours and she rang the doorbells of over a hundred doors. Three books the first evening wasn't bad. On a Monday, besides. Things usually went better later in the week, when people were in a better mood.

Now she was done with Kungsmarken anyway, the most notorious of rental districts in Karlskrona, where there were a lot of Swedes but primarily people and families from other countries. The three books were all purchased by immigrants. Tomorrow she would head to Mariedal, an area bordering Kungsmarken that consisted mostly of single-family homes. It wasn't so easy to peddle there, either, she thought. It wasn't the most fashionable residential area of Karlskrona, but at least it was people who could afford to live in houses. Jenny hoped she would reach her weekly goal of twenty books on Friday evening so that she wouldn't have to work at it over the weekend. She decided she would start already in the afternoon because many people came home from work early on Fridays.

She unlocked her bike, put on her mittens, and pulled up the zipper of her winter jacket. It was cold, and the wind was blowing from the southwest. It would be freezing cold when she passed the Sunna canal. She looked at her watch as she got on her bike. Seven thirty. In a half-hour, everyone would be gathered in the basement room. George announced that he would be revealing to the whole inner circle the most important reason for creating the Trummenäs Headquarters. She rode quickly, filled with excitement about getting there. She didn't even feel the cold. It was only the specially chosen ones who were called, and it felt really good that she and Daniel were among them. Daniel came home from Copenhagen earlier than planned. He became Clear a month ago, and now he was down there taking preparatory OT courses. Åsa wasn't one of the chosen few, unfortunately. Daniel and Jenny talked with Peter about it, but Peter thought she was unstable and had a whole lot of auditing left before she would be ready to be invited in.

"But if she continues showing the dedication she has shown thus far, it won't be long before she's included," he said.

It was a tough winter, both living out at Trummenäs and with work for the church, even though it was also fun. It simply wasn't easy to live so far out from the city. It took at least twenty minutes to drive in, and both she and Daniel were substitute teachers and had varied work hours. It was like doing a puzzle to get it all to work, because they couldn't afford to have two cars. But because more people also moved out there, they could carpool, and that meant it worked out in spite of it all. The cold was the worst of it, Jenny thought. It was a cold and windy winter, and the cottage was drafty even though the owner told them it was winterized.

Her relationship with Daniel was still strong, even if the honeymoon period was ending. It started to become a problem that they didn't have much time for each other with their teaching jobs during the day and work, studying, and auditing at the Scientology Center in the evenings and on weekends. For the past few months, Jenny had been commuting to Copenhagen and been gone for several weekend in a row, sometimes for weeks. Daniel wasn't as energetic with his auditing. He liked it, but he thought it was just as fun to work for the movement, and he really liked the camaraderie at the center. He wasn't as goal-oriented as Jenny. There were many late nights because the members usually went to each other's homes to have an evening coffee, sitting and chatting for a couple of hours. Now even more had moved out to the promontory, and only a few people were still looking for places to live there.

She arrived frozen through at the center, which was on Bryggaregatan at Möllebacken in central Karlskrona. She locked her bike, stepped inside, and hung up her coat. There was not a soul in sight; it was exactly eight o'clock. She hurried down the stone stairs, down to the warmth of the basement area. Everyone was already seated on sofas and in armchairs. The lights were off, but candles were flickering on the tables. Some were eating pizza, others drinking hot cocoa. An armchair stood in the middle of the room, and next to this armchair was a small table with a tape player. George sat sunken into the armchair. He smiled at Jenny.

"Welcome, Jenny!" he said ceremoniously in English. "Take a seat, please."

Jenny caught sight of Daniel, who made space for Jenny on one of the sofas. She slid in and Daniel poured tea for her.

"How did it go?" he whispered.

"Pretty good. Sold three."

Daniel gave her a kiss on the cheek just as Peter stood up.

"Ok! Now we're all here. Welcome to this very special evening, which we've all looked forward to so much!"

He turned towards George and smiled when he said the last sentence. George smiled and nodded.

"It's now been almost six years since George decided to move here to this godforsaken place, and I know that many of you have wondered why he chose to move here, of all places. Well, besides that he fell in love with Maria, of course. And the latter is, by the way, something I've wondered about many times," he said, and everyone laughed. Laughing herself, Maria tossed a book of matches at him.

"But jokes aside," he continued in a serious tone. "It's not only because he fell in love with Maria that he decided to start a Scientology mission here. There is another very special reason. Something that was decided a long time ago."

He paused for effect, letting his gaze wander around the room at everyone who sat there.

"Just like it's not a coincidence that you are all here today," he continued, his gaze fixed on Jenny. "That you all decided, twenty or thirty years ago, to be born right here. That was also decided a long, long time ago."

Jenny felt butterflies in her stomach. So George did have a hidden agenda. She held Daniel's hand tightly.

"It's taken a few years, but now George feels that you who have been called to this talk have come so far in your spiritual development that you are ready to know why you are here in this basement, in this city, right now."

Peter fell silent and walked to the table where he set his mug. He picked it up and took a sip of coffee before returning to his place.

"George has, therefore, recorded a series of talks on tape that we will all be able to listen to," he continued. "We'll start tonight with the first, which is an hour long. It's in English because George feels most comfortable in his mother tongue." Peter turned towards George, who puffed on his pipe and nodded.

"I'll just say one more thing before George turns on the tape player," Peter continued. "What you will hear tonight must stay in this room. You are not to speak of this with anyone else. Not other members of the Church of Scientology, not friends outside of the movement, not with your parents, not anyone. Other people aren't ready to hear this; they won't be able to understand, and it will only harm us if it gets out."

He turned towards George.

"So, George, go ahead."

George pushed the button to play the tape. The lecture went on for an hour and a half. He sat there in the armchair, smoking his pipe. A faintly sweet scent of pipe tobacco surrounded the ten young people who sat spread out in the basement room, listening devotedly to George's fascinating and powerful story.

"Many are the philosophers throughout history who have tried to understand the meaning of life," he began. "The pessimists among them believe that human consciousness is a tragic mistake of evolution. They claim that the fact that humans are the only creatures on this planet that are conscious of their own existence is proof that it is a mistake, and that we should not actually exist. They have not understood anything. L Ron Hubbard, on the other hand, has. His discoveries and research on human consciousness and existence is revolutionary. They give us the explanation for why we are here. Not just why most people walk around on earth, on this gutter at the edge of the Universe, thinking they are their bodies which, in a best-case scenario, will be buried in the earth after eighty or a hundred years. His research shows that we are prisoners, not only here on earth but also in our bodies. I've built on Ron's discoveries and, through my own research, have been able to find answers to the question of why we who are sitting in this basement are sitting right here, right now."

He continued to explain in his leisurely, monotonous English. He was glad that the most important members of his original clan had now finally gathered. He was proud that everyone in the group had, in such a short time, come so far in their mental readiness that they were prepared to hear the truth. After seventy-five million years, they were finally together again. He said that seventy-five million years ago, he had been their leader on one of the seventy-six planets that the Intergalactic Dictator Xenu ruled over. Through his intelligence work, George found out about Xenu's plans. He was going to take all of the inhabitants of the planet, including George and his group members, prisoner and place them on a prison planet at the edge of the Universe. Not only that, they would be placed in physical bodies. It would be like being in a prison with a double lock. When George found out about this, he sent a patrol from his home planet to Earth in advance. With them, they had a vehicle, a spaceship, that they were commanded to hide carefully. With the help of this ship, the group could get out of their prison at a later time.

And that time was now.

28.

The investigators of the Blekinge Police experienced the worst summer in the history of the force. The investigation of the April murder of an eight-year-old Palestinian girl named Yara meant all planned vacations were cancelled. The case sparked enormous media interest, and Karlskrona was overrun with journalists from the moment the murder hit the presses. The only event to surpass this murder in terms of media coverage was when the Russian submarine U137 got stranded in the eastern archipelago thirty-three years earlier.

Jonna Gustafson stood in her office with her head resting against the cool windowpane and looked on as one of the Öresund trains left the station. She'd asked to be excused from the Yara investigation, and the request was granted. Astrid was in the same class as Yara, and the girl's murder impacted Jonna in a way she'd never experienced before despite that she'd seen a whole lot since graduating from the academy in Växjö nine years earlier. She didn't want to subject herself to the pain of immersing herself in the case. Sitting through extended interrogations with the suspected perpetrators, Yara's uncle and his wife, looking at photos of the badly abused, defenseless girl, meeting with the girl's confused parents. An empathetic boss made sure she wasn't part of the investigating team, but at the same time it meant she was obliged to take on all other cases, and she was forced to work a lot of overtime.

She looked at the clock. Eight-thirty. She went back to her desk chair and sat down. It was Thursday evening and her husband David was in Copenhagen for work, as usual. She sent her mother a silent thank you. She was at home in the apartment, taking care of Astrid and three-year-old Simon. David would come home on Friday evening as he always did, but she wasn't looking forward to it. She realized over the past few months that she was in a situation she swore she would never end up in, and she was cursing herself for letting it happen. After nine years of marriage, her relationship with her husband was dead.

The whole time, he had been working in Copenhagen, where he had a lucrative job at a pharmaceutical company. He lived there for weeks at a time and was only home on the weekends. Slowly, they drifted apart. Jonna couldn't remember the last time they had sex. She suspected he satisfied that need when he was in Denmark. The thought that she could also be with someone else popped into her head now and then over the past year. She'd longed to feel another body this summer. She began fantasizing about going to bed with a man just to satisfy the desire. Without any questions, before or after. Without involving any emotions. But her moral compass struggled with the idea. She didn't see herself as an unfaithful person. She didn't *want* to see herself that way. If she were to have it in black and white that David was catting around in Copenhagen, that'd be a different story. Then her hesitation would cease. She had plenty of opportunities, but she hadn't yet met anyone she wanted to go down that path with. Until Saturday evening, that is, when Luke Bergmann piqued her interest.

She suppressed these thoughts and continued writing the email she was going to send to the IPO, the Unit for International Police Operations, at the National Police. Loman asked her to check whether Luke Bergmann had a criminal history in the USA. The IPO took that type of inquiry to the authorities in other countries.

She didn't know what to think about the tall American. Her instincts told her that he was a good person. She could see it in his eyes. Loman also liked him at first, but now he seemed to have changed his mind. At their morning meeting on Monday, he said he didn't believe his story and that's why he wanted Jonna to investigate his background.

Jonna had a great deal of respect for Loman. He was smart and experienced, and she liked him a lot. They'd worked together for a good two years and started in the division at approximately the same time. Loman was originally from Karlskrona, and worked as an officer in the city until 1994 when he applied for and got a job with the Swedish Security Service in Stockholm. He moved back to his hometown after finding out he had colon cancer.

The first course of treatment went well, but after a year, the cancer came back. Jonna thought it was sad. Loman told her about it early on, but they hadn't brought it up at all since then. He was clear with her that she was one of few at work he told, that he didn't want to talk about it, and that it shouldn't impact their work relationship. Meanwhile, he disappeared for periods to undergo treatment, both radiation and chemotherapy. This was one such period. After the morning meeting on Monday, Loman said he would be gone for a few days for treatment, so now Jonna had to take over the Spandel case as well as the investigation of Bergmann breaking into the apartment. Jonna couldn't understand how Loman had the energy to work between courses. The treatment must be incredibly draining.

She read through her email to the IPO one last time and clicked "send." She sat there for a moment, looking at the screen and thinking about her meeting with Luke Bergmann in Viktor's apartment and about what he said. About the book-burning. She googled the local newspaper's archives, wrote "Viktor Spandel" in the search field, and got several hits. The most recent ones were various headlines connected to a company called Twain Technology. She scrolled down in the list of hits. Viktor had clearly been an excellent fencer when he was young. There were several articles about him on the sports pages.

Finally, she found what she was looking for. On April 2, 1994, the newspaper published a long article about Viktor Spandel and another defector from Scientology. On the front page was a large picture of the two young men, standing on either side of an impressive pile of burning books in a gravel area behind Östersjöhallen in Karlskrona. In the article, they told their story about how they were pulled into the cult and become increasingly brainwashed. But they'd had enough, were able to get out, and wanted to warn other young people about Scientology which, at that time, had clearly been very active in Karlskrona. Jonna read through the article carefully and was especially transfixed by one quote from Viktor Spandel:

> "We've searched for every single book we could find. In our own homes, of course, and then we've also traveled around southern Sweden rifling through secondhand bookstores and buying anything we could find. We ended up with quite a bit, as you can see. We wanted to make a grand bonfire out of this dangerous trash."

Well, wouldn't you know, Jonna thought. He did burn all of his books. But maybe he changed his mind after a few years and became interested in the teachings of Scientology again. She remembered the computer that the technicians took from the apartment and that she saw lying in Loman's office. If she were lucky, maybe Viktor Spandel took photos in his living room with the bookshelf in the background and saved them on his computer.

She stood quickly and went to Loman's office to get the laptop. She called Jonas, the division's IT specialist, and found out that he had already hacked his way in and removed the password. Smooth sailing. Just start it up and get going, he said. Once she was in, Jonna had to look around for a bit in various photo folders before finding one that contained personal photos. There were nine hundred and fifty-nine photos in the folder. She sighed. It would take a couple hours to go through them. She decided to take one hour now and continue the next day if she didn't find what she was looking for.

Only fifteen minutes later, she clicked on an image of the daughter, Agnes, dressed up as a princess and dancing in front of the camera. Behind her was the bookshelf. Jonna noted that the photo was taken on June 21, a full week before they died. Jonna took out the technicians' photo of the bookshelf and laid it next to the computer. The section where the yellow Scientology book stood was clearly visible in the photo on the computer. She zoomed in. The image was so sharp, she could almost read the titles on the spines. She leaned forward and looked carefully at the books.

The yellow Scientology book was not there.

29.

The door was locked. Luke rang the doorbell a number of times, with no response. Looked at his watch. Quarter to nine. He went to the other apartment door and rang the bell. The nameplate said "Hansson." After a minute, there was a rustling sound at the door. The security chain rattled and the door was opened by an older women in a green blouse and white skirt. She looked suspiciously at Luke.

"Excuse me, do you have a key to Maria Palm's apartment?" Luke asked. "I think she's sick in there."

The woman shut the door without altering her expression. Luke shook his head and took out his phone, selecting the Eniro app. Diana Palm. There couldn't be too many people with that name living in Stockholm. As long as she wasn't married and had changed her name, he thought.

Luckily, there was just one. Fiskaregatan 14. Luke called her and she picked up immediately.

"Are you Maria Palm's daughter? Who lives on Kungsholmen?" he asked.

"Yes," she answered. "Why do you ask?"

"I'm standing outside your mom's apartment and I think she may have had an accident. There's music coming from inside but no one is coming to the door. How long ago did you last talk to her?"

"Um, I talked with her yesterday, I think. But wait, who are you?"

"I can't explain all of that right now," Luke answered. "Do you have a key to her apartment?"

"What happened to her?"

"I don't know. Can you come here?"

"Yes, but not until you tell me who you are. Why are you there? Do you know my mom? How can I be sure you're not trying to pull one over on me?"

Luke thought for a few seconds.

"I'll send you a telephone number right away," he said. "For a police officer in Karlskrona named Jonna Gustafson. She'll vouch for me. Call back when you've talked to her."

They hung up and Luke sent Jonna's number to Diana. After a couple minutes, his phone rang again.

"I'll be there in twenty minutes," Diana said.

Then Luke called 911 and said there was a dead woman in the apartment. He gave the address and his telephone number and was told that a unit would be there within twenty minutes. Then he sat on the steps to wait. His phone rang. It was Jonna Gustafson. He silenced his phone and let it go to voicemail. He didn't want to have to explain to her what he was doing in Stockholm. He'd do that later. The motion-sensor light in the stairwell turned off and he sat there in the dark, listening to Chick Corea's electric keyboard and the guitarist's distorted solos. His phone display lit up again. Jonna didn't give up, but Luke wasn't about to answer.

He listened to the music, trying to find some sort of melody. He thought in hindsight that he could pick out a theme. It was fluffy, the notes from the piano sounded happy, like a babbling brook in springtime. Strange name, he thought. "Theme to the Mothership." Mothership, like a UFO. Science fiction. Space music for Luke was Star Wars music. Grand and pompous. Why did the murderer decide that Scientologists should die to this spasmodic music? Did the idea of a mothership have something to do with Scientology? The one true all-encompassing belief? Are they being murdered because they left? Viktor left the movement so long ago. Over fifteen years. Why wasn't he murdered then?

When the song restarted for the third time and he'd almost begun to like what he was hearing, the door down at the entrance slammed shut and immediately after, the lights in the stairwell turned on. A young, red-haired woman in a green hoodie and black running tights came bounding up the steps. She was clearly in excellent shape, hardly out of breath at all when she got to Luke.

"I took the subway to Central Station and ran here," she said. "It was quickest."

She introduced herself and Luke saw that "Coastal Jaegers, Sweden" was printed in a circle around a gold trident on the chest of her hoodie. Naval special ops. Her curly hair was intensely red, she had broad facial features, beautiful green eyes.

"I called the police," Luke said. "They should be here any minute."

Diana held a keyring in her hand. She flipped through for the right key, found it, and inserted it into the keyhole. Luke laid his hand on her arm. He'd put on his gloves.

"Are you sure you want to go in?" he asked. "It might not be pretty."

Diana looked at him resolutely. Turned the key.

Before she could grab the door handle, Luke stopped her. He set his hand on it instead and looked at Diana.

"We don't touch anything with our hands when we've gone in," he said. "Okay?"

Diana nodded without looking at him, and when Luke opened the door, she went quickly ahead of him.

Luke noticed right away that the person who lived there had expensive, minimalist taste. All of the walls were white; three large silver candelabras stood on the dark wood floor in the foyer. On the wall hung a gigantic, colorful oil painting. Luke followed Diana quickly in the direction of the music. Before he could see anything, he heard Diana scream. He ran the last few yards to the doorway of the living room.

From the opening, he could see Diana holding the legs of a woman who was hanging from a noose. The woman's face was tinged with blue and she was hanging just as Viktor did, on a door with the noose tied around the door handle on the other side. This time, the door was to one of the bedrooms. On the floor, a bucket lay on its side. Just like in Viktor's apartment, all the shades were down. The woman looked like she was in her forties. White blouse, black jacket, and a tight black skirt. It stank of feces, and urine had run down her legs, forming a puddle on the floor.

Luke ran forward and pulled the rope along the edge of the door so Diana could lift her mother down and lay her on the floor. He could see in her face that there was no point in trying to revive her. Diana knelt next to her mother, moaning and rocking. Luke went quickly into the bedroom and found a white piece of paper on the pillow. The exact same message as in Viktor's apartment. He went back to the living room and sat on the expensive white sofa, in front of a laptop computer he suspected was playing music from a CD. The music streamed through small speakers placed throughout the room.

He then strode into the kitchen, took a dishtowel, and held it while he opened cupboards and drawers to find a pair of rubber gloves. He found a pair in the cupboard under the sink, put them on, and went back to the computer in the living room. He pressed a key and the computer came to life. He clicked on the email program, which was open. He scrolled quickly through the latest emails, which were all work-related. He took the list of names he got from Anna Adams and searched for them in the inbox. He got a hit on Max Billing. She recieved three emails from him a few weeks earlier. One of them was long, he realized. Then Luke's phone rang; it was an officer saying they were standing outside.

Luke clicked "print" and heard sounds from a printer that came to life in the bedroom. He looked at Diana, who was still on her knees next to her mother. She was in shock and hadn't noticed any of what he was doing. Luke closed the email program, let the music continue, and went in to get the printed email.

30.

When George's voice went silent, he leaned forward and pushed the button to turn off the tape player. He looked up and smiled, studying his audience with his calm, penetrating gaze. It was completely quiet. No one said a peep for several minutes. The air in the basement wasn't only filled with smoke from George's pipe and cigarettes. It was electrified. Camilla was the one who broke the silence.

"Fantastic, George. Completely fantastic." George smiled and nodded.

"It's a great story indeed. But best of all, it's true." He got up from the armchair, packed up the tape player, and reached out his hand to Maria, who came quickly to her feet. They walked silently up the stairs.

Jenny felt on the verge of fainting as a result of what she just heard. She looked around the room again at the friends sitting around her. Peter, Fredrik, Camilla, Viktor, Max, and the others. Slowly, the realization dawned on her. She was with them at the beginning of time. That was why she felt drawn to them so strongly already the first time she met them in Stefan's sister's apartment in Ronneby. That was why she felt such a strong feeling of belonging with them. It was something greater than love. It was something *original*. Something that originated in the very innermost core of existence. They were split apart but searched for and finally found each other. After eons, they were finally together again. Still trapped in their prisons. In their bodies, on Earth.

Now they were going to get out. Escape.

Jenny grew dizzy from a warm, wonderful feeling inside when she thought about it. What a guy George was. How lucky she was to be one of the chosen. Who got to be part of this. At the same time, she understood it wasn't luck. It was meant to be. They *chose* to be born close to each other. She smiled, imagining them as soap bubbles sailing around in the atmosphere above Karlskrona, searching for suitable bodies to dive into. As Daniel described it when they told each other about their auditing sessions.

Jenny thought it was too bad that George and Maria didn't stay. Many of them had questions for George, and she would really have liked to hear more. But George always distanced himself from the rest of the group. George really only talked to Peter and possibly Fredrik. They comprised an unofficial leader group. Peter was definitely George's right-hand man, and he was also the one who took over when George left the building.

"I suspect there are a number of questions bouncing around in your little heads right now," he said, smiling widely. "Should we talk about them right away? I can't promise I'll be able to answer all of them. It depends on if I think you'll be able to take the answers."

Jenny turned to Daniel, who hadn't made a sound since George turned off the tape player.

"What do you think, Daniel?" she whispered. "Unbelievable, right?" Daniel squeezed her hand and nodded. Jenny saw that his eyes were shining and realized he was having a hard time talking. Daniel was unusually easily moved and very sensitive. It was one of the reasons she loved him.

"How on earth does George know all of this?" Camilla asked Peter. Her cheeks were red, probably both from the warmth in the space and in excitement over what she just heard. Jenny liked her. She wasn't the smartest person in the group, but she was a passionate Scientologist. She had a charming sort of childlike naïveté. Open as a book. And she wasn't afraid of asking stupid questions.

Peter looked at her and smiled.

"Have you heard of something called 'memory'?" he asked.

"Don't be mean," Camilla said.

"George is one of the Scientologists in the world who has got highest up on the bridge," Peter continued. "And he was one of the first who did OT III, the Wall of Fire. He cleared away a bunch of junk on the timeline, and during auditing for OT III, the memories came."

Now Daniel cleared his throat.

"You've done OT III, too," he said to Peter. "Did you also get this same story there?"

Peter nodded.

"Yes. Largely. Fredrik did, too. We'll have to see what happens with you when you do it."

"Why did we choose Karlskrona?" Daniel continued.

"The entrance to the spaceship is here," Peter answered. "Out at Trummenäs."

"What?" Camilla said.

Peter looked very pleased. All the others sat there with their mouths agape. All except Fredrik, who clearly already knew all of it.

"Why do you think George and Maria bought exactly the lot they bought?"

No one said anything. Jenny sensed what was coming.

"Seventy-five million years ago, this planet didn't look like it does today," Peter continued. "The patrol that hid the ship placed it in a location that would be well-hidden. They probably chose the northern part of the globe for that reason. They made sure the entrance to the ship would be easy to access and put a puzzle lock on the door that leads into the ship."

"So it's buried?" Viktor asked.

"Well, it's not like they had spades and shovels with them, exactly," Peter said. Everyone laughed. "At that point, most of northern Sweden was partly covered by a shallow sea. I would think they placed it on the bottom. Then the sea level dropped, and since then it's been covered by different layers of rocks over all these millions of years."

"How big is it? Do you guys know?"

"It's big," Peter answered. "It's less a saucer than a cigar. The entrance is in the middle of the ship, which reaches from Kristianopel in the east to Ronneby in the west. According to George, it's more than forty miles long."

"Dear lord," Jenny said. "That's gigantic."

Everyone sat silently for a moment, contemplating the enormous space-craft that lay there under their feet, just waiting to be able to break free and take them away from the earth. Jenny thought what a shock it would be for the residents of Blekinge when the ship exploded through the earth's surface.

"Does George know where the entrance is?" Viktor asked.

"Yes," Peter answered. "He did a sort of position-related auditing and was out at Trummenäs lots of times a couple years ago. He finally located the door, found out who owned the land, and offered to buy the lot. Luckily, it was part of the planned residential development for the area. But at first, the farmer didn't want to sell. He intended to lease out several lots, includ-ing this one. But George isn't an OT for nothing. The farmer didn't have a chance. Without him even knowing how it happened, he agreed to sell to George—and for an amazing price, too."

Jenny could just see how George, with only his strong intention and strength of will, made the farmer say things that he didn't actually want to say. Incredible, she thought. I have to get on with my auditing.

"Where exactly is the entrance to the ship?" Max wondered.

"It's about seven yards underground, about five yards southwest of George and Maria's house," Peter answered. "And only George will be able to open the lock. But if he's going to be able to do that, he has to get even farther on the bridge. He has to do both OT VII and OT VIII. These cost almost forty thousand dollars, and he doesn't have that kind of money today. We have to help him get that money."

If any outsider were to have stepped down into the basement on Bryggaregatan in Karlskrona that dark, cold Friday evening on February 19 just then, they would have been able to feel the electricity in the air. Ten rosy-cheeked young people in a candlelit, smoke-filled basement room who just heard that they comprised the core of a creation history that beat the Christian one by a long shot. That they were chosen, that they belonged to an ancient clan that had now found each other again, that their billions of years of double imprisonment would soon be over. They only needed to get seven yards down, into the ship, and leave all of the poor, lost, spiritually blind people behind, to their great surprise.

There was a lot of love in the room. Jenny had never experienced such a strong sense of belonging. Never in this lifetime, at least. She thought of the word "affinity," which was one of the three foundational factors in Ron's theory of communication; attraction, the desire to occupy the same place as another being in the physical universe. The definitive expression for a true and genuine love.

That was what she felt in this moment.

31.

The police patrol quickly established that Maria Palm was dead. And when Luke gave his witness statement to one of the policemen, he said that a person in Karlskrona was found in exactly the same way the previous Monday, that both were Scientologists in their youth in the same congregation in Karlskrona, and that he suspected it was murder in both cases. The policeman conferred with his colleague for a moment and then decided to call in a investigator and a forensic technician.

One of the policemen now tended to Diana in the kitchen. The other policeman asked Luke to remain in the apartment to wait for the investigator. Luke sat on the sofa in the living room, waiting, when his phone rang. He had eight missed calls. Luke looked at the clock—quarter to ten. He pressed the green button on the display.

"Hi, Jonna. Do you always work so late in the evenings?" he asked, getting up from the sofa and going out into the hallway so he could talk undisturbed.

"What the hell are you doing?"

Her voice was ice cold.

"Right now, I'm standing in the hallway of an apartment in Stockholm," Luke said.

"I got a call from a woman a while ago who was asking if I could vouch for you," Jonna said. "I don't know why I did it."

"Because you have unusually excellent judgment," Luke said.

Jonna ignored his joke.

"She said you asked her to come and unlock the door to her mom's apartment on Kungsholmen in Stockholm," she continued. "Are you at the home of that corporate lawyer you were talking about?"

"Yes," Luke answered.

"How is it you have the nerve to continue your own private investigation after what happened on Saturday?"

"I understand this might look strange," Luke said. "But I had the feeling there was something odd about the whole thing. And it turned out I was right."

"How's that?"

"Maria Palm is also dead," Luke said. "Hanged in exactly the same way as Viktor, the same music playing and same poem on her pillow."

It was silent on the other end of the line.

"Are you still there?" Luke asked.

"So there are three who died in the same way," she said. "The local police in Olofström called my colleague, Mattias, at the intelligence unit tonight," Jonna said. "They found a dead man in their district this afternoon."

"His name is Max Billing," Luke said.

"Was he also on your list?"

"Yep. Where did they find him?"

"In an abandoned building somewhere outside town," Jonna answered. "Hanging on a door, the same message and music. It was pure luck that we found out about it. If Mattias hadn't been friends with one of the guys in Olofström and they hadn't chatted with each other about it, it would have probably been written off as suicide, too.

"By the way, you were right about the Scientology books at Viktor's house," she continued. "They weren't on Viktor's bookshelf two weeks ago."

Luke sat down on a slim chair next to the large painting in the hall.

"There are more names on my list," he said.

"How many?"

"Five. And it's possible more should be on it."

"Give them to me. Time for you to leave this to us, now," Jonna said.

Luka rattled off the names for her. Three with both first and last names, two with only first names.

"Do you only have the names? No other information?"

"No. Nothing," Luke said. "One thing I was wondering about is the fact that Viktor and Max Billing took several trips to Russia over the past two years, to St. Petersburg and Kaliningrad. I don't know if others who went on these trips, too, or if it has anything to do with this. But could be worth checking into."

A round, balding man in his forties stepped into the hall along with an older man in glasses and a blue shirt with a bag in his hand.

"Gotta go," Luke said to Jonna. "A couple of officers just came into the apartment."

The slightly heavier man introduced himself as Håkan Jonsson, investigator at Stockholm's downtown police district. The man with the glasses was the forensic technician.

Håkan Jonsson walked ahead into the living room, spoke for a moment with the two officers who arrived first, looked around, and went to Maria Palm's body.

"Sad," he said, crouching down and examining the body.

"I hope you haven't touched anything in here?" said Håkan Jonsson to Luke as he stood up.

"Not other than taking down the body. Diana couldn't bear to see her mom hanging there."

"Let's go into the kitchen," Håkan Jonsson said, and Luke followed him.

Håkan Jonsson introduced himself to Diana, who was sitting at the white, oval-shaped kitchen table.

"Are you the daughter?"

Diana nodded.

"How are you feeling? Do you need a doctor?"

She shook her head.

"No, I don't think so right now," she answered. "If I need to, I can get that support through my job."

"Where do you work?"

"I'm a lieutenant in the Amphibious Corps," she answered. "Coastal Jaeger."

He sat in the chair across from her.

"I didn't know there were female coastal jaegers."

"Now you do."

Håkan Jonsson cleared his throat.

"I know you've both already given your witness statements, but we need to hear the circumstances in a little more detail," he said. He looked at the clock. "And because of that, I have to take you down to the station, but it's a little too late to do that tonight. I'll be contacting you about it, probably tomorrow. Will you still be in town?"

"Yes," Diana said.

"I'll be here tomorrow, too," Luke said, "but I was going to head back down to Karlskrona as soon as I can."

Håkan Jonsson checked with both of them that he had their contact information, then Luke and Diana left the apartment. They walked quietly down the stairs. When they came out onto the street, Diana stopped and turned towards Luke.

"Can you tell me what this is all about?"

"Is there somewhere we can go to talk?" he asked.

Diana looked across the street towards Hotel Amaranten.

"We can head to Mom's usual spot," she said. "The bar at Amaranten. I need a whisky."

As they crossed the street to the hotel, Luke took out his phone and dialed the number for Anna Adams, who answered immediately despite it being eleven o'clock in the evening.

"Max Billing and Maria Palm have been found dead. Murdered in the same way as Viktor. There are five names on the list that I got from you, and they're probably in great danger. For two of them, you only had the first names, Åke and Jenny. We need to come up with their last names. Do you know anyone at all who would know that or who might be in contact with them?"

Anna was silent for five seconds, then said, "Give me a half-hour. I'll call you."

"Besides, you thought there could be more. Check that out, too."

Luke hung up and they went into the hotel. People began to scatter, and they found a pair of armchairs at a table in the corner. Luke went to the bar and ordered two double whiskies. He took his glass and downed the whisky in one gulp.

"Why do you think someone murdered my mom?" she asked.

"Did you know your mom had been a Scientologist when she was young?"

Diana nodded.

"My dad was, too. Is he also in danger?"

"What's his name?"

"George Knightly."

"His name is on the list," Luke said. "How involved was he in Scientology?"

"He was the one who established the movement in Karlskrona. He's been living in Florida for years. I don't have any contact with him at all."

"If I were you, I'd try to get in touch with him," Luke said.

"I haven't talked to him in eighteen years. He just abandoned me and mom. He got in touch a few times when I was little, but then there was just nothing."

She stood up.

"I need one more," she said. "Want one?"

Luke shook his head. When she came back, she said, "Now you have to tell me. In what way does this have to do with Scientology?"

Luke started at the beginning. It took him twenty minutes to tell her the whole story.

"The whole time, I've argued that Viktor's death wasn't suicide," he concluded. "Now that your mom and Max Billing have died in the same way, there's not a shred of doubt remaining. What worries me is that there are at least five people left who might be targets for the murderer. I've given the names to the Karlskrona police, but I'm not sure they're doing everything they can to get hold of them."

He fell silent and looked at Diana. Throughout his whole description, she sat quietly and listened with her gaze fixed on him.

"I also have a hard time believing that my mom would take her own life," she said. "She's had her ups and downs, but now she was looking forward to being able to move away soon, to Greece, where she has a house. She's been working like crazy these past few years to save up enough money for it. She was nagging me to go with her. Now she won't be able to experience it."

Her eyes filled with tears, and the floodgates opened. The realization that her mom was dead, murdered, seemed to have sunken in. She cried violently. Luke went over to her and embraced her. After a moment, she sat up, wiped her face with a tissue.

"I'd like to make sure we find those five on the list," she said, a determined look in her teary, red eyes. "Now."

"Now?"

"Yes," Diana answered. "We can borrow one of the computers in the lobby. I won't be able to sleep after everything that's happened anyway. And if it's true that someone murdered my mom, no one can stop me from doing everything I can to find out who it was and to make sure that person gets the punishment he deserves."

They got up, went to the lobby, and sat at one of the three computers available to guests.

"What do you know about your mom from the time when she was a member of the Church of Scientology?" Luke asked as they started up the computer.

"She was a member when I was born. Had been for many years. I was named after L. Ron Hubbard's daughter, Diana. Hubbard is the guy who established the cult in the first place. Mom left it when I was only about a year old. But that was over twenty years ago. So you're saying someone murdered her because of something that happened so long ago?"

"I don't know," Luke answered. "But this is one of two clues I have now. Do you know if your mom had any contact with any of the others who were in the cult?"

"I have no idea. If she did, she didn't tell me, anyway. What's the other clue?"

"Do you know if your mom took any trips to Russia in the past couple years?"

Diana shook her head.

"I don't think so. I would've known. Why are you wondering about that?"

"Viktor took several trips to St. Petersburg and Kaliningrad in the past year," Luke said. "Along with another former Scientologist, Max Billing. Trips he didn't want to tell me about. Is Max Billing a name you recognize?"

Diana shook her head.

"I heard you say that name when you were on the phone earlier on the street," she said. "I've never heard it before."

Luke took the list of names out of his pocket and showed her.

"Here are the rest of the names of the people who are supposed to have been in the cult at the same time as your mom," he said. "Do you recognize any of these names?"

Diana took the paper and studied the names. She shook her head.

"No, unfortunately. I've never heard of them."

Luke's phone rang. It was Anna Adams.

"Thank god for Facebook," she said. "Found one of my old friends on it who, just like me, was just a member for a short while and who I hadn't been in touch with all these years. And now I've talked to her, and she refreshed my memory."

"That's great," Luke said. "What did you remember?"

"Åke's last name was Hansson, but he changed it to Fleming," Anna said. "There can't be many with that name. I guess he changed to an old family name a few years after he left Scientology. My friend has had sporadic contact with him through the years and thinks he lives somewhere in Skåne. She didn't know where, and she doesn't have a phone number, but it shouldn't be hard for you to get hold of that. She also remembered two people I completely forgot: Camilla Svensson and Micke Andersson. And Jenny's last name was Eklund."

Luke thanked Anna and turned to Diana.

"We've got a name that probably not many people have. Åke Fleming. Lives in Skåne, supposedly."

"Fleming," Diana repeated. "That's old nobility, if I'm not mistaken. Shouldn't be too hard to find it."

Diana began searching on Facebook for Åke Fleming. Luke went to the reception desk and asked if they had a single room available for the night. They did, and he booked it. When he came back, Diana said, "It's too late, Luke."

Luke saw that Diana had found Åke Fleming's Facebook page, and at the top of the status updates was an obituary that someone named Eva Fleming photographed from Skånska Dagbladet. Åke Fleming died on May 15, a month and a half before Viktor and Agnes. Diana scrolled down. A lot of people commented on the page; there were pictures of some people who lit rice paper lanterns and someone who sent money to the sea rescue service in Åhus, which Åke Fleming had been active in.

"Can we see if we find some of the other names on the list in his Facebook friends?" Luke asked.

"He has three hundred and thirty-one of them," Diana said. "And they're not searchable. We'll have to scroll through his entire friends list."

She was scrolling through the list when Luke's phone rang. It was Jonna. He stood up and went over to sit by one of the other computers in the lobby.

"Are you awake?" Jonna asked. "Where are you?"

"Sitting in a hotel lobby, talking to Maria Palm's daughter," Luke answered. "I know you don't like it, but she knows things that are worth listening to."

"You are completely impossible," Jonna said. "Weren't we in agreement that you would lay off and let us do our job?"

"Jonna, don't you understand that there are five more people on the list who could be in grave danger?" Luke said. "We have to act quickly. Can't you just let go of your pride for a minute and try to see that I can actually contribute something of value to this?"

"What is it she knows?" Jonna asked.

"She's just found one more," Luke answered. "Åke Fleming. Died on May 15. The obituary was posted on his Facebook page."

"That's six weeks before Viktor and Agnes."

"The risk is that the murderer is getting close to the end of the list," Luke said.

"I've also been looking around on Facebook," Jonna said. "And I think I've found one more who might still be alive. Found him through Viktor's Facebook page. He was friends with someone named Peter Ek in Malmö. Probably the Peter who's on your list. Max Billing was also friends with him. Peter Ek doesn't seem to be particularly active on Facebook. His last status update was in March."

Luke was quiet for a few seconds. Why hadn't he thought of using Facebook? He had an account, but he didn't use it.

"I'm sitting at a computer," he said. "I'll go in and look."

He started up the computer and went in to Viktor's Facebook page and was met by a large picture of a smiling Viktor with Agnes in his arms and a ton of wall posts from Viktor's friends, expressing their grief. He had to steel himself so he wouldn't stop. Clicked on Viktor's long friends list and scrolled down to Peter Ek.

"I see him now," he said to Jonna. "That should be him. But he looks older than Viktor. How can we get hold of him?"

"There are four people in Malmö named Peter Ek," she said. "Checked on Eniro. I'll call them tomorrow. It's too late now.

"Viktor was popular," Jonna continued. "He had over a thousand Facebook friends. The others on the list may well be there, but I have to head home now. We'll have to continue tomorrow."

"What did Loman say when you told him?" Luke asked.

"He mostly seemed irritated over the fact that you are still going about your private investigating," she said. "He's going to be calling you. He's putting together a group that will work on the investigation, and he asked if I were interested. I am."

32.

The phone call came at eight o'clock the next morning. The night's sleep was deep and dreamless, but the day arrived abruptly. Luke forgot to silence his phone.

"Are you still in Stockholm?"

It was Loman. Luke sat up in bed and cleared his throat.

"Did I wake you?" Loman asked.

"Yes," Luke said. "It was a late night."

He leaned forward, opened the small door to the minibar, took out a bottle of water, and drank.

"Should I call back later?"

"No, this is fine," Luke answered.

"A colleague from the City Police in Stockholm called me just this morning. I assume you know why?"

"If your colleague's name is Håkan Jonsson, yes, I know," Luke answered.

"Correct. This is a damn mess, all of this," he said, giving an audible sigh. "We found one more in Olofström yesterday. Named Max Billing. Three dead. Besides Spandel's daughter. Same method."

Luke realized Jonna hadn't had the chance to talk to Loman.

"Four," he said.

"What?"

"There are at least four now. Åke Fleming in Kristianstad. He's on the list I assume your colleague told you about. But the name there is Åke Hansson. He was part of the same Scientology group as Viktor and Maria Palm were in the 90s in Karlskrona. Changed his name a few years later. He died on May 15. I'd bet he was hanged, that there was the same suicide note, and that 'Return to the Mothership' with Chick Corea was playing when he was found. Might be worth checking." Luke heard Anders Loman taking notes.

"How did you find him?"

"Facebook."

"How do you know he was in the same group in the 90s?"

Luke thought. He didn't actually know if he wanted to give Loman more information.

Clearly, Anders thought the answer was taking too much time.

"Luke. I'm responsible for this investigation and..."

"Oh? Is it an investigation now?" Luke answered. "What type of investigation?"

"...and I expect you to cooperate with the police. If you're in possession of information that could be valuable for us, it would be best if you gave it to us. And I would appreciate if you'd lay off the smart remarks."

"So you've changed your mind now?" Luke asked. "Do you agree that Viktor was murdered?"

"I'm not excluding any possibilities at this point," Anders Loman answered. "Considering how things have developed, it could turn out that your theory may very well be right."

Luke realized that this might be the closest to some sort of acceptance he would be able to get Anders Loman. He described the meeting with Viktor's former colleague, the visit to Anna Adams, and the list of names of some of the members.

"I got the names on your list from Jonna Gustafson," Anders said when Luke was done. "But we haven't had the chance to start looking for them yet. Up until now, I've been the only one on this case, but I'll get reinforcements today. We'd like to meet you as soon as possible so that you can give us all the information you have. How soon can you get down to Karlskrona?"

Luke did a quick search online and found a flight.

"If there's a seat on the eleven o'clock Blekingeflyg flight, I could be in your office by one."

"Good. I'll inform the group so they'll be present," Anders said, hanging up.

Luke booked his flight online, called the hotel reception, and asked for a taxi immediately. He quickly threw his things together and ran down the steps to the waiting car.

At exactly one o'clock, Luke stepped into the police station in Karlskrona. Jonna met him at the reception desk. Her hair was wrapped into a bun at her neck, making her look young. Young and impossibly beautiful. Luke guessed she was about thirty-five. Old enough to have significant life experiences, yet young enough to still be curious about life. She stood leaning against the reception desk and looked at him differently from when they were sitting in the interrogation room on Saturday.

Luke stumbled and pretended he was about to fall. Jonna ran to him and took hold of his arm.

"What's happening?" she asked.

"I don't know. I saw you and suddenly became completely weak in the knees," he said.

The thing was, her smile honestly did make Luke's knees weak. She let go of him and took a step back.

"That was unexpected," she said. "You're quite the comedian. I didn't expect that of you."

"Come on," she continued, starting for the door next to the reception desk. "We're going up to our little conference room. Anders and Mattias are waiting for us."

"Are you going to be there?" Luke asked.

"Yes. I'm part of the group that's going to be working on this case," she said as they went up the steps. They came up to the second floor and walked silently next to each other down the long hallway. Jonna rapped loudly on the door of the conference room and then walked right in ahead of Luke. Inside, Anders Loman was sitting at the table along with a young guy with a crew cut in jeans and a T-shirt, laptop on the table in front of him. He introduced himself as Mattias Palander. On the table was also a thermos, four mugs, a few small cookies, and napkins.

"Mattias, and Jonna—whom you already know—are part of this hastily thrown-together investigating team," Loman said. He got up, took the thermos, and began pouring coffee into the cups.

"The goal of this meeting is primarily for you to provide us with all the information you have gathered over the course of your own private little investigation, Luke. I trust that won't be a problem?"

Luke shook his head.

"No problem at all," he said. "I'm glad you've finally realized that there's a murderer at work here."

"Yes, well, I don't think we should put the cart before the horse," Anders answered. "We have to stick to the facts. What we know today is that several people with a believed connection to each other have been found dead, and that they have died in what appears to be the same way. Whether it's another person who killed them or whether they did it themselves, we simply don't know at the moment."

Luke stared at him.

"You mean that you still believe that all four killed themselves?"

"Seven. Seven people have been found dead now, besides Agnes Spandel," Anders said. "With Jonna's help, Mattias has now found Peter Ek, Fredrik Ek, and Camilla Ek today. Can you say more about that, Mattias?"

"Of course. It wasn't difficult. All of them were on Facebook and were friends there. And all three of them were all Facebook friends with Viktor Spandel and Max Billing. Peter Ek, forty-seven years old, was single and lived in an apartment on Möllevångstorget in Malmö. The neighbor found him hanging from his bedroom door on June 12. The music was on, but we haven't yet been able to find out if it was the same song as with Viktor, Max, and Maria Palm. But the same suicide note was in the apartment. His brother, Fredrik Ek, five years older than Peter, and his wife Camilla lived in a townhouse in Växjö. One of their adult children found them on May 13. They were found with the same props as the others, but there was only a suicide note in this case. And..."

Mattias stopped and flipped through the pages in his notebook.

"...it seems all three were still active Scientologists. And also Åke Fleming. I haven't been able yet to find three people on the list yet: George Knightly, Jenny Eklund, and Mikael Andersson."

He looked up at Luke. "Seven people dead in the same way and you still believe they've committed suicide? All seven? You have to be joking."

Luke looked at Anders Loman as if he truly hoped he would admit he were kidding.

Anders leaned forward and gave Luke a grave look. "The only thing we have is your claims that these people belonged to a cult in Karlskrona a full twenty years ago. And *if* that's true, then suicide isn't a completely unreasonable explanation. This isn't really particularly unusual for that cult. I've done my research, too. You'd be surprised if you saw how many suicides have been committed by Scientologists over the years. Mostly in the USA, but also here in Sweden."

Luke looked at him suspiciously. Anders continued.

"What does rebirth mean? Reincarnation?"

"What are you getting at?" Luke asked.

"If you believed in rebirth, would you be afraid to die?"

Luke didn't say anything.

"No. You wouldn't." Anders answered his own question. "There are several examples of other crackpot cults that committed collective suicide. In 1997, thirty-nine members in a cult called Heaven's Gate committed suicide in California when they believed a comet was going to crush the Earth. They drank phenobarbital, the same drug Viktor's daughter took. And then we have that jungle sect in South America led by Jim Jones. There, the parents forced their children to take the poison before they drank it themselves. Over nine hundred people died. And there are other examples, too. Take the Muslim suicide bombers..."

"Stop. That's enough," Luke interrupted him. "Do you mean that Viktor and the other six committed a long-distance collective suicide? And not simultaneously, either. There were several weeks between deaths. Viktor, Max, and Maria Palm weren't even in the cult anymore. I'm sorry, but I still can't believe you're seriously committed to this theory." Luke looked at Jonna for support. She just looked back, not saying anything.

"Calm down," Anders said. "The only thing I'm saying is that we can't rule it out. Enough about that. We called this meeting to have a discussion with you about what's going on. We want more information. I want Mattias to be able to get started as soon as possible investigating the connection between these people to see if your theory fits."

"I think it's more important for you to concentrate on trying to find the three people left on the list, isn't it?" Luke asked. "There's a chance they're still alive. But if they are, it's probably not for long."

Then Anders Loman exploded.

"We don't take orders from a former mafia gangster!" He stood up so quickly, the chair fell backwards and the coffee cup tipped over. Black coffee ran out in a little puddle on the table. "Who do you think you are? You're not going to come in here and tell us how we should work! You can be damn sure of that!"

He stood up and pointed threateningly with a long, narrow finger towards Luke. His blue eyes were wide in his weathered face. Mattias Palander hurried to wipe up the spilled coffee. Both Luke and Jonna looked at Anders Loman in surprise. The room went quiet. Anders Loman looked sharply at Jonna.

"You take over. Report to me on Monday morning at eight o'clock. I expect that you two will be working over the weekend on this."

He walked towards the door with quick steps, then stopped and pointed at Luke again.

"And you end your private investigation. From now on, we're taking over."

He turned on his heel and slammed the door.

"Shit," Mattias said. "He's not feeling well."

Jonna looked questioningly at Luke.

"What did he mean by 'former mafia gangster'?"

Luke cleared his throat.

"He's been checking into my background," he said. "For a couple years in my youth, I was mixed up in the Israeli mafia in New York."

"What? How so?"

"I worked as a security guard for their boss, Johnny Attias," Luke said. "I needed a job, and that job was damn good pay."

Both Jonna and Mattias sat quietly, looking at him, waiting for more details.

"That was a long time ago," Luke said. "Not something I'm proud of, but it's in the past and completely resolved. I'm not suspected of anything. I'm completely clean. Like the driven snow. But I wonder how Anders got that information."

"He told me he checked you out," Mattias said. "He has contacts with the FBI that he made when he was training in the USA twenty years ago. He claimed the FBI had a whole lot of information about you."

"I testified in a trial in exchange for my freedom," Luke said. "And for witness protection in another country. The prosecutor also agreed that the material would be classified for thirty years because some people didn't like that I was cooperating with the police. Clearly, that classified stamp wasn't worth much."

33.

The woman sitting across from Jenny was in her thirties. Ingela was from Malmö and was short, large-busted, frumpily dressed, and looked friendly. She was one of the participants in a special course, a weekend short course in auditing arranged by the movement and intended for people who recently took the communication course. Eleven people jumped at the chance, and Jenny was one of the members working the course this weekend. It was nice to have a break from the digging and building out at Trummenäs. They'd been at it since early May, almost three months now, building a new house and helping dig. This time, they were working on Peter's house. He'd come upon one of the lease plots and bought a prefab cottage from Västkuststuga that the seller promised would be delivered complete. But it turned out not to be that easy. A lot of work was left to do once the house was delivered.

The main responsibility for digging down to the ship fell on Åke. He had an associate's degree in engineering and was the only one in the group who had any sort of technical education. They bought an old excavator second-hand for fifteen hundred dollars, and Åke sat on it, digging a large hole in the ground next to George and Maria's house. Jenny and the others used wheelbarrows to haul away all of the dirt and gravel. Everyone in the group had to work during the day to earn enough money to cover not only their own auditing, but also a portion of George's. Some sold newspapers in the early morning, others taught Swedish to refugees, one sold cakes. The building and digging was mostly done on the weekends. Because the excavator made a horrendous racket, they told the neighbors they were building a pool on George and Maria's lot.

They worked in shifts; every other weekend, one group worked out on the promontory and the other took care of the activities in the center of town. This weekend, Jenny's group was in town, working with the Dianetics course. The goal with it was, of course, to lure people who were curious about auditing into buying the larger auditing course. Before they came, they all had to read L. Ron Hubbard's book, *Dianetics: The Modern*

Science of Mental Health, and in the morning, they had to perform various exercises. Now it was time to apply their knowledge in short auditing sessions. Because there was an odd number, Jenny had to volunteer to have Ingela as her therapy buddy.

Jenny was having a hard time concentrating. She was thinking about Åsa, Daniel's sister, and was sincerely worried about her. Two months ago, she again entered a deeply dark state. She received several auditing sessions and became stuck in an engram, Peter explained. He finally took over the auditing from Mikael, who couldn't guide Åsa through these difficulties. He didn't say any more than that, just assured Daniel that it would work out. If Peter couldn't fix it, he would make sure George went in and took over. George was one of the best auditors in the world, according to Peter. If anyone could fix it, it was him.

Åsa closed herself off more and more and became very quiet. Depressed. Finally, George took over and had now been performing intensive sessions for a week, but Åsa wasn't getting any better. Daniel was really worried. On this particular day, Åsa didn't show up at the center for her auditing and didn't answer her phone. Daniel went to her apartment, where he had a key. But she wasn't there, either.

"Hello?" The woman across from Jenny leaned forward and looked at her encouragingly.

"Oh, sorry. I was lost in thought. What was your question?"

"We're doing loss. Imagine a time when you lost something or someone."

"Oh, right!" Jenny thought. They'd been instructed not to do serious or deep topics. The exercise was mostly so that the participants could see how it felt to sit in a session.

"Last week, I lost my wallet when I was putting gas in my car at the gas station," Jenny said. "I put it on the top of the car and drove off. When I realized what I'd done, I drove back but couldn't find it."

"Good. Now it's your turn to guide me," Ingela said.

Jenny took out her course binder and checked.

"Okay. Let's do headaches. Think of a time when you had a headache."

Ingela thought for a moment.

"It was last night," she said. "I woke up because my guy was snoring, and snoring turns me on. So much that I have to masturbate, and I can't stop until the snoring stops. He snored all night long. And into the early morning hours, I had a crushing headache. I always get one when I'm at it for that long."

She stopped and looked at Jenny, who needed to work to control herself and not lose the neutral composition of the auditor. Ingela leaned towards her.

"It's such a pain," she said. "He snores every night."

"Okay. Can you tell about the event in more detail?" Jenny asked.

Before Ingela could begin to describe, there was a knock on the door. It was Peter, the course leader that weekend.

"I'm sorry to bother you, but Jenny, I need you. It's Åsa."

Jenny understood that it must be serious; Peter would never interrupt an auditing session otherwise. She got up right away and went out. Daniel was standing at the reception desk, looking pale. He was about to put on his overcoat.

"Åsa's been in a car accident," he said. "She's in one piece, apparently, but a witness saw her get out of the car and then began taking off all of her clothes. Completely naked. A few people took care of her and called the police. Now she's in the psychiatric emergency ward. I have to go there. Now."

34.

The rustic and brightly-styled kitchen in the apartment on Alamedan 25 felt like a dark Thai-scented isolation cell. The silence was only broken by the metallic sound of silverware hitting plates. It was Saturday evening, the day after the meeting with Luke at the station.

The children had tossed dinner down their throats as usual, and left the table, and it was now completely silent. Jonna realized it had been like that for most of her marriage with David. During the three first years, he was the same man as when they met. In love, considerate, creative, and open. He was intelligent and good at his job. Earned good money. But at the same time as his brother died and he got the upper-management job at the pharmaceutical company in Copenhagen, something happened. He slowly disappeared mentally from her life, went quiet. And that's how it was for the past six years. In the beginning, she tried to talk to him about it. But she couldn't get anywhere. He didn't think he'd changed and just grew irritated when she brought it up. When the children were born, he re-blossomed, and she thought he'd come back. It only lasted a short time, though, and then he withdrew again.

David didn't come on Friday evening as promised. He called and said that he was going to go out to the bar with an important client and that he would come home first thing the next day. He arrived on the train after lunch on Saturday. Crabby, hungover, and without his wallet, which he lost sometime during the night. He went immediately to the bedroom to take a nap. Jonna had to take the children to the playground to Admiralty Park for a couple of hours. David was sensitive to sound and would have been furious if he was woken up. When she made dinner, she tried to be as quiet as possible.

Now here they sat, eating Saturday dinner together. Neither saying a peep. Jonna tried to start up a conversation. Asked if he had a nice time with his client the previous evening. David just nodded without lifting his gaze and continued eating. Then Jonna told him about the investigation of the suicide of Viktor Spandel and his daughter, that there was now a theory the deaths were murder. This piqued his interest, and he asked a few questions about it. But after a while, they fell silent again. When David was done eating, he laid his silverware down, leaned back, and put his hands behind his neck.

"In three weeks, my work friends are coming up from Copenhagen for our usual summer party. I've told you, right?"

"No, but it sounds really great!" Jonna said.

She meant it. She liked several of his colleagues, all guys she got to know at these summer parties. They hung out with some of them as a family, too. When just the guys got together, they turned into teenagers and could come up with the craziest things. Jonna giggled.

"Not Santas stripping on the nudist beach again, I hope?"

Two summers in a row, after downing a few cases of beer, they dressed up as Santas, and in the middle of the afternoon, they rowed over to the nudist beach where they performed an advanced striptease. Right before the eyes of many angry, naked sunbathers. The second time, someone called the police, and Jonna had to work hard to convince her colleague it was just a boyish prank.

"We seldom do the same trick three times," he said. "We're more creative than that."

Jonna thought about the times things went too far. They partied hard, and when they were drunk, they pushed each other to outdo themselves. This resulted in several wild fistfights at the bar with other guests who reacted to the group's provocative concoctions. But she also remembered the days after the partying. When they had good conversations, singing, good-natured competitions. And lots of laughter. This group of friends possessed incredible humor and warmth. Jonna usually took care of where they stayed, food prep, all the practical stuff. She liked it, despite how much work it was.

"It'd be really fun to see them again," she said, taking a large bite of rice drenched with Thai sauce. "Should we sit down someday and plan the food and activities?"

"Wait a minute now," David said. "I said 'my' work friends. I want you to stay in town this time with the kids. I'll take care of the logistics myself."

Jonna stared at him. David gazed back, expressionless.

"What do you mean?" she asked. "I've always been there."

"Yes, but the last few times, you've been so embarrassing," he said. "Even though I asked you to stay in the background last summer, you babbled on like always," David said. "I don't like it. This will be way better. Then you won't have to do all of that work and can do something fun with the kids instead."

Embarrassing.

Jonna couldn't believe it. He was forbidding her from seeing his friends. Because *she* was embarrassing. She clenched her teeth. So mean. She didn't know what to say. If she should say anything at all. She didn't have the energy for the conflict. She got up, took her plate, and began clearing the table.

She had basically already disconnected him from her life, and concentrated on having a good life with Astrid and Simon during the week. She just tried to survive the weekends. She decided she would endure it; she really didn't want the kids to become the children of divorce like so many of their friends' children. She was ready to give up a part of herself just to give them a good childhood.

She set the plates and glasses on the counter, went to the bedroom, and closed the door. She heard how he took care of things in the kitchen and then went to the dresser outside the bedroom where they kept their exercise clothes. After a few minutes, the front door closed. He'd gone out for a run, as he typically did when recovering from a hangover. Astrid and Simon were playing in their room, and Jonna got up to go back into the kitchen. She couldn't stop thinking about what he said.

Damn, what an asshole he was, she thought. On the way to the kitchen, she heard the telephone on the wall by the refrigerator ring. She walked over and answered it. It was a woman. She had an English accent and asked for David.

"He is not home," Jonna responded in English. "Who are you?"

It was quiet for a few seconds.

"Tell him I'm the girl from last night," said the female voice. "He left his wallet here."

"Where?" Jonna asked.

She didn't get an answer. The woman hung up. Jonna quickly checked the number and wrote it on a piece of paper. She grabbed her laptop, went in to Eniro, and found a link to the equivalent Danish directory assistance site. She quickly typed in the number, and the result appeared immediately. The number was connected to someplace called "Romantica." Her pulse quickened. She clicked on the website and, slowly, a red-and-black webpage opened with the picture of a woman in fishnets and a string bikini,

160

looking at the camera with bedroom eyes. Jonna clicked on "The Girls" in the menu, and then a page appeared with more than a dozen women.

David left his wallet at a brothel.

Twenty minutes later, she heard the front door open. She went immediately out into the hallway. David was sweaty and flushed from the effort.

"Your wallet has been found," Jonna said. "At a brothel in Copenhagen. The whore you fucked called a little bit ago."

David looked up at her. For once, he looked unsure of himself.

"Oh, David. What a pig you are."

He still didn't say anything, just stood there, sweating, looking stupid.

"You don't have to say anything," Jonna said. "I don't want you to say anything. I assume you'll be taking care of the kids tonight. I'm not going to be home."

Before David could react, she left the apartment, slamming the door behind her.

35.

Time stopped. The air over Admiralty Park was still. A solitary gull circled over the beautiful old clocktower that stood at the top of the park.

It was Saturday evening, July 12, 2014. Just after eight o'clock. Jonna sat in her car next to the park, which was steaming in the evening sunlight. A long-awaited rain began around four, but now the sky was blue again. Jonna had rolled down both windows. The air was filled with oxygen.

She was deep in thought. She knew this day would come. Yet now that it was here, it felt unexpected. Like when an aging parent finally dies. You know it's inevitable but it's impossible to completely prepare yourself.

The decision was irreversible. It was over now and she felt free. Free, relieved, and angry. That asshole had been with prostitutes.

She sat in the car for ten minutes. Then she made her decision. Got out, went back into the building, down to the storage space where they kept a small supply of wine. She took a woven basket and set one bottle of red wine and a corkscrew in it, an old wine glass, and a threadbare blanket. She took out her bicycle and rode east towards one of her favorite places on Trossö, a small green space high up on Björkholmen. The green space was comprised of exposed stone slabs, wild grasses, and a grove of trees. Below this spot was a small harbor, and on the other side of the inlet lay Saltö fishing port. Jonna lay the blanket out, opened the bottle, and filled her glass. She stood up and looked towards the sea. A large, dark rain cloud looked like it was parked over Hasslö. She heard faint music from the Hasslö festival. She knew Ulf Lundell was set to play that evening, but she couldn't determine whether it was his music traveling the almost four miles across the bay to her.

Two glasses of wine later, she took out her phone. David hadn't tried to reach her. She searched for Luke's cell phone number. She knew he lived on Björkholmen.

She wrote, *What are you doing? -Jonna*

The answer came quickly. *Nothing in particular. At home taking it easy. Are you working?*

Want a glass of wine? I'm sitting on a blanket in the green space on Björkholmen

Two minutes later, she got a response.

Coming

Dusk had begun to fall over Björkholmen when Jonna saw a tall figure in a grey hooded sweatshirt and jeans come climbing up over the exposed rock from the quayside. She stood up and handed him the glass without saying a word. He accepted it and took a sip. Jonna pointed out towards the sea.

"Is there anything more beautiful?"

Luke turned around and shook his head. They stood together in the dusk and looked out over the sea, surrounded by the scent of rock moistened by rain and warmed by the day's heat, past Saltö and out towards Hasslö where the streetlights glittered like stars in the sky. The rain cloud over the island remained, creating a fascinating naturescape.

Jonna bent down, picked up the wine bottle, and reached her hand out to him. Luke took it and she led him to a bench that was out of sight of the apartment buildings nearby.

"Sit down," she said, filling the glass. She took a drink and then handed it to Luke.

"Cheers," she said.

"Cheers." Luke raised the glass and drank.

"To Darwin," she said.

Luke almost choked on the wine but was able to swallow it without having a coughing fit. He looked at her inquisitively.

"You've captured my interest, Luke Bergmann," she said, sitting on his lap. She leaned forward and kissed him. Intensely. He responded, their teeth hitting each other and her tongue playing wildly with his. The first, fantastic kiss. The new, unfamiliar mouth. New hair, taste, smell. They kissed long and hard.

Luke dropped the glass next to the bench. The sound of breaking glass seemed like lighter fluid for Jonna, who ripped off Luke's hoodie and T-shirt as if they were on fire. She unbuttoned his pants and sat on top of him. She took off her panties while waiting for him to come. Jonna was like a woman possessed. Luke sat on the bench with his legs outstretched, breathing through her hair as her body worked on his. The experience was earth-shattering, profound. She'd had sex many times before, but never like this.

Afterward, they sat tightly intertwined for a long time. Jonna remained with her legs on either side of Luke, holding him tightly.

"God, how I needed this," she whispered in his ear. "Thank you."

36.

The silence in Karlskrona. Luke loved it. He was on his way down towards the quay on Björkholmen after the encounter with Jonna. Despite it being Saturday evening, the only discernible sound was the faint cries of seagulls. In the distance, he could feel more than hear the bass drums from Hasslö. He tiptoed carefully down the little path in the darkness.

Giddy.

And confused over Jonna's sudden intensity and hunger. He didn't stand a chance. She knew what she wanted. And he loved it. There was something irresistibly independent about her. He saw it the first time he met her, in Viktor's stairwell.

They sat entwined for a long time afterward, not saying anything. Then she got up and picked up her blanket, basket, and wine. Luke gathered the broken glass. She gave him a warm kiss, took her bicycle, and left him.

He stopped, standing still and listening to the silence. A gust of wind brought an intoxicating smell of honeysuckle. Possibly elderflowers, too. He thought about how fortunate he was. When, seventeen years earlier, he moved to a city in the frozen North, almost four thousand miles from home, he'd felt like he imagined Vietnam veterans felt when they were sent home after months at war.

He found peace and quiet.

After twenty-four years in a constant state of war, he came home and was able to rest. When he was little, there were constant arguments and violent fights between his mom and dad, and it continued until he was ten years old and his dad disappeared. Then he was pulled into the Devil's Rebels, which found itself at war with rival gangs in Brooklyn. The Williamsburg police were always on their heels. It didn't get any better when he became Johnny Attias's right-hand man. He was forced to be on his guard 24 hours a day so he wouldn't end up in the eternal sleep.

Movement was Luke's best friend. From room to room, building to building, street to street, neighborhood to neighborhood, from one hell to another. In Karlskrona, he found peace and could stop moving. Until two weeks ago.

He hoped he wouldn't need to do anything more to find Viktor's and

Agnes' murderer now that the police were putting more resources into the case. But he wasn't sure. And it didn't feel good at all that Anders Loman got hold of information about his former life.

Still reeling from the events up on the hill, Luke opened the door to his little yard. Two figures stepped forward from the shadows into the beams from the streetlights. Two men. Big men. One was just as tall as Luke, the other, a little shorter and rounder. Purposeful. The big one wore a denim vest with ripped-off sleeves. Probably to suggest that no clothing could fit around his swollen arm muscles. He was enormous. The slightly shorter one had on a black leather vest with a swastika tattooed on his temple. He was as wide as a steroid-laden East German discus thrower with that hard, massive flesh that is almost, but not exactly, muscle. Luke saw that both held brass knuckles in their right hands. They were clearly not there for a friendly visit.

The shorter guy had shifty eyes and was twitchy. His head jerked involuntarily at random times. He seemed to be on some sort of drugs.

"You should've called," Luke said. "I'd have come home early and put on the coffee. I like having friends over."

"Shut up," the short one said.

"Listen, fatty," Luke said. "What sort of language is that? It's not polite for a guest to talk like that. Haven't you learned any manners?"

"We don't like foreigners," the big one said. "We want you to leave."

Luke stood so he was two yards away from them. He would have rather had the big one to his left because his right fist would then have a little longer to travel and the force of the blow would be harder. But he didn't have any problem taking the shorter one out first.

"Unfortunately for you, you're the ones who are leaving," Luke said. "From this yard, at least." He took a step towards the shorter man.

"Hey, fatty. I'm going to give you a choice."

"What sort of choice?" he asked. Angry. Surprised.

"You get to choose the variety."

"What?"

"That was clearly a hard word for you. Don't you know Swedish? Even a foreigner like me knows what 'variety' means."

Luke saw that the fat one was preparing to strike.

"Wait a minute," Luke said. "I'm going to explain what I mean. You get to choose how you're going to leave my yard. Because you are leaving, that's

165

a fact. You can choose whether you leave on your own, or your overgrown friend here can push you out in my wheelbarrow."

"Oh, is that so?" the fat one said.

"I'll count to three, and you have to make your decision before then. Do you understand?"

Luke started counting before the shorter one had a chance to react.

"One." No reaction.

"Two." No reaction.

But Luke lied. He didn't count to three. Immediately after saying "two," he took a quick step forward and head-butted the fat one. He lashed out with his upper body from his waist up and rammed his forehead directly over the guy's nose. It was a perfect head-butt. Perfect timing, force, and aim – old skills brought back to life.

No one expects a head-butt. A punch with the right fist or maybe a kick. But no one thinks a person will use their head in a fight, especially not as their very first move. And Luke's forehead was unusually thick, like it was made of concrete. So it could just as well have been a bowling ball flung right into the face of the shorter man.

The guy crumpled like a house of cards. His brain stopped working in the moment Luke's forehead crushed his nose and caved in his cheekbone. Blood gushed from his face, and the back of his head struck the pavement with a heavy thud.

Luke turned towards the taller man. He seemed not to have understood what happened at first. He looked at his companion lying unconscious on his back. Then he went on the attack. Arm muscles as thick as the ceiling beams in Luke's cottage, enormous thighs, fists as big as basketballs. But now he was blind with rage. He ran towards Luke with jerky steps and prepared his right arm to crush Luke with a single blow. And if the blow had made contact with Luke, he probably wouldn't have survived. But Luke's head wasn't where the brass-knuckled fist landed. Instead, Luke answered the attack by throwing himself forward and ramming his elbow horizontally right into the man's forehead. It had the same effect as if this beast ran straight into a speeding freight train. The man lost consciousness immediately and he, too, fell backwards onto the pavement, landing next to his unconscious friend.

Luke stood there panting for a few seconds. He shook off the adrenaline rush and felt how his legs were about to give way. He bent down and searched through the men's pockets but found nothing except a couple of car keys. He then dragged the two out onto the street, a bit from the gate, and laid them on the sidewalk. He didn't want to have this garbage in his yard. He went back to his cottage. The door had been forced open, and it looked like the two had plenty of fun in his house. They'd rampaged through it like berserkers. One of them found Luke's baseball bat and broke most of what was inside. Luke picked up his phone and called Jonna.

"Still not satisfied?" she asked.

"I could've gone all night," Luke said. "Are you home?"

"No."

"Do you want to come here? There were a couple of guys here waiting for me. They weren't very friendly."

"Where are they now?"

"Lying in a heap on the sidewalk. I didn't want them in my yard."

"Are they alive?"

"They were when I dumped them there. But they need a few band-aids. Possibly brain surgery. Maybe you could call for an ambulance? Or two. They were pretty big."

"What did they want?"

"For me to leave the country. They destroyed my whole place to show they mean business."

"I'm coming," Jonna said. "Don't touch anything in your house. I'll make sure my colleagues send a unit, too."

37.

"Mikael and I will go with you," Peter said to Daniel. "We have to make sure she doesn't see any psychiatrists, because things will go downhill fast. They'll look in her file and then start in with the whole battery of drugs."

Daniel looked at Peter. They discussed Åsa's mental state and her situation two years earlier, when she attempted to take her own life. According to Peter, it was because her parents made sure she was admitted to the emergency psychiatric unit and the doctors stuffed her full of psychotropics. Her doctor labeled her "manic depressive." Peter pronounced the entire psychiatric field as quackery and said that Åsa had now finally found her way home. With the help of therapy within the movement, she could quickly find the root causes of her problems and become a happy, cheerful person.

Daniel didn't say anything, but Jenny saw in his face that he was nervous and hesitant. He put his jacket on. They decided to go to the hospital in two cars. Jenny went with Daniel and Peter. Mikael went in Peter's car.

When they arrived at the hospital's emergency entrance, Peter wanted them to first sit in the foyer to go through what they should do. They found a seating area with a blue sofa in a corner facing the reception desk. Before them stood three rows of wooden chairs arranged as if they were in a cinema. A handful of people sat spread out on the chairs. Jenny sat next to Daniel.

"Because she isn't hurt physically, they will probably set her up with a psychiatrist quickly," Peter said, looking intensely at Daniel. "But they can't admit her unless she agrees on her own. You have to make sure to talk privately with her and convince her that the best thing for her is to come with us. We'll make sure she gets healthy again. We'll start heavy auditing for her immediately. Tell her that. The risk is that right now, she doesn't have the ability to see clearly and to realize what's best for her. But you have to get her to agree to it, otherwise she'll just be drugged again, and you know what happened last time."

Daniel was looking down at the table the whole time Peter was talking.

Jenny understood he was nervous, and that he was doubtful about what Peter said. He just sat there silently, not saying a word.

"What are you thinking about, Daniel?" Peter asked.

Daniel looked up at Peter.

"Damn it, I don't know, Peter. It all just feels so awful. I'm scared for her and want her to get better."

Peter lay his arm around him.

"I understand. I'm scared, too. But think of the alternative. There's even the risk that they'll decide to give her electric shocks. We have to make sure she gets out of here. We'll take her to my apartment and make sure someone's with her all the time. Then we'll put her in a program immediately. There are treatment plans for when situations like this arise. It's diet and therapy in combination. Believe me. This is the right solution. The only solution."

Daniel nodded and stood up.

"Okay."

"Good. Then I suggest you go to the desk and ask to speak to the doctor whose care she is under."

Daniel went to the desk, introduced himself as Åsa's brother, and said that he wanted to talk to her doctor. He was told that Åsa was still in the emergency room and that the receptionist would see if she could contact the doctor. After thirty minutes, the doctor came out—a young woman who introduced herself as Anna Larsson. She had a handwritten name tag on her white coat. Next to her name, it said that she was a resident. She sat on an available chair next to the seating area. In her hand was a folder, which Jenny realized was Åsa's file. Daniel said that he was Åsa's brother and that the others were her friends.

"How is she doing? Daniel asked. "Can we see her?"

"Physically speaking, she's unhurt. Apparently, she drove into a car that stopped at a red light, and she wasn't going fast. On the other hand, she doesn't seem to be well, psychologically speaking. She is apathetic and says very little. But when she does talk, she seems confused. We've made the decision to admit her to our psychiatric ward to do an examination. Now we're just waiting for the all-clear from them."

Daniel gave Peter a quick glance.

"We, or rather, I, would like to take her home. Right now. If that's okay?"

Anna Larsson raised her eyebrows.

"Really? Why is that? My diagnosis is that she needs psychiatric treatment. She is not well."

Daniel hesitated, not knowing what he should say. Peter broke in.

"Well, what's going on is that Åsa doesn't believe in psychiatric treatment. And we don't either, for that matter. And from what you see in her file, she's had experience with that sort of treatment, and it didn't go so well for her last time, isn't that right?"

Before the doctor could say anything, Daniel stood up and interrupted.

"I would really like to see her. Now. Along with Peter. Can we do that?"

The doctor looked up at him.

"Yes. We can arrange that. But before we do, I'd like to see your ID. I have to confirm that you are indeed her brother."

Daniel took out his driver's license. The doctor looked at it and noted that he had the same last name as Åsa. Then she walked ahead of Peter and Daniel through the hallway. She stopped at a closed door. She opened it and went in to Åsa.

"Åsa, you have visitors. Your brother, Daniel. And two friends. Is it okay if they come in?"

Åsa nodded, and the doctor opened the door, letting Daniel and Peter in.

"I'll be back in fifteen minutes and we can continue talking then," she said, leaving the room.

Åsa lay on her back in bed. Her long, black hair lay spread out on the pillow. She looked thin and pale. Her large, beautiful brown eyes were filled with tears. Daniel ran to the bed, knelt, and embraced her.

"Åsa, Åsa. What's going on?"

Åsa didn't react. She just lay still with Daniel over her. She didn't move. The only thing that moved was the tears running down her cheeks. They lay like that for a few minutes. Then Peter stepped forward, sat in the chair next to the bed, and rested his hand on Daniel's back. Daniel stood up, wiped the tears, and took Åsa's hand. Peter leaned towards Åsa.

"Åsa," he said.

Åsa carefully turned her head towards him.

"Hi, Åsa. We're going to get you out of here. Away from the hospital. You have to get help, and we're the only ones who can help you. If you stay here, the doctors will just give you a bunch of drugs that will cut you off from everyone, and you will never be able to uncover the real reasons you feel so bad. Do you understand that, Åsa?"

Åsa looked at him with an empty gaze.

"Yes," she said weakly.

"That's good," Peter said. He looked up towards Daniel.

"Then we'll do what we talked about, Daniel. We'll make sure she gets out of here as quickly as possible. I'll go and find the doctor, and tell her Åsa wants to be discharged. Maybe you could help Åsa get dressed."

Peter stood up and left the room. Daniel took Åsa's clothes from a closet, helped her up, and got her dressed. After a few minutes, Peter came back with Doctor Anna Larsson. She looked worried, and she went to Åsa, who was sitting up in bed, fully dressed. She took a chair and set it in front of Åsa. She took Åsa's hand and looked her in the eyes. Åsa sat completely still, staring at her knees.

"Åsa. Is this really what you want?" Anna Larsson asked. "Don't you want to stay here so we can help you? We have really excellent psychiatrists at the hospital, and I'm sure they can figure out what you're suffering from and how to help you."

Åsa didn't react. Peter went around the bed and stood next to the doctor.

"I asked Åsa before I went to find you, and she said she wanted to be discharged. Or, more precisely, I asked her if that was what she wanted, and she nodded. Isn't that right, Åsa? You want us to take you away from here, right?"

Åsa nodded hesitantly. Anna Larsson stood up from the chair and looked at Daniel and Peter.

"Could I speak with both of you out in the hallway?" She walked quickly out of the room. Peter and Daniel followed. Daniel closed the door.

"I strongly advise you not to remove her from the hospital," she said, looking at Daniel. She nodded towards Åsa's file, which she held in her hand.

"Considering her previous depression and suicide attempt, I believe there's a great risk she will make more attempts in her current state. If that happens, the responsibility for it falls on you two. I hope you understand that."

"That is exactly why we have to take her away from here," Peter said coldly. "If you read carefully in the file you're holding in your hands, you will see that Åsa tried to kill herself *after* you stuffed her full of psychotropics. Do you think it's that unreasonable for us to be reluctant, to say the least, to let you make the same mistake again?"

"I can't take responsibility for..."

Peter interrupted her brusquely.

"Did you know that one hundred and fifty people die on this planet every day because of psychotropics? That's 24,000 people each year. It's as if two packed jumbo jets crashed two days a week, all year long. All caused by the biological view of the psyche, which has its foundation in Nazi Germany. That was when this all started. German psychiatrists murdered 250,000 mental patients and people with cognitive disabilities in the years before the war, and their knowledge was then used during the Holocaust. They were consultants for purposes of genocide. But they were never punished—instead, they were given lucrative positions at universities and hospitals around the world where they could continue developing their biological psychiatry which is based on the idea that we humans are just piles of flesh and that if someone feels bad, you fix it with poisonous chemicals and electric shocks."

Anna Larsson stood silently, looking at Peter. She realized she would never get this man to agree to leave Åsa here.

"Okay," she said. "Then I'll just arrange the logistics of the discharge. You can take her out into the foyer by the reception desk, and I'll come out with the paperwork." She turned on her heel and left them.

Peter looked at Daniel with a pleased expression.

38.

The sunlight moved slowly through the room, reaching Jonna's eyes five minutes before nine on Sunday morning, and she was flung out of her dreams and into reality. She turned her head and saw Astrid's and Simon's golden curls on the pillow. Images from the previous evening appeared in her consciousness. It was a tumultuous Saturday. One of the most eventful in all her thirty-four years.

She didn't regret seducing Luke on Björkholmen for a second. It was better than she imagined. She'd love to do it again, actually.

He was a special man. The two men he left lying half-dead on the sidewalk outside his house would probably agree with her. They'd survive, but one would probably spend a long time in the hospital. And the question remained if he'd ever be normal again.

She lay silently, listening. It was completely quiet in the apartment. Where is David? Then she remembered. When she came home after having been with Luke the second time, he was lying on the sofa, sleeping. A suitcase stood packed next to him. She didn't have to throw him out of the bedroom. Astrid and Simon must have woken up in the night and crawled in next to her.

Jonna thought about their marriage, realizing that they had fundamentally different ways of relating to life, and that this was why they wouldn't work in the long run. It wasn't actually about him having been with a prostitute. It ran deeper than that. David wanted to have everything, own everything. His entire life was based on it. That was why he would never even consider looking for a job in Karlskrona. There was no company that could pay the salary he needed to have, he often said. He had to earn a lot of money in order to buy everything he wanted to have. A boat, a summer cottage, nice cars. It was the same with people. After he won Jonna over, he owned her. Had her. And now he had a family, too. And when he had something, he lost interest in it.

For Jonna, the owning part wasn't important—it was the opposite. She wanted to experience things, she wanted to be changed, develop. Love wasn't something you possessed but something you did. Jonna tried to talk with David about this, but he didn't understand what she was talking about in the least.

He'd chosen to turn his back on her and the children. The forgotten wallet at the brothel was just a drop in the already-overflowing bucket. Now it was definitely over. He had to get out of her life. Having made the decision made her feel strong. And she didn't think the children would be harmed too much by a divorce. They'd grown up with a mostly-absent father. This wouldn't mean any great change in their daily life.

She snuck out of bed, put on her robe, and went out into the living room. The sofa was empty. He was gone. Probably went to the cottage. She gave a sigh of relief. She had to work today, and she wouldn't want or have time to talk with David about whether she wanted a divorce. She'd have to do that later. Instead, she took a quick shower, made breakfast, and woke Astrid and Simon up. One hour later, she dropped them off at her mother's house, and at exactly ten o'clock, she stepped into the police station.

She and Mattias split the job between them. Mattias would first search for the three remaining people: George Knightly, Jenny Eklund, and Mikael Andersson. Jonna would go through all the material one more time. But she started by calling the hospital to check on how things were with the two who jumped Luke. The shorter man had regained consciousness, but the doctors put him into a medically-induced coma because the pressure on his brain, caused by extreme blood loss, was too high. The bigger one received a serious concussion and also had suspected bleeding on the brain. Both would have MRI scans later that day. Jonna asked if they had established the identity of either man, but the nurse Jonna was talking to said neither of them had any identification on them.

Jonna took out her cell phone. She noted the license plate number of the car that stood parked outside Luke's cottage. She did a quick search and found a name and social security number. The car belonged to Mats Cederberg, thirty-six years old, address in Spjutsbygd, a village twelve miles north of Karlskrona. She recognized it and quickly clicked to a folder on the Intranet labeled "The Force Soldiers," a criminal biker gang whose clubhouse had been located in Spjutsbygd for a few years now. They backed the Revenge Crew in Kalmar, which was one of the Bandidos' supporting organizations.

She flipped through the list and pictures of members until she came to Mats Cederberg. It was the shorter of the two whom Luke sent to the hospital. It would be interesting to interrogate him about the motive for jumping Luke Bergmann. If he would ever be able to talk again, that was.

She wondered if Luke's background in the Israeli mafia could have anything to do with it, but she thought that was probably a long shot. An answer would hopefully reveal itself.

She changed course and took out the folder that contained all of the material pertaining to Viktor and Agnes. She went through the forensic investigation. Nothing out of the ordinary there. Only Viktor's, Agnes', and Luke's fingerprints in the apartment. On the jar of powdered poison, only Viktor's fingerprints. No others. The potential murderer had been clever about hiding his tracks. She wondered about Anders Loman's theory about collective suicide. Could he be right? She googled the word "Scientology," both in Swedish and English. She got almost 200,000 hits in Swedish, and 4.5 million in English. For reference, she searched the word "Buddhism." Nine and a half million hits. Scientology was bigger than she thought. She found a site that described its overarching tenets. Reincarnation was a significant part of their worldview, she realized. Then she searched Scientology and suicide. Found a site that described a number of suicides committed by Scientologists. Seemed mostly to be people who were pressured by the church to pay a bunch of money or who ended up in depression after therapy sessions within the church. Even the founder's twenty-two-year-old son took his own life, it turned out. But she didn't find anything that indicated there were Scientologists who committed collective suicide.

Jonna needed coffee. She went to the coffee maker in the kitchen and filled a cup. When she came back to her office, she took out the autopsies for both Viktor and Agnes. The autopsies were completed by the National Board of Forensic Medicine in Lund. Viktor died from suffocation caused by the hanging. She read further in Agnes' report. She died from the veterinary poison phenobarbital, which knocked out her central nervous system. Her breathing eventually stopped. Jonna continued reading but stopped short at one sentence, "An injury was observed on the girl's vagina of the sort that indicates an object was pushed into it with force. Probably a bottle or other object with a similar form. No sperm or other bodily fluid can be found on or in the body."

39.

Jenny and Daniel each held one of Åsa's arms the whole way out to the car. Peter and Mikael followed behind them. Åsa walked with small steps and her head bowed.

"It'll all be fine, Åsa. It'll be fine," Daniel said several times during the walk to the car. No one else said anything.

"Jenny, you drive Daniel's car. We'll put Åsa in my car, and Daniel will come with us," Peter said when they got to the parking area. "We'll drive to my apartment. Åsa can stay in the guest room for now, and we'll take shifts. She can't be alone for the first bit here. Is that okay, Åsa?"

Åsa didn't answer, and Daniel helped her into Peter's car. Jenny sat behind the wheel in Daniel's little red Fiat and waited for Peter to exit the parking lot. She sat there watching Peter's blue 745 and thought, was it right of them to take Åsa from the hospital? She knew that she would never be able to question it in front of the others. Only in front of Daniel. She decided to talk to Daniel when they got home. If they even went home together, that was. She knew Daniel was worried and that he would probably want to stay with Åsa all night.

And that's what happened. As soon as they got to Peter's apartment, they put Åsa in the bed in Peter's guest bedroom, and Daniel stayed with her. She was completely apathetic. Daniel sat at her bedside and held her hand. Jenny took the key to Åsa's apartment in order to get clean clothes and her toiletries. When she came back, Daniel, Peter, and Mikael were in Peter's kitchen, talking.

"She's sleeping now," Daniel said to Jenny, who sat at the kitchen table. Peter had set out tea and sandwiches, and she gratefully accepted a steaming cup.

"Luckily, Ron has produced a method of dealing with exactly the type of state Åsa has ended up in," Peter said. "In his earlier research, he was very interested in psychotic states, and in January of 1974, he released a bulletin in which he shows in detail how to treat people who have this type of problem. He called the method 'Introspection Rundown', which is a series of auditing processes that aim to find the cause of the problem. There is an event or an engram on Åsa's timeline that has been triggered for some reason and is causing her to become sick. And we can find that engram or event with the help of Introspection Rundown."

"It is doubtful that she will be receptive to auditing in the state she's in now," Daniel said. "She's completely apathetic. Doesn't even react when she's spoken to. How would it be possible to audit her?"

Jenny heard in Daniel's voice how stressed he was.

"I agree, Daniel. First and foremost, we have to make sure she gets properly rested. And at the same time, we're going to put her on a special diet that will make her feel better—bread, fruit, calcium-magnesium supplement, and vitamin C. Lots of vitamin C. Nothing else. We'll do that for five or six days. Someone has to be with her 24 hours a day. But we can't talk to her. She has to be completely isolated. We'll take shifts. I don't want you to be with her, Daniel. This won't work if you have an emotional bond with the person. You can help with the groundwork, but you can't be with her during this period. Okay?"

Daniel nodded.

"Who will conduct the Introspection Rundown on her?" he asked.

"I will," Peter answered.

During the following days, the members of the movement took turns keeping watch over Åsa in Peter's apartment. They kept careful log books about her diet and behavior. After three days, she refused to eat or drink, and her guards would have to force-feed her. She lay in her bed and slept a lot. When she was awake, she was apathetic and violent in turns. She tried to hurt herself a few times, throwing herself head-first into the wall and scraping up her face. She clawed at her arms and body with her nails. Peter called a doctor in Malmö who was a Scientologist and convinced him to write a prescription for valium, which made Åsa calmer. A few times, Daniel tried to convince Peter to let him visit her, but Peter was adamant. It would jeopardize the whole rehabilitation, he said. Åsa would be emotionally moved if she saw Daniel, and then they'd have to start over again. On the fifth day, Peter began the Introspection Rundown. Peter audited her in short sessions several times a day.

The tenth day, it was Jenny's turn to sit with Åsa again. The previous time she was with her, she was completely apathetic. Jenny had to force the two bits of bread and juice into her. Several times, she lay down and cried completely silently. Peter's auditing hadn't achieved much so far.

Jenny put on a warm top and took her bike. Despite that it was still August, a chilly wind pierced her clothes and she was frozen through when she locked her bike on Vallgatan outside Peter's apartment. She rushed into the stairwell and hurried up to the second floor. She met Mikael in the hall. He had blood on his shirt and hands. Before Jenny could say anything, he said, "It's okay, Jenny. It's okay now. Something happened here this morning. She found Peter's shaving kit in the bathroom and cut her wrists. Lucky, it had just happened when I went to her. I was able to stop the flow of blood. Peter's in with her now."

"My god!" Jenny screamed, rushing past Mikael and running into the guest room. Peter was sitting on the edge of the bed Åsa lay in. She looked like she was sleeping. Blood covered the bed and there was a large red puddle on the floor. Peter turned around as Jenny came into the room.

"It's okay now, Jenny," he said. "But it was damn lucky that Mikael went into her room so early today. Otherwise, who the hell knows what would've happened. Mornings are risky—the overnight dose of Valium stops working by then. We might need to start waking her up in the night and give her a little more so she will be calm when she wakes up. I've given her Ansopal, so she's going to be sleeping like a log for a few hours," Peter said.

40.

"Why didn't you tell me?"

Jonna flung the autopsy report on the conference table in front of Anders Loman, who looked at her with surprise. Mattias Palander looked at Jonna in confusion.

"What?" Anders said. "That Agnes was sexual assaulted?"

"Yes. Or raped."

Mattias' mouth gaped open. "Raped? You have to be joking," he said. "Let me see." He leaned over the table and scratched together the pages of the report.

"An object had been shoved up her vagina," Jonna said, turning towards Anders again. "Why didn't you say anything about it?"

Anders leaned back in the chair.

"What good would it have done?" he asked. "Telling her mom and grandparents that Agnes' dad raped her before he killed her? It would've been twisting the knife a few times in their wound. Would you have wanted to see them suffer even more?"

"Oh, Christ." Mattias was reading the doctor's description. "What an animal."

"What good would it have done? This isn't about the good it would do. It's about the truth," Jonna said. "Even if you didn't tell her family, you should have told us, obviously. I don't get it."

"How many work days have passed since Max Billing and the woman in Stockholm were found dead?" Anders asked.

"Two."

"Not even. They were found on Thursday evening. And the decision to form this investigation team was made on Friday. How could I have told you this earlier? This is the meeting where we'll go through all the material. I would appreciate it if you would think a little before you open your mouth."

As he finished his sentence, he opened the folder in front of him and turned towards Mattias.

"Now then. How have things gone for you?"

Jonna sat down, slightly humiliated at the same time as she cursed herself for not being able to keep from throwing the report in front of Loman before the meeting even began. When she sat in her chair, it struck her that there hadn't been anything about it in the report he himself wrote about the suicide. He might have a point about keeping the assault from the family but he shouldn't have left it out of the report. Even so, she decided not to say anything about it. To be safe, she would read through the report one more time to make sure she really had a leg to stand on. Then she would inform the Chief of the Criminal Division.

"I've found one more death," Mattias said, laying a picture of a man with a mustache and thinning hair on the table. "Mikael Andersson, fifty-three years old, living in Gothenburg. Was found hanged at his workplace, Schillerska High School in Gothenburg on Monday, May 9. But the two others, George Knightly and Jenny Eklund, I can't find. George Knightly lived in Karlskrona until 1993. According to Luke Bergmann, who talked with the daughter of Stockholm victim Maria Palm, he's the former husband of Maria Palm and father to Diana. He moved to Florida a number of years ago. I got a telephone number from Luke, but no one answers when I call."

"Jenny Eklund," Anders said. "Did you find anything about her at all?"

"Yes, I found a Jenny Eklund who graduated from Chapman School in 1991, with top grades. It might be her. But after that, she's just gone. I've searched in every single registry we have access to."

"She's probably moved, got married, and changed her name," Jonna said. "We have to find her social security number. Have you been able to find anything that supports that they were all members of the Church of Scientology in Karlskrona in the late 80s or early 90s?"

"It's not easy to find any proof of that," Mattias answered. "That church isn't active in the area anymore, and we don't know if they had a membership registry. But I got hold of a woman who was a close friend of Camilla Svensson during this period, who wasn't a member herself but knew this group. She recognized several of the names, and according to her, it was an exclusive group that only hung out with each other."

Anders looked through his documents and took out a paper with a list on it. It was a copy of Luke's list, Jonna saw.

"So we have eight confirmed deaths," he said. "The same M.O., and all were probably members of this reincarnation cult twenty-three years ago."

"In different places, except two," Jonna said. "The married couple in

Växjö, Fredrik Ek and Camilla Svensson. You'll have to excuse me, Anders, but the idea that they all committed collective suicide feels a bit far-fetched."

Anders pushed his glasses up to his forehead and looked at Jonna with his piercing gaze. Suddenly, he smiled.

"How long have you been a police officer, Gustafsson?"

Jonna decided not to waver. She looked at him with a steady gaze.

"Ten years. Why?"

"Where did you get your degree?"

"Växjö."

Anders smiled widely.

"Then it all makes sense," he said.

"What makes sense?" Jonna felt the anger bubbling up inside her. So damn mocking and unpleasant.

Anders leaned over the table towards Jonna.

"I understand why you're asking such stupid questions and showing your deep lack of insight into basic police work."

He still had a faint smile on his lips.

"Didn't you learn up there in the forests of Småland not to eliminate anything before you have the facts on the table?"

Despite that Jonna was on her guard and understood this man was a snake, she wasn't ready for such an attack.

"Maybe Sergeant Gustafson is so titillated by the tall American that she can't see clearly? Completely understandable, but not acceptable."

He turned to Mattias.

"Should we continue?"

Jonna thought feverishly how she should handle the situation. She fought the impulse to simply get up and leave the room. Then Anders turned towards her again and lay his hand on her arm. She jerked it away.

"I hope you aren't upset," he said, with seeming sincerity. "But sometimes it can be good to hear the truth. Until now, I've only heard good things about you, Gustafsson. Let's see if we can have a good collaboration as we go along. Okay?"

He sat up in his chair, laid his hands on the table and turned to the two of them.

"I am completely aware that the most likely scenario is that we have a serial murderer on our hands. But," he turned his head towards Jonna, "we cannot, we must not, eliminate other possibilities, isn't that right, Gustafson?"

Jonna felt forced to nod her head.

"Good. Let's think about the other scenario," Anders continued. "That is, that we've got a serial murderer here. Palander, what do we know?"

Mattias flipped through his folder and took out a few documents.

"We know that the first murder—if it is the first, since we still have a couple of names on our list—was committed in late April this year. Three months later, eight people have lost their lives. In seven different places."

"He, or she, must have prepared carefully in order to be able to do all this," Anders said.

"The MO is almost identical for all eight," Mattias continued. "Music on, likely the same song—I haven't completely confirmed this yet, but it's probably true. A computer-printed message with exactly the same wording. And then the hanging. In the bloodstream of at least three of the eight dead adults, an opiate was found. Flunitrazepam. I haven't been able to get the autopsy report from the five remaining adults, but it's probably present there, too. Because the deaths were classified as suicides by hanging, it isn't a given that the pathologist would look for such substances. Besides, we have the connection to the Church of Scientology. We have to check on that further." He stopped talking and looked at Anders.

"I assume you haven't been able to talk to any family members yet," Anders said. "So we don't know if any threats were made against any of them?"

"No," Mattias answered. "We have a bit to do in the coming days."

Anders leaned back in the chair, put his hands behind his neck, and looked up at the ceiling.

"What sticks out here is Agnes," Jonna said. "That she was murdered. She wasn't a Scientologist twenty years ago and so her potential murder probably wasn't planned." Jonna looked at Anders and emphasized the word "potential."

"She had a poison in her system, not the opiate like the others. And also, the murderer or murderers—we don't know if it's one or more—clearly raped the little girl with some object. And if we work based on the assumption that it wasn't the dad, where do we end up?"

She looked at Mattias.

"Well, where we end up is that we have to try to find a motive for

182

someone, or a few someones, to murder a whole group of Scientologists," Mattias answered.

"And force themselves on a little girl," Jonna added. "Either it's a completely insane murderer who also enjoys torturing people or he, or one of them, is a sadistic pedophile. I have a hard time believing it's a woman we're talking about here."

"Aren't all murderers insane?" Anders asked.

"Sure, but there are degrees of mental illness. Someone who isn't satisfied with just taking the lives of their victims but also wants to see them tortured likely has a greater degree of psychological disturbance."

"The question is whether that was what drove the murderer to force himself on the girl," Mattias said. "The information we have so far doesn't indicate that the victims were harmed in any other way than that they were hanged. No objects shoved anywhere."

"We have to check that out," Anders said. "Can you take that on, Mattias?"

Mattias nodded and made a note.

"If we assume that it's only Agnes who was subjected to this, it might be a sign that the murderer is sexually deranged," Jonna said. "From what I know, only at Viktor's was a child present." She looked at Mattias, who nodded.

"In all of the other cases, it was only adults," she continued. "The murderer probably hadn't counted on there being a child at Viktor's. Agnes was actually supposed to be with her mother that evening. When she showed up, the murderer couldn't resist the temptation."

Anders nodded, stood up, and went to the window that faced the city's indoor pool building. The square outside was empty. It was summer vacation, steaming hot, and those Karlskronites who were outside were probably on some beach or at their summer cottages. He turned towards the other two.

"This is too big for the three of us," he said. "We need reinforcements. I know that Malmö is completely overwhelmed with work, so we'll have to check with the National Police to see if they can spare anyone. At least a profiling expert. I'll call them right after this meeting."

He went back to the table and sat down.

"Meanwhile, we have to get going with what we can do ourselves," he said. "We need more facts. I want to have complete information about the victims, both about their assumed connection to Scientology and whether they were subjected to any violence similar to what Agnes suffered. I want the victims' computers gone through. Hopefully they're still around. Inventories of crime scenes can sometimes take a while. Whether they were murdered or decided to commit suicide simultaneously, we might find proof of that in emails or via that Facebook thing. Get help through police resources in the districts where they were found. I'll make some calls and start beating the bushes right away. If you run into any problems, tell me."

He turned around to face the room.

"So let's get going. Okay?"

Mattias looked uneasily at Jonna and cleared his throat.

"Shouldn't we start by trying to find the last two on the list?" he asked. "They might still be alive."

"It could also be one of them who's behind the murders, if it is murder," Jonna hurried to add.

"That's right," Anders said. "We still have them."

"How does it look with the timeline of deaths, Mattias?" Jonna asked.

Mattias took out his notes.

"The first we know of took place on April 30," he answered. "That was Åke Fleming in Kristianstad. After that, it's about two weeks between deaths."

"The last must have been Max Billing," Jonna continued. "That probably happened last Thursday, July 10, is that right?"

Mattias nodded.

"If this is a serial murderer on the move, and if he or she is following some sort of plan, that means that we have about a week before the next murder will happen," Jonna stated. "If the last two aren't already dead, of course."

"Okay," Anders said. "One of you focus on finding Jenny Eklund and George Knightly. You do that, Mattias. Jonna, you gather facts via the other police districts. Let's get this moving."

41.

Daniel lifted Åsa to a sitting position in the bed. She had bandages wrapped around both wrists. Her face was scraped up as a result of the struggle when Mikael was trying to stop the flow of blood. Now, Daniel and Åsa sat there, holding each other. Both were crying. Åsa didn't say anything to her brother. She just cried. Peter and Mikael stood next to the bed.

"She has to go to the hospital, Peter," Daniel said between sniffles. "We have to get her to a doctor."

Peter crouched down next to Daniel and laid a hand on his shoulder.

"If we send her there, you know what will happen to her," Peter said. "Drugs and maybe even electric shocks."

"But what in the hell should we do?" Daniel screamed at him. Jenny jumped from the unexpected outburst. Peter stood up hastily.

"Hey, hey, hey. Take it easy, Daniel," he said. "We have to act reasonably now. What I could see is us taking her to Malmö. I know a doctor there who's a Scientologist and member of the Malmö church."

"What sort of doctor is he?" Daniel asked suspiciously.

"A general practitioner. He works at the main clinic in Limhamn. He's very capable and smart. I'll go call him immediately."

Peter left the room to call the doctor and came back after five minutes.

"That's what we'll do," he said. "Olof Hansson is the doctor's name, and he'll see us as soon as we get there. He has his own private clinic at his home in Limhamn. If we leave right away, we can be in Malmö in two and a half hours."

They decided that Daniel and Mikael would come along in the car. Jenny got Åsa dressed. She and Daniel helped Åsa out to Peter's Volvo. Åsa held Jenny's hand tightly. She felt how Åsa's entire body was trembling.

Åsa fell asleep in the car and slept almost the whole way down to Malmö. They quickly found the doctor's large house in Limhamn and were welcomed in. Åsa had to go in to see the doctor alone, with a nurse assisting him. After an hour, Olof Hansson came out to Peter, Daniel, and Mikael and said he had taken some blood and urine samples to send for analysis.

He could say immediately that she was suffering from dehydration and malnourishment. They had to put her on an increased vitamin treatment and make sure she was consuming enough fluids and food. He was against all types of drugs and said that they should continue doing Introspection Rundown on her. Åsa's problem was obviously psychosomatic. He couldn't find anything physically wrong with her, and he didn't think the tests would show anything, either.

On the way home, they stopped at the Ekeröd rest stop to eat. Åsa sat and poked at her food. Daniel tried to talk to her, but she gave only one-word answers, unwillingly. She sat and looked down at her plate, avoiding his gaze. Daniel suspected she was scared of Peter. When Peter went to the bathroom, it felt like Åsa relaxed. But as soon as he returned, she tensed up again.

They arrived in Karlskrona just after eleven in the evening, and Daniel helped Åsa into the guest room of Peter's apartment.

"I don't want to go in there again," Åsa said quietly to Daniel as they stood outside the door to the room. "I want to go home. I don't feel well."

"But my sweet Åsa, you have to get healthy. Peter is going to help you get healthy again. And you have to have treatment. The doctor said so, too. Now we can be sure this is the right thing to do."

Åsa didn't say anything else but let Daniel help her into the room, where she crawled into bed.

The next morning, Jenny was supposed to come early to help with the breakfast duty. Daniel told her about the trip to Malmö and the doctor visit. He seemed to be a little calmer. Now at least a doctor had examined Åsa, and Daniel thought he had more of a connection with her on the way home.

When Jenny stepped into the apartment, Peter was in the kitchen washing dishes. Jenny took out two pieces of white bread, a banana, a glass of water, and vitamin C and magnesium tablets.

"We're going to increase her vitamin treatment," Peter said when he saw the tray Jenny had put together for Åsa. "I'll arrange more vitamins today."

Jenny took the tray and went to the guest room. She knocked carefully before opening the door and going in. Åsa lay unmoving in the bed. Jenny set the tray on the table next to the bed and pulled up the blinds to let light into the room. Jenny looked at Åsa. The covers had slipped down to her hips, and Jenny realized how thin she'd become. She was only skin and bones. Åsa didn't react to the light, so Jenny bent down and said her name quietly to get her to wake up. No reaction. Then Jenny laid her hand on Åsa's shoulder and shook her gently as she said her name a little louder. Still no reaction. Scared, Jenny called Åsa's name loudly and shook her harder. But Åsa remained lifeless. Jenny panicked and screamed for Peter, who came running into the room.

"She's not waking up, Peter! Help me!" Her voice didn't hold, and she felt how the fear spread through every cell in her body. "She can't be dead!"

Peter didn't make a sound. He bent over Åsa and shook her. Then he shouted her name and pressed two fingers to her carotid.

"She has a pulse," he said. "Go get a pitcher of water, Jenny."

Jenny ran as fast as she could out into the kitchen, filled a pitcher with water, ran back to the guest room, and gave it to Peter. He carefully poured water on Åsa's face, but she still didn't react. He bent over her again and put his ear to her mouth.

"I can feel her breathing," he said. "Strange that she's not waking up."

He stood up again and looked at Jenny.

"Stay here with her. I'm going to call George and consult him."

Jenny went to the bed and sat on the edge. She took Åsa's hand and squeezed it tightly. She pinched her skin. No reaction. After five minutes, Peter came back.

"George said we should try to get food into her. Get her to chew and swallow. That might make her wake up. He's on his way here to check on her."

Jenny thought it was strange that they would try to get her to eat when she seemed to be unconscious. But Peter asked Jenny to hold Åsa's head. He opened her mouth and pushed in a bite of bread. She got it down into her throat, which presumably made it so she couldn't get any air. She coughed suddenly and spit out the bread and saliva onto Peter's hands. Peter took a new bite and pushed it into her mouth, despite that she was coughing and gagging. Jenny felt hopeful. She was showing signs of life, at least. After a moment, when Åsa had swallowed a little bread, Peter stopped. She seemed to be breathing better, but they still couldn't get a reaction from her. Her eyes were closed, and she didn't answer when they called her name.

Suddenly, Jenny realized that George was in the room. He went to the bed and sat at its edge. He didn't say a word as he laid out her arms along her sides.

187

"Åsa, I'm going to conduct a touch assist on you now," he said to her, despite that she didn't seem to hear anything. "I want you to concentrate on the point where I put my finger. Concentrate with everything you've got on the point where you feel my finger. That's all you will do. I want you to confirm when you've felt my finger. Say okay or just nod so that I know you've felt it."

Then he put his left index finger on her left temple and said, "Feel my finger."

He held his finger there for a brief moment. Åsa didn't react. George didn't bother waiting for the confirmation. Instead, he quickly moved it to the corresponding point on the other side of her head.

"Feel my finger."

Then he continued in the same manner over her whole body all the way to her toes. He moved his finger to corresponding points on the other side and repeated the same words. Then he started again from the beginning, at the temples, and conducted the procedure five times. Åsa had neither moved nor given any sign of feeling his finger at any point in the process.

When George was finished, he leaned forward and raised Åsa's eyelids to look into her eyes. He said her name, but he got no response. He stood up and turned towards Jenny and Peter.

"Now her eyes are open, at least," he said. "I'm going to conduct another form of assist on her, too. How do you say 'unconscious' in Swedish?"

Peter told him, and George sat down again on the edge of the bed.

"Åsa, now I'm going to conduct an unconscious-person assist on you."

He paused briefly.

"Give me your hand."

No reaction. George took her hand and held it in his for a moment.

"Thank you," he said, laying her hand back down.

"Give me your hand."

The same thing was repeated. Åsa didn't react. George picked up her hand and said thank you. Laid her hand back down. He repeated the same procedure at least twenty times. Finally, he stood up.

"I feel a difference," he said to Peter and Jenny. "Now she's resisting slightly when I take her hand. I want you to continue conducting this assist on her until she wakes up. She will, if you just do exactly as I did. This assist was developed by Ron in the 60s, and it's helped loads of people who ended up in a coma to wake up. There are even cases where Scientologists have got people who were recently pronounced dead to come back to life with its help."

When George left the apartment, Peter told Jenny that L. Ron Hubbard began developing different forms of assists already in the 1950s, and that it was primarily about getting the thetan to come into contact with its body and the present. When that occurs, a miracle happens.

Over the coming days, the members conducted several different assists on Åsa. Foremost the unconscious-person assist, but also the touch assist and another that was called the contact assist. They sat for hours on the edge of her bed and repeated their commends. They fed her with bits of bread, crushed vitamins, and magnesium tablets in water, and tried to get fluids into her. Amazingly, her chewing and swallowing reflexes seemed to work. She didn't take much in, but a little bit went down. At one point, Mikael came running out to the kitchen where Daniel, Jenny, and Peter sat having tea. Mikael was sure he felt a movement, that Åsa pressed his hand. Not hard, but it was a distinct pressure. But it only happened once, then everything was just as before.

"Damn it, Peter. We have to take her to the hospital," Daniel said. "Three days have passed since she went into a coma. This isn't working."

"Patience, Daniel," Peter said. "We have to be patient. This will work out if we just don't give up. The pressure that Mikael felt might have been a sign that she's on her way up out of it. We have to give it a couple more days. I've talked with George about it, and he's in complete agreement."

Daniel stood up so suddenly that the chair flew backward and hit the stove before it landed with its back on the floor.

"But she's only skin and bones! Look at her! She can't weigh more than ninety pounds! I can't let this go on. I'm taking her to the hospital myself."

He walked with determined steps towards the guest room. Peter nodded to Mikael and both stood up and ran after him. Peter positioned himself in front of Daniel.

"Now you're going to calm down," he said in a firm voice, looking Daniel straight in the eyes. "You're almost OT, Daniel. Act like it."

"But what the hell, Peter! My sister is about to die in there!" He turned to the side and slammed his fist into the wall so hard that two books tumbled down to the floor next to them. Peter gripped Daniel's arms firmly.

"You're going to calm down now, Daniel!" Peter shouted. Jenny had never heard Peter raise his voice before. It was unpleasant.

Daniel seemed to resign himself after Peter's outburst and let Peter guide him back into the kitchen. Jenny sat next to him and held him. She saw now that tears were streaming down his cheeks.

"What am I supposed to say to my parents?" he asked Peter. "They're asking what's going on. Åsa used to call our mom several times a week, and now they haven't heard from her in two weeks. I can't lie to them any more. They have a right to know their daughter is sick."

"What have you been telling them?" Peter asked.

"That she's taking a course and it's taking all of her time. And that she's completely wiped out in the evenings and doesn't have the energy to talk. Dad is furious. He doesn't believe me. He doesn't like that we're Scientologists at all. He has threatened to go down to the Center and see what's going on there, he said. It wouldn't surprise me if he actually did it, either. And then he'll see that Åsa isn't there. What do we say to him?"

Peter didn't say anything. He poured more tea.

"Peter," Daniel said pleadingly. "I believe in the technology. I've invested tens of thousands of dollars into it, damn it. But I'm so damn worried about her. Maybe we're not doing the right thing, or maybe she needs something else. Something isn't working, anyway. You must see it yourself, right? Nothing's happening. She's just lying there, wasting away." His voice broke and the tears flowed again.

"We can do this, Daniel," Peter said. "I'll check with Olof Hansson, the doctor in Malmö, again. Maybe he has the results of those tests. And if he wants to look at her again, we can drive her down there one more time. Does that feel okay?"

"Hell if I know," Daniel said. "What he said the last time didn't help one damn bit."

"No, but now her condition has changed," Peter said. "Olof has the medical knowledge, just like doctors at the hospital have, *plus* our technology. I don't believe Åsa could have more qualified help than that."

Daniel gave in, and Peter went into his bedroom to call the doctor. He came back after a few minutes and said that Olof Hansson thought they should bring her to him immediately. Daniel carried her out to Peter's car and laid her in the back seat. Peter drove, and Daniel went with them. Jenny told him that she was going to go home to her parents' apartment, which was empty because they were on a week-long vacation in Tenerife. She didn't have the energy to go to the Center even though she felt her mind was more at ease now that they'd taken her to someone who was medically competent. She carried the innermost hope that the doctor would make Åsa healthy again or make sure that she was admitted to a hospital.

In the apartment, she ran a warm bath and lay there for at least an hour before she got out and sat in front of the TV. Two hours later, the phone rang. It was Daniel. He was on the verge of a breakdown. Jenny couldn't understand what he was trying to say. He was alternately crying and screaming. Finally, Jenny screamed at him to calm down and tell her what had happened.

"Åsa's dead!" he screamed.

42.

Jonna and Mattis both helped connect the computers in the slightly larger room they'd been granted so they could sit together as they worked on the investigation. They decided to sit facing each other.

"Damn, Loman was nasty to you," Mattias said, connecting his large screen to his laptop.

"Really unpleasant," Jonna said. "I don't understand why he had to be so mean."

Mattias sat down in his office chair and turned on his computer. Jonna did the same.

"So the only thing Loman was going to do, besides contacting the National Police, was to call around to the other districts and 'beat the bushes'?" Jonna said. "We have a shitload of stuff to check on. And so damn little time."

"He's only been working half time since he got the cancer diagnosis a year or so ago," Mattias said.

Jonna looked at him.

"So you know about it, too?"

"He told me yesterday. How long have you known about it?"

"A long time. It's probably been a year since he told me. But since then, we haven't talked about it. Did he say anything about how serious it is?"

"From what I understand, it's over. He didn't say it himself, and I didn't want to ask. But Adelsvärd, who worked with him before, told me so at coffee yesterday when I asked him. He has a year left, max. He probably won't live long enough to retire. Maybe that explains his bad mood."

"How old is he?"

"Sixty-three."

Jonna sat quietly. She tried to think about how it would feel to know that she only had one year left to live.

"It must be terrible to know you're going to die soon," she said. "I don't understand how he can bear to work at all, really."

They decided to go and get a cup of coffee in an attempt to wave off the thoughts of cancer and death. Then they sat each at their own desks to make a prioritized to-do list.

"We have to put a lot of energy into finding the last two on the list," Jonna began. "I don't care what Loman says, that has to be our priority. The background information, connection to Scientology, and connection between victims, that stuff we'll have to take up later. I want to proceed as if all that were true."

Mattias nodded.

"We have a few clues for Jenny Eklund that I've started working with," he said. "I'll continue with those."

"I also want us to concentrate partly on the perpetrator," Jonna continued. "We do have something to go on there. We have to assume that this is murder. If it were suicide, which I don't believe for a second, we can't do anything anyway. But if it's murder, we can maybe prevent more. I'll check on that."

They got started immediately. Jonna did searches through the registry of reported crimes, RAR, for all reports of sexual assault of a child during the past ten years. First only in Blekinge and, with Mattias' help, she also gained access to RAR in Kronoberg and Kalmar county. In all, she got over eight hundred and thirty-six hits. She was astonished by the number of reports. Over eighty reported pedophilic crimes per year in southeastern Sweden. Eighty children who, each year, were damaged for life because a few deranged people couldn't keep themselves from living out their sick fantasies.

She filtered her search and typed in the code for gross sexual assault of a child. One hundred and seventy-seven hits. Still an incredible number. She tested for rape of a child. No hits in Blekinge, but some in Kalmar and Kronoberg. Five hits in all. She noted the social security numbers of the people accused of the crimes. She opened up the PMF, another registry that functions as a portal to numerous other registries the police have access to. Now she could see more information about the crimes. She cross-checked with the Federal Corrections registry and could eliminate three of the five because the perpetrator was still behind bars. But two remained. She realized their perpetrator could have previously committed crimes in other counties in Sweden, but this was a start in any case. She could re-do the searches for the entire country later if it was needed.

Two names left. She began with Magnus Abrahamsson, born in 1963 in Sävsjöström in Småland. Sentenced in 2005 to ten years in prison for two cases of first-degree rape of children, three rapes of children as well as child pornography. He had also, on probable cause, been suspected in two cases of murders of children who were also raped in the late 90s, but was acquitted. He was institutionalized in Kalmar and released in 2012.

Jonna noticed a note far down on the page: "Was attacked by unknown assailant/assailants in his apartment in Karlskrona on March 8, 2013. Badly assaulted and penis severed."

Someone wanted revenge, Jonna thought, clicking on the next name–Hans Holmquist, born in 1965 in Mörrum in Blekinge. He was sentenced in 2001 to life in prison for the murder of a four-year-old girl. Holmquist worked as a preschool teacher and lured the girl into the forest with him where he raped her and then struck her in the head with a stone, hiding her body under some pine branches. The body was found four days later, with Holmquist participating in the search. Holmquist's DNA was found on the girl's body. The police also found child pornography, both films and images, on Holmquist's computer. His sentence was reduced to eighteen years in 2010, and he was released three years later after twelve years in prison.

Even though Jonna had two names to work with, she was disappointed about her meager results. She hoped to end up with a few more potential perpetrators after the search. She realized she would have to do the same thing again, but for the whole country. She also hoped that Anders' request for reinforcement by a profiling expert would give a quick result.

Jonna leaned back in her chair, lifted her gaze over the computer screen, and looked at Mattias.

"How's it going for you?" she asked. "Are you finding anything on Jenny Eklund?"

Mattias tossed down the pen he was using to take notes and slouched down in the chair.

"Yeah," he said. "I got hold of a couple of her old classmates who remember her well. One of them knew she was a member of the Church of Scientology at the end of her high school years. She also said something tragic happened in her life a couple years after they graduated. A family member died, she thought. And immediately after that, Jenny left Karlskrona. She didn't know where Jenny moved to, and she also didn't have any idea where she is today."

"So we know it must be the same Jenny who's on the list, at least," Jonna said.

Mattias stood up and stretched. He looked at the clock.

"It's getting late. I have to head home in a little bit. I've called Chapman School to get her social security number. If I can just find that out, I'll be able to trace her. But the person who can give that information to me is gone for the day. I'll have to go back to it tomorrow."

The desk phone that rested on the table between them rang. Mattias leaned forward and took the receiver. He introduced himself and was then silent for a few seconds. Then he said, "Wait one moment. I have my colleague here. I'm going to put you on speaker so she can also hear."

He laid his palm over the receiver and turned to Jonna.

"It's the investigator with the City Police in Stockholm, Håkan Jonsson, who's working on the investigation of Maria Palm's death. He has a relevant piece of information for us, he said."

Mattias leaned over and pressed the speaker button, then setting the receiver next to the phone.

"We're both listening, Håkan," he said.

"Okay. Hold on to your hats," Håkan Jonsson said. "We have a DNA hit in Maria Palm's apartment. We found strands of hair that we knew didn't come from the apartment's resident so we had them analyzed. It turned out that the hairs belong to a convicted pedophile and suspected murderer who lives in your area. His name is Magnus Abrahamsson."

43.

"Can you get it up a little higher?" Mikael fought with the wheelbarrow. He tried to get it under the boulder that was hanging a bit above the surface of the ground. Viktor and Max were helping to move the stone in over the wheelbarrow. Jenny pulled on the rope with all her strength and lifted the stone enough for Mikael to push the wheelbarrow in under it. The sweat poured down her face. It was hot for a late September. The warm summer had heated the sea, which was now returning the favor generously.

"Now," Mikael said. "Let go slowly, slowly."

It hurt her fingers, despite Jenny's work gloves. She released her grip slowly, letting the rope slip through her gloves. She was completely weak in the arms and her fingers hurt. It was three in the afternoon, and they began early this Saturday morning, just like all the other Saturday mornings of late. Åsa's death had paralyzed all of them, and all work lay undone for several weeks. Now a month had passed since her death, and this was the first day Jenny was helping out.

The stone came to a rest in the wheelbarrow. Mikael went around it, took the handles, and carefully backed down the gangway of boards that they laid out heading towards the pit, which was large—at least five yards by five yards.

The excavator was broken again. This time, it was something with the bucket that locked up. Åke had to order a truck to come and take it to a shop. It was the third time since they bought the excavator that it was away for repair. Getting down seven yards into the ground wasn't as easy as they thought at first. When Åke dug two yards down, he hit some large boulders. He got some of them up with the bucket, but it was too much for the old excavator, which then broke. That was the first time. The second time, there was something wrong with the hydraulics. And now the bucket.

George was frustrated that everything was going so slowly, so he decided they would work by hand, pulling up stones and digging with shovels until the excavator was repaired.

Today, six people were working. One of Jenny's duties was to tend the "giant," a three-legged manual crane. Åke built it. Three powerful joists, each over two yards long, were bolted together with hinges at the top so the three legs could be spread in a tripod. At the top, he attached a pulley through which ran a thick nylon rope. Viktor and Max dug away dirt and sand around the stones. Mikael and Jenny each had a lever, which they bound around each stone so it could be laid bare and moved near the edge of the pit. They helped each other fasten the rope around the stones, and then Jenny, using the pulley, would pull the stone up high enough for Mikael to push the wheelbarrow underneath. They were able to lift up some really large boulders with it. Camilla and Peter dug and carried smaller stones by hand up to the collection pile that was ten yards away. It was tough work. Camilla was not enjoying herself.

"Shit," she said, wiping the sweat from her face. "You can hardly tell we've been at it for five hours."

"Come on, now," Peter said. "It's only a few weeks' physical labor so that we can take it easy for a billion years."

"Check it out." Viktor stood, looking down into the big hole that remained from the large boulder they just removed.

The others went to him. The hole was filled with water.

"That must be groundwater," Viktor said. "It seems to be incredibly high here. How in the hell are we going to be able to dig five more yards if it fills with water all the time? It's just going to be a water-filled pit."

Jenny was already doubting the whole story and doubting George and Peter, especially after Åsa's death. But she didn't dare admit it to anyone. Not even to Daniel. Not with how he felt after what happened with Åsa. He was completely crushed.

Åsa stopped breathing in the car on the way to Malmö, Peter told Jenny. Somewhere around Lund, they noticed that she was completely lifeless. Daniel panicked and started screaming. Peter stopped at the first opportunity and tried to bring her back to life. There was no point. Peter rushed to the emergency room in Lund. There, they confirmed she was dead. There was nothing they could do.

When Daniel heard the news, he first called Jenny then ran out of the hospital and disappeared. Peter and Mikael drove around Lund for two hours, looking for him. Finally, they found him lying on a park bench in the main city park. His eyes were completely glazed over. They took him to the car and drove home to Karlskrona. When he came home, he took off his clothes, laid in his bed, and did not get up for two weeks. He didn't say anything, and he only ate if Jenny brought food in to him.

On the day of the funeral, he got up, dressed, and sat through the ceremony as pale as a corpse. His parents would not allow anyone from the Church of Scientology to participate in the funeral. The dad didn't want Jenny to be there, either, but Daniel's mom convinced him. When the funeral was over, Jenny thought Daniel began to recover a bit. He started talking with her about what happened, and he didn't lie in bed as much any more. He also participated a few times, working with the pit and with Peter's house.

After the first shock of Åsa's death subsided, the parents reported the church to the police, saying they bore the responsibility for Åsa's death. They filed the police report the same day the autopsy was sent to them. Åsa died of a clot in her left lung that was likely caused by dehydration in combination with a long period of bed rest. According to the parents, the Church of Scientology in Karlskrona caused their daughter's death. Daniel took both the results of the autopsy and his parents' reaction hard. He fell back into a deep depression, and since the report came a week earlier, he started lying in bed again. He didn't want to talk to anyone and refused to see Peter and George, who wanted to help him out of his depression. He didn't want to see his parents, either. Jenny didn't know what she should do besides try to stay close to him and make sure he had food and water.

On certain days, he was a little better. A little more communicative than other days. But then he would just fall back into complete silence the next. Jenny was worried he was in the same state as Åsa. Maybe it was hereditary, this depression thing. She hardly dared to leave him alone. She felt completely powerless and just hoped that it would soon pass.

This morning, Daniel seemed to be more energetic and said that he was going to walk down to George and Maria's house during the day. But he didn't come.

Jenny folded up "the giant" and Mikael helped her carry it to the storage shed where they kept the tools. It was almost six in the evening, and they decided to continue the next day. If they could even continue, considering that water began filling the hole. They hoped George and Åke would have some solution to the problem.

"We're going to have dinner at George and Maria's tonight," Mikael said.

"Do you think you could get Daniel to come? I think it would be good if he got out of the house and spent some time with other people."

Jenny set her end of "the giant" on the ground inside the shed, and they carefully laid the whole apparatus down.

"That would be nice," she answered. "He seemed okay this morning. It might work. I'll be in touch if it will."

They exited the shed.

"Is it okay if I leave you with the rest?" she asked the others, who were also about to finish up. "I'd like to get home to Daniel right away."

It was no problem. They would take care of the rest. Jenny took her bike and rode quickly home to the cottage. It was a little chilly now; fall was on the way, but Jenny didn't give the weather a thought. Her thoughts circled around all the awful things that happened over the past month–Åsa, Daniel, his parents, and she wondered how everything would turn out. It overshadowed everything else, even the digging project.

She was sweaty when she rested her bike against the corner of the cottage. She saw there weren't any lights on, but she didn't think about it. Daniel was probably still in his bed, just as he was when she left the cottage that morning. She opened the door and heard music. She was happy. He's listening to music, she thought, smiling. She hoped it was the first sign that he had begun turning his attention elsewhere, away from himself and his grief over Åsa.

She heard it was Chick Corea he was listening to. They listened to a couple of his records to try to understand his music. Chick Corea was a dedicated Scientologist, and many of his albums and lyrics contained Scientology-focused messages. Daniel had finally begun liking it, though Jenny could never quite get used to it. She took off her shoes and hung up her jacket. She went into the kitchen and stiffened. Through the opening to the living room, she could see Daniel.

He was hanging from a noose on the bathroom door.

44.

Jonna knocked once on the door, without any result. She stuck her head in the door to Anders' colleague, Göran Adelsvärd, who was in the room next to their shared workspace and asked if he'd seen Loman. He went home, Göran said. He left a few hours ago, in a big hurry.

"Maybe you know about his illness?" he asked.

Jonna nodded.

"These past few weeks, he hasn't been at work much," Göran continued. "He doesn't talk much about being sick, but I have the sense they stepped up his chemo, and that's taking a toll on his strength." He shook his head. "Some people just can't get a break. Anders is one of them."

Jonna went into the room.

"Mattias said you worked with him already twenty years ago, before he went to Stockholm. So you know him well?"

"We were partners for many years," Göran said. "Then I got a position in Kristianstad and moved there, and we lost contact. A few years later, both of his children died at about the same time. The boy committed suicide after his sister died from some illness. I didn't know anything. I only found out about it when I came back here three years later. By then, Anders was divorced and had moved to Stockholm."

He leaned back in his chair and gave a deep sigh.

"To lose your children must be the worst thing that could happen," he said. "And now he's got cancer."

When Jonna came back to her and Mattias' room, Mattias gave her a questioning look.

"Loman has left the building," she said.

"And turned off his phone," Mattias said. "He's probably at a treatment. Or feels like shit."

Jonna sat down in her chair.

"We'll have to go ahead ourselves," she said. "We can't wait for him."

"I did a search in the national registry for Magnus Abrahamsson while you were looking for Loman. 'No known address'. Searched on Eniro and a couple of other sites, too. He's nowhere. He also isn't in our surveillance registry. He's like a ghost."

"Damn," Jonna said. "He has to be somewhere. I found him in the registry when I searched for convicted pedophiles in southern Sweden. He lived in an apartment in Karlskrona on March 8, 2013."

"Why is that info in the registry?"

"It was the date when he was attacked and castrated."

"Aha. That's the pedophile in Kungsmarken," Mattias said. "I remember it. I wasn't part of the investigation, but the morning after the attack, the jokes about castration were flowing freely through the hallways by the coffee machines. A lot of people were singing the praises of whoever did it."

"So his apartment was in Kungsmarken?"

Mattias nodded.

"If I remember correctly, he moved there when he was released from prison in Växjö," Mattias answered. "Or was he in Kalmar? Anyway, he was clearly trying to hide from whoever later caught him. Must have been someone close to one of his victims."

"I wonder why this doesn't sound familiar," Jonna said.

"It was pretty quickly silenced by brass. We weren't allowed to talk about it. The perpetrator's intention was likely that Abrahamsson wouldn't survive. And the newspapers weren't informed of the sensitive detail of the missing body part. The whole thing just became a regular news item."

Mattias fell silent for a few seconds.

"So he's the murderer on the move, then. Interesting."

He looked quickly at the clock and flew out of his chair.

"It's late. I have to get home to my family. Can we continue with this tomorrow?"

"You go home," Jonna said. "I can continue myself for a bit. My mom is at home putting the kids to bed."

"If I were you, I'd check on who led the investigation of the attack," Mattias said as he walked towards the door. "That person should have a whole lot of information about him."

Jonna had already located Magnus Abrahamsson's social security number and opened DurTvå, the archive of all crime investigation reports. She clicked through to the attack on Abrahamsson. He moved to Karlskrona when he was released from prison in Kalmar in February 2012. A full year later, on March 8, 2013, he was attacked in his apartment in Kungsmarken. A neighbor heard the screams and called the police. One officer happened to be nearby when the call went out and got there quickly. In the apartment, he found Abrahamsson lying on the floor in a pool of his own blood. The perpetrators had beaten him badly, cut off his penis, and probably taken it with him as a sort of a trophy. It wasn't found in the apartment or in the area around the building, at least. If the police officer hadn't happened to be nearby, Abrahamsson wouldn't have survived. The officer was able to stop the flow of blood until the ambulance came.

Jonna had seen many terrible crime scene pictures in her career, but these made her feel truly sick. She had to turn her eyes away from the pictures of the bloodied apartment. So terribly awful, she thought, as she fought the nausea. Could this really have been done by a normal person? A parent? It must have been a paid job. Someone hired a professional.

She didn't know how she would react if a pedophile assaulted any of her own children. She'd often thought about it when she read about pedophiles who attacked small children, and she thought she would probably be prepared to commit murder herself if anyone were to do that to Simon or Astrid. But was there a line she wouldn't be able to cross when it really came down to it?

Jonna froze when she read further. Anders Loman had led the preliminary investigation of the case. She picked up the phone and called him again. Still no answer.

45.

At exactly ten o'clock, Jonna stepped through the door to the police station. She left the house this morning without waking Simon and Astrid, who were up late the night before.

David knocked a few minutes after she came home the previous evening. He was presumably sitting in his car outside, waiting for her to get home. When Jonna's mom left the building, he went in and presented Jonna with a large bouquet of red roses and a present. Wanted to apologize. Jonna said it was too late, refused the flowers and the present, and asked him to leave her alone. She needed time before she would be willing to talk to him. Then she shut the door in his face. It felt good.

So typical of him to buy expensive presents and then think that everything would be fine. He did the same thing with the kids. Always bought expensive, trendy brands and expensive toys. He bought his way out of that pesky bad conscience he had from being gone so much. Jonna realized how much it impacted them when Simon refused to wear a particular shirt one morning just because it wasn't Lacoste.

She hated that superficial attitude towards life. People who valued themselves and others according to what gadgets or clothing they had. Who saw bookshelves only as decorating details, who could name all the decor magazines that were published, and who furnished their homes like sterile, soulless copies without having any taste of their own. They laughed at people who didn't know what Burberry was at the same time as they thought *The Red Room* was a new furniture series at IKEA. She didn't want Simon and Astrid to inherit that view of people and realized that this alone was enough reason to break free.

She said goodbye to her mom after they had breakfast together. It was a teacher training day at the preschool, so the children were off and grandma was going to stay with them all day. Jonna snuck away with a heavy conscience. She hadn't spent all that much time with the children in recent months. First, it was the reconnaissance job with the kids and the hash pushers, and now the murder investigation. She would take a few days off when this investigation was over, she decided. She needed to be with the kids. And she needed to sleep. This past night, she hardly slept a wink. The thought of Magnus Abrahamsson sat like a tick embedded in her frontal lobe, and she couldn't relax.

She punched in the code to the inner security door and came out into the hallway where Anders Loman's office was. She went to his door and knocked. She waited a few seconds and then opened the door carefully. It was empty. She took out her phone and dialed his number as she looked at the clock and walked to the coffeemaker. It was ten after ten. Loman didn't answer. Because it was summer vacation, most offices in the building were empty. Checking in with Loman was one of the more important things to do today. She just had to get hold of him. Not least because he was the lead for the preliminary investigation into the attack on Abrahamsson and maybe knew where he was.

She had just sat down when Mattias Palander came into the room, breathless. Before he was able to sit down in his chair, Jonna told him about the attack on Abrahamsson and that Loman led the preliminary investigation. They went through all the material one more time and then split up the work that lay before them. Mattias would continue hunting the administrator at Chapman School to find Jenny Eklund's social security number. He'd also try to contact the families of the others who were found dead to establish a connection to Scientology and to try to gather as much information as possible about the activities they were engaged in. In all probability, he thought, that was where the motive for murder lay.

Jonna started tracking Abrahamsson. It seemed pointless to continue trying to get hold of Loman. He probably either felt really sick or was in the hospital for radiation or chemo. When he turned on his phone, he would see and hear that she was looking for him and then he would hopefully call back.

She clicked into the property registry to see if Abrahamsson owned some summer cabin where he might be hiding, but she didn't find anything. She went into the national registry to see if she could find any family she could contact, and there she caught a break. Magnus Abrahamsson's dad had passed away, but his mom was still alive. Karin Abrahamsson, 72 years old, still living in Sävsjöström.

Jonna went quickly into Google Maps and checked how far up in Småland that was. Around 70 miles, so an hour and a half to get there by car. She weighed the decision of whether to call first, but if Abrahamsson were hiding there, calling would ruin everything. She made up her mind and told Mattias she was going to drive to Sävsjöström. Wrote down the address, went down to the garage, signed out one of the service cars, and drove north.

She talked with Anneli on the phone almost the whole way. Anneli was her best friend, and they hadn't talked in several weeks. She needed someone to talk to about what happened between her and David. Anneli was smart and a good listener.

At two o'clock, she drove into the little community.

46.

Thomas Svärd took the mug out of the holder on the dashboard and slurped the coffee he bought at the Preem gas station at Bryggarberget before he drove to the Wämö Center. He grimaced when the liquid hit his taste buds. It was cold and tasted terrible. He sat in his car in the parking lot for almost an hour, waiting. He'd arrived just in time to see the woman go in. It wasn't difficult to recognize her. The photo in the folder looked like it was taken in the same place he was sitting. Attractive and young-looking for her age, he thought. He was sure many men stared wistfully in her direction.

He positioned his car so he had a full view of the entrance to the adult psychiatric clinic. When the woman came, she parked her car right next to Thomas. He bent his head and looked down at his lap when he realized she was going to pull into the spot next to him. When the door closed behind her, he moved his car a little bit further off to another parking spot to reduce the risk she would recognize him when he followed her.

He picked up the folder to go through all the details again. Her movements each day were almost mechanical. Where she shopped, when, where, and how she worked out. Therapy on Tuesdays at eleven, and then she usually shopped at Willy's on Pantarholmen before she went home to her house on Långö. She apparently had a special someone who didn't live with her but often slept over at her house. But he didn't on Tuesdays, typically. Today was July 15. Only a week since the previous assignment. He actually preferred to have more time between them, but this time, the prerequisites were relatively simple. For two of the murders, it was close to going to hell in a handbasket. He was forced to muster the furthest extent of his creative abilities and his acting prowess.

This time, he would be the chimney sweep. He was amazed at how naïve people were. Suddenly, the doorbell rang and there stood a guy in a coverall who said that he was from the chimney sweeping company, sent to conduct a fire safety check. Worked every time. He didn't even need to show his fake ID card. And in three of the cases, he was offered coffee, which was really lucky. He hadn't even needed to exert himself to get the drug into them. He was lucky. And he hoped he would be this time, too.

47.

The only sound in the room was Jenny's crying. The tissues were almost gone. The box sat there on the round birch table in the small room at the Adult Psychiatric Clinic at Wämö Center every time she was there that summer, fifteen times in all. She never cried, but she was making up for it now. It had been twenty-one years since she found Daniel hanged, but her grief over him welled up like storm waters within her. Or maybe it was feelings of guilt coming to the surface. She didn't know which. Maybe both. The therapist, Rolf, let her wracking sobs come. He just sat there, waiting them out.

"What are you feeling now, Jenny?" he asked quietly in his soft, Scanian dialect when she calmed down enough to breathe somewhat normally.

Jenny blew her nose hard and immediately took a new tissue.

"I think it's both grief and guilt," she said. "I never got to grieve properly over Daniel's suicide because there was such a ruckus afterward. And all these years, I've felt so guilty over what happened. Because I didn't realize what was about to happen. Because I didn't make sure he sought professional help when he was depressed after Åsa's death. How in the hell could I be so blind that I thought he would just be able to deal with it himself because he was Clear and well on the way to becoming OT IV?"

She fell silent. Suddenly, she laughed. It was a hollow sound.

"And how could I believe that George's story about the flying saucer? It's sick. I've been so ashamed about that. Haven't told anyone about that in all these years. It's really embarrassing."

"What do you think?" Rolf asked. "How could you all—as I understand it, a group of friendly and, as it seems, smart young people—suddenly start believing such things?"

Jenny looked at him, her eyes bloodshot from crying.

"A refined form of brainwashing," she said. "With the same mechanisms that explain how the German people could act as they did against the Jews," she said. "Blind belief in authority and groupthink. Plus a human need for control, explanations, and meaning. All these things, which create conditions that are ripe for religions to grow in."

She was quiet again, looking for a formulation she read somewhere that struck her. She found it.

"Religion is a cognitive parasite that eats into your brain and blunts critical thinking," she said. "Someone creates an idea, a delusion that there's a light at the end of the tunnel. That's what religion sells. It profits off of human illusions, of our need for life to have significance, a higher meaning. Believing in the delusion of the flying saucer isn't actually any stranger than believing that there was a man two thousand years ago who could walk on water. Or that there's one God who rules over us. It's all abstractions, fantasy. And when enough people believe the same delusion, they can get it into their heads to act in the strangest of ways. Like taping bombs around their bodies and detonating them in large gatherings of people. Burning women on bonfires, murdering followers of other religions. Digging for flying saucers."

She looked at Rolf as if to gain his approval of the theory.

"I hope you aren't religious," she said. He shook his head.

"Evil and narrow-mindedness come from those who believe they're sitting on the truth," Jenny continued. "They've stopped questioning and only exist to defend their beliefs. Anyone who thinks otherwise is an enemy, and in extreme cases, should be destroyed. At any cost."

She sank deep into her thoughts as she rolled the tissue in her hand.

"Dear Lord," she said. "I was an easy target. I was only nineteen years old. I only wanted to do good things, and I was completely convinced that what we were doing was right. But it ended up being so wrong."

She broke down again. The sobs didn't come as forcefully this time. It felt good to just release the sorrow. Rolf left the room and got a new box of tissues. When he returned, Jenny was calm. Rolf lay the box of tissues carefully on the table in front of her and sat back down.

"What happened next?" he asked. "After Daniel took his own life?"

"It became complete chaos," she said. "Someone within the church clearly tattled to the Office of Special Affairs, the OSA, in Copenhagen about what we were doing. The OSA was the Church of Scientology's security division and belonged to the Sea Organization. A gang of uniformed Scientology police came up and did a round-up in our church. They even went to people's homes."

"Uniforms?"

"Hubbard was a former Navy officer and organized the church according to the model of the American Navy. The most dedicated belonged to the 'Sea Org' and had to wear uniforms. The ones in the security division, too. That was the organization's secret police, the KGB of Scientology."

Rolf nodded.

"They never came into the cabin Daniel and I shared because the police were there," Jenny continued. "George and the rest of the leaders were found guilty of having trying to harm Scientology through squirreling, which was a Scientology expression for heretical activities. They had to decide between being exiled and declared Suppressive Persons, the worst punishment a Scientologist could receive. This means that you're labeled as an enemy of Scientology, you can't practice Scientology, and other Scientologists can't have any contact with you. Or they could instead choose to go to Copenhagen and submit to RPF, Rehabilitation Project Force, I think that stood for. Penalty duty. Some picked that and had to live in shabby rooms at Hotel Nordland in Copenhagen, cleaning both the hotel and the AOSH space. There was a rumor that they had to scrub floors and toilets with toothbrushes."

"What happened to you?"

"I'd had enough. As luck would have it, my contract ended and I could sneak out the back door. The OSA people were focusing completely on the leaders in Karlskrona, and a few of us could get out of it all without anyone else noticing. Luckily. I escaped to Båstad, where I got a job at a bar. I tried to heal my wounds there for a few months before I applied to college in Örebro."

"What happened with Daniel's suicide and his parents?"

"The mom went into a deep depression. The dad went on the warpath and filed a police report against the church for having also driven Daniel to death, but the prosecutor pulled the plug on the preliminary investigation. But he was able to carry the case with Åsa to court. I was called as a witness one year after her death. It was terrible. I still shudder to think about the day I sat there. I'll never forget the hateful look of Daniel and Åsa's father. But the charges were dismissed later. It was something like they couldn't prove that the blood clot was caused by dehydration, I think. It could just as well have been formed in the car accident."

Rolf glanced at the clock that hung on the wall behind Jenny. She turned around and realized that time had run out.

"Oh, has an hour passed already? What should we do now?"

"We have to end this session, Jenny. But I recommend that we continue. Today you've come a long way, and a lot has happened within you. I think you need to dig a little deeper to figure out how this period of your life is impacting you today."

They made an appointment for the following week. Jenny thanked him, took her jacket in her hand, and left the building. She felt lighter. Sad, but lighter.

She stopped on the steps as she came out. She pulled the warm, fresh air into her lungs with a deep inhale. A blackbird sat singing very close by and high up. She looked up to see where it was sitting. She caught sight of it at the top of the red brick building across the way. It was sitting on the roof ridge.

An image of Daniel appeared in her mind. That's him. The thought came without her being able to control it. She realized how deeply her experiences from Scientology sat inside her. But now, she allowed the thought to settle inside her, letting it rest there, welcoming it. She found a sort of peace and quiet in thinking that it was Daniel singing up there, singing for her. That he was nearby, watching over her. After all these years. She stood still, looking up and listening to the bird when it sang. She decided to stay there, listening to the song until it flew away.

48.

Restless in his bones. Like that time in May of 1989 when he was seventeen years old and lying in Wyckoff Heights Medical Center on Stockholm Street after being attacked and shot at six times. One in the stomach from close range, four in the legs when he tried to run. One shot missed, apparently, but he only found that out afterward. He collapsed and the perpetrator ran forward, aiming the pistol at his chest. It clicked. If it had been a revolver magazine with seven bullets, he would be dead.

Two weeks after the attack, when Luke was still in the hospital, his gang gathered heavy weapons, stole a van, and set into motion Revenge Operation Tet, named for the Vietnam offensive in 1968. Their version of Tet went on for three days, during which he received no information about how it was going and whether they were alive or dead. The uncertainty plagued him almost as much as the wounds in his body. It was the same feeling he had now. The police were hunting for the murderer and he wouldn't hear anything about it. Nothing.

Luke sank down onto his black leather sofa, frustrated, took out his phone and was disappointed. No missed calls, no texts. He had fought the past two days with himself, trying not to call Jonna. After Saturday's double challenge, she was completely silent. He was incredibly curious about how the investigation was going, whether they'd found the last three on the list: Mikael Anderson, Jenny Eklund, and George Knightly. He decided to let that sit until the next day.

On Sunday, he dedicated several hours to cleaning up his cottage after the two men's rampage. After work on Monday, he rented a car and trailer at the Preem gas station and made one trip to the dump with his wrecked TV and other garbage. He made quick stops at Elgiganten electronics superstore, where he'd bought a new flat-screen TV, and Luddwe's in Nättraby for a new bathroom vanity. It took the whole evening and half of Tuesday, but now he was happy. He decided to go to the gym.

He tossed his workout gear in a bag, locked the door of his cottage, and went out towards the street. When he rounded the corner of Norra Smedjegatan and Ronnebygatan, his phone dinged. He hoped it would be a text from Jonna and quickly clicked through to the message. It was from Anna Adams.

"Jenny Eklund's last name is now Dahl," she wrote. "Thought you'd like to know. XOXO!"

Luke wrote a quick thanks, clicked the message away, and dialed Jonna's number. It was busy. Tried Anders Loman. No one answered. Instead, he called information and asked for the phone number and address of Jenny Dahl in Karlskrona. Lucky strike—there was only one person with that name. He had the details texted to him and clicked immediately on the phone number. It rang several times, but no one answered. He looked at the street address: Ordensgatan 51. A quick search on Eniro showed it was on Långö, just past the bridge. Not far away, max one mile.

He looked at the time. Just after one in the afternoon. She was probably at work. He googled her name plus "Karlskrona." If he were lucky, she had a job that would make her name pop up. But he didn't get any hits.

He decided to forget about working out and head to Ordensgatan instead. He turned on his heel and started walking towards Långö. After a few minutes, he realized he had started jogging lightly. He ran and walked in turns the whole way and arrived at the old Långö bridge ten minutes later. Three kayakers were gliding along on the still water under the bridge. The beautiful old wooden buildings lay before him in a charming patchwork as if they were tossed aimlessly over the whole island. He walked quickly through the residential area to Ordensgatan. Ten two-story townhouses in a long row. In one of them lived Jenny Dahl. The side of the row that faced Skolgatan, where Luke stood, was the back, strangely enough. Every townhouse had its own small, rectangular yard. He decided to go around the row to the front side. He went past the first seven townhouses and stopped a bit from the eighth. A sign on the door said "5J." The kitchen was on the lower floor, and its windows faced the front. Further in was the living room.

Luke went towards the door and simultaneously looked in the kitchen window. He saw two coffee mugs on the kitchen table. A man dressed like a chimney sweep came walking down the steps and went into the living room. Luke decided to ring the doorbell and see what was going on. He took a step forward and rang the bell. The signal was clearly audible inside the house. But that was the only sound, everything else was silent. He pressed the button again. Luke took two steps to the side and peered cautiously in the kitchen window. He saw the contour of the man in the large living room. He was standing still as a statue by the steps, turned towards the front door and the kitchen. Quickly, Luke pulled his head back. He thought for two seconds. Then he pressed the doorbell one more time. Took two steps back, looked up at the window on the second floor and then went back along the row of townhouses. He walked without turning around and looking at the house in the hope that the man would believe he'd given up.

When he came around the corner, he sprinted to get around to the other side. He noticed that, on several of the houses, windows on the back side were either fully open or at least cracked due to the heat. He hoped Jenny's was one of them. When he got to the house two away from Jenny's, he stepped over the fence and crept along the wall. He moved quickly to the fence that separated Jenny's yard from her neighbor's. He stood pressed against the wall and looked over the edge of the fence. The window was closed.

49.

With a quick jump over to the other side of the fence and two strides, Luke was against the wall and kneeling on the wooden bench below the windows. There wasn't a sound. He cautiously raised his head and body. Looked in. Saw that the shade in the kitchen was now pulled down, making the living room dim, but he could see that no one was there. He walked in a crouching position to the balcony door and carefully tried the door handle. It wasn't locked and he cautiously opened the door a crack. He put his ear against the gap and heard nothing. Then he pulled open the door, glanced around the room and up the stairs. It was still completely silent. He went in, stood on the doormat, and closed the door as quietly as he could. Now he could hear someone whimpering. It was coming from upstairs.

He quickly took off his black boots so he could sneak soundlessly up the stairs. Simultaneously, he looked around the room for something to use as a weapon. He caught sight of a fireplace poker leaning against the wall by the fireplace. That would do. He took it and went up the stairs on the far right of the steps to minimize the risk of creaking sounds. The stairs led up to another living room with a sofa and a large TV. From the upstairs living room, a hallway led to three doors. Two of the doors were closed, but one was open. That's where the sound was coming from.

Luke walked with quick, silent steps to the doorway. He stood pressed against the wall and exhaled. He heard the whimpering clearly. It was a woman. Luke took a step forward, peeked into the room, and pulled his head back again. The woman was lying on the bed, her mouth taped shut. Her arms were tied behind her and her eyes were wide with panic and fear. She whimpered again. A white bucket stood in front of the door and a noose hung over the edge of the door. The man in chimney sweep's clothing stood with his back to the door as he worked on a pair of speakers atop a desk by the wall at the end of the bed. A phone dinged inside the room. Luke took the chance that it was the man's phone and that he would stop to look at it, allowing Luke the chance to take another glance. The man was still standing with his back to Luke, his head bent, typing something into his phone. Luke couldn't see any weapon on him. He gripped the handle of the poker firmly, took a few quick steps into the room, and whacked the man on the neck with the poker. He never knew what hit him and crumpled to the floor. Luke went to him, crouched down, and laid the poker down.

He went through the man's pockets. No weapons. Just two bottles, one containing a clear, transparent liquid, the other a hazy one. They were marked with letters: a P on one bottle and a Z on the other. Suddenly, the woman on the bed began making loud, jerky sounds. Luke turned his head and saw a tall man dressed all in black in the doorway. He had a ski mask over his head and black gloves on his hands. All that was visible was his blue eyes, which were fixed on Luke.

In the second that followed, time stood still. It was all the time that was needed for the sight to be transformed to an interpretation of the situation. Then everything went very fast. Luke looked quickly to the floor to find the poker, gripped it, and jumped to his feet. When he looked at the doorway again, it was empty. The man was gone. Luke ran after him and saw his back disappear down the stairs. He realized he had to concentrate on Jenny and decided to let the man go. Instead, he returned to Jenny and took away the tape over her mouth.

"Hi, Jenny," he said. "My name is Luke Bergmann."

Jenny looked at him. She was shaking.

Luke released her wrists and helped her to her feet. But her legs couldn't hold her and she sat down on the bed.

"Did he make you take any drugs?" Luke asked.

Jenny shook her head.

"There are two coffee mugs on the kitchen table. Did you offer him coffee? Did you drink anything yourself?"

"Yes," she answered.

"Might he have put something in your coffee?" Luke asked. "Was he ever alone in the kitchen?"

Jenny looked confused.

"Um...I don't remember. I don't think so." She turned around and looked at the man who was still lying on the floor, unmoving.

"Who is he?" she asked.

"I hoped you could tell me that," Luke said.

"He was going to kill me." She looked up at Luke, who nodded.

"You would've been the ninth. He and his partner have killed eight of your old Scientology friends."

"What? Why is that?" she stammered.

"I don't know," Luke said. "Do you?"

Jenny shook her head.

"It was so long ago," she said. "Over twenty years ago."

"What was it that happened then?"

She looked at him uncomprehendingly.

"Something must have happened to make someone decide to kill all of you twenty years later," Luke said.

Jenny still looked confused, her mouth half-open.

"I have no idea. I don't get it."

"It must be something," Luke said.

He interrupted himself when he heard a groan from the man on the floor. Walked over to him and lifted him up onto the bed. He hit him in the face and the man woke up.

"Did you give her anything?" he asked.

Svärd shook his head.

"Didn't have to."

"Who are you and who is your partner?" Luke asked.

"Go to hell," Svärd said.

Luke hit him in the face again.

"Do I need to do that a few more times?"

The man looked up. Blood was flowing from his nose.

"Be my guest. Hit away. I like it. Hit me as much as you want. I'm not going to say anything anyway."

Luke looked at him and realized he probably meant what he said. He leaned over him and rifled through his pockets. Found a wallet, phone, car keys. In the wallet he found several ten-dollar bills, a Visa card, and a driver's license.

"Thomas Svärd," Luke said, casting a glance at him.

Svärd looked at Luke with a mocking smile on his lips. Here sat Viktor's and Agnes' murderer, right in front of him. Grinning. Luke felt the rage building up inside of him, and he couldn't stop it. He leaned down, took hold of the neck of Svärd's coverall, jerked him up to standing, and pulled him close.

"You pig. You murdered my best friend and his daughter."

Svärd was still smiling.

"Oh really? You and Viktor Spandel were friends? Interesting. He pissed himself when I kicked the bucket away, did you know that?"

Luke lost control. He pulled his knee up with all his strength into Svärd's midsection. Svärd released a sighing sound and sank to the floor. Luke let him lie there. He looked at Jenny, who sat stiff and with her mouth agape far back on one corner of the bed.

"Sorry. I couldn't stop myself," he said. "Are you okay?"

She nodded.

"I'm going to call the ambulance and police soon," he said. "But first I have to check these things."

He picked up Svärd's belongings, which he tossed away when he dragged Svärd from the bed. He laid the wallet on the bed, stuck the car keys in his pocket, and held the phone. He saw that a new text had come in.

"What's happening?"

Luke realized it was the man in black. He thought for a moment. Resisted the impulse to call him. He called up the number. There was no name associated with it, only the number. Luke took out his own phone and called Jonna. Still busy. Loman didn't answer. So he called the police operator and asked to be connected to Mattias Palander, who answered immediately. Luke explained what had happened and asked him to make sure an ambulance came to take care of Jenny.

"Svärd is presumably Magnus Abrahamsson," Mattias said. "His DNA was identified in Maria Palm's apartment." He chose not to say that Abrahamsson was a pedophile and what he did to Agnes before he gave her the poison. He thought Luke might kill him on the spot if he did.

"There's no doubt this is the right man," Luke said. "But only one of them. There are two, and the other one just sent a text to Svärd's, or Abrahamsson's, phone. Can you search for the number?"

He gave Mattias the number and waited.

"It's not a listed number," Mattias said after thirty seconds. "Must be a prepaid phone."

"OK. Do you know where Jonna and Loman are?" Luke asked. "I've tried to call them several times, but neither is answering."

"Jonna headed to Sävsjöström in Småland where Abrahamsson's mom lives," Mattias answered. "Loman is sick."

They ended the conversation after agreeing that Mattias would try to get hold of Jonna as well as send an ambulance and a squad car with technicians to Jenny's house.

Luke stood still for a moment, looking at the text in Svärd's phone. Then he decided. He started typing in an answer.

217

Was able to escape.

The answer came instantly. *Where are you now?*

Luke wrote, *In the car.*

Drive to the bunker.

OK, Luke sent back.

He leaned over and lifted Svärd, who came to. He grimaced from the pain in his belly. Saliva ran from the corner of his mouth to his chin.

"Where's the bunker?" Luke asked.

Svärd didn't answer.

Luke turned to Jenny.

"Svärd's friend wrote in a text that he wanted Svärd to drive to a bunker," he said. "Do you have any idea what that could be about?"

Jenny shook her head.

"There are loads of bunkers out in the archipelago," she said. "I see them everywhere on those little islands."

"Okay," Luke said to her. "Stay here. An ambulance and police officers are coming."

Luke took Svärd in his arms, stopped at the bedroom door, pulled down the noose that Jenny was to be hanging by. He needed something to tie Svärd up with. Then he dragged Svärd out of the house.

50.

When they came out onto the street, Luke pressed the key fob and hoped Svärd's car would be one of the ones parked closest. He was lucky. A white Opel Astra flashed its lights. Luke set Svärd against the front of the car and tied his hands behind his back. He tossed him into the back seat, pulled the rest of the noose around Svärd's neck, and tied the rope tightly to the headrest so he wouldn't be able to move.

"I can hardly breathe," Svärd hissed.

"If you don't tell me where the bunker is, it won't be long before you won't be able to breathe at all," Luke said, pulling a little harder without completely strangling him.

Svärd sat completely still, fighting for air, Luke went behind the car and opened the trunk. It was completely empty. In the back seat, next to Svärd, was a bag containing several bottles identical to the ones Luke found in Svärd's pockets. There were also two ropes already tied into nooses, tools, duct tape, and some clothes. On the floor were McDonalds wrappers, empty soda bottles, and other garbage. On the front passenger seat lay a green folder.

Luke sat in the driver's seat and quickly flipped through the contents of the folder. Someone had prepped very thoroughly for the attack on Jenny Dahl, he realized. There were descriptions of her habits, daily schedule, and a drawing of her home. In the folder he also found a map of central Karlskrona on which Jenny's house was circled. Luke opened the glove compartment on the dashboard and took out everything that was inside it. The car's manual, a little garbage, and one more map. A map of Sturkö, one of Karlskrona's largest islands, that lay eighteen miles east of the city. The title of the map read "Defense Fortifications on Sturkö." There were a handful of symbols printed on the map, among them six round yellow rings along the southern coastline. "Fortifications on the Per Albin Line" was the explanation of the yellow symbols. One of them must be the bunker, Luke thought. I have to take the chance.

He turned towards Svärd, who sat there gasping for breath. Held up the map.

"There went your chance to get out of the noose," he said.

219

Svärd tried to say something through his clenched teeth. Luke didn't hear what he said.

"Save your breath. Let's go," Luke said, starting the car. He drove quickly towards Björkholmen. He needed a weapon.

He turned off at the sports arena and, one minute later, stopped outside his place. He went in with quick strides and looked around in his closet for a special box. In it lay the macana. It was the only weapon he had—a little clumsy, but incredibly effective when you knew how to use it. Luke had a scar from it, on the back of his thigh, from a street fight with the Latin Knights in the mid-1980s. If he hadn't been lucky enough to see the blow coming out of the corner of his eye, he probably wouldn't have a right leg today. A macana can cause terrible injuries. It was an old, primitive weapon the Aztecs produced and used. Looks like an angular baseball bat with razor-sharp pieces of obsidian attached to the edges, harder than razors but just as sharp. The Latin Knights produced their own macanas, and when Luke's gang later joined the Latin Knights, Luke trained with the weapon. He had a sheath made for it that was worn as a backpack and meant he could, with a quick grab, draw the macana up over his head. He hadn't used it for many years and realized he was a little rusty, but it was the only weapon he possessed.

Luke hastily pulled the macana from its sheath and tested the glass shards. Still sharp. He pushed it back in and returned to the car. Svärd seemed to have found a position that enabled him to get enough air. He sat completely still, intently looking straight ahead. Didn't make a peep.

"Now let's head to Sturkö," Luke said.

Then he called Mattias Palander and said he was on his way out to Sturkö to find a bunker and that he'd taken Svärd with him.

"I think you should let us take it from here, Luke," Mattias said.

"How's that?" Luke asked.

"You stop the car, I send a couple of squads to Sturkö and they take over," Mattias answered.

"That won't work, Mattias, Luke said. "You don't know where you're sending them because there are six bunkers on the island, and we don't know which one it is. There's a big risk we'll lose Svärd's friend, who's on his way there right now. We don't know what he looks like, and if he sees a ton of squad cars driving around the island, he'll retreat immediately."

"You don't know which bunker it is, either," Mattias said.

"No, not yet. But I'll find out soon enough," Luke answered. "And when I know, I'll call you back."

He hung up and called Jonna's number. Now it was ringing, but she still didn't answer. He left a message, describing in brief what happened, that he was on his way to a bunker on Sturkö, and asked her to call him as soon as she got the message. He thought for a moment and then dialed another number. His call wasn't answered.

They crossed the last bridge, the one that went from Senoren to Sturkö, and were now on the island. After five minutes, they arrived at the first big crossing, which was in the middle of the island. Luke drove to the edge and stopped. He took the map, got out of the car, and opened the back door where Svärd was sitting and gasping for air. Luke knelt so he would be on the same level as Svärd's face. Held up the map in front of him.

"Now you're going to tell me which bunker it is that your friend wants you to meet at," he said calmly. "If you do as I say, I'll loosen the rope a little. If you don't, I'll pull it harder."

"Loosen it," Svärd hissed.

"First, you're going to tell me which bunker it is," Luke said. He pointed to the northernmost bunker and looked at Svärd.

"Is this it?"

Svärd shook his head.

"The southern one," Svärd said.

Luke pointed at the yellow ring furthest to the southeast.

"This one?" he asked.

"Yes," Svärd hissed.

"If you're lying, you can count on me hanging you exactly the same way you hanged Viktor," he said as he loosened the rope around Svärd's throat a little. Svärd coughed and cleared his throat as the pressure on his windpipe released.

"He's ten times smarter than you," he said. "You won't have a chance."

Luke didn't bother answering. He sat in the front seat and looked at the map. Only one road went the whole way to the bunker. He started the car and turned to the left at the crossing. After a few hundred yards, he turned to the right onto a gravel road. He remembered he promised to tell Mattias where the bunker was when he found out. He picked up the phone and called him. No signal. Luke swore. He knew there were problems out on the islands with cell phone coverage, above all with Telenor's network. He

221

took out Svärd's phone. He also had Telenor. He tossed both phones into the passenger seat. He'd have to deal with this himself.

It grew lighter between the pines up ahead. They were approaching the sea. Luke slowed down and was on the lookout. No sign of another car yet. Weighed the possibility that Svärd's partner took another route and gone through the forest. But he realized there probably wasn't a reason for him not to take the fastest route. Hopefully, he thought he and Svärd would meet at the bunker. Luke stopped the car and looked at the map. It wasn't far now. He didn't want to drive all the way there even if they were in Svärd's car. The element of surprise would be completely lost.

He looked up and saw a little tractor path into the forest on the left, and drove in on it. He went fifty yards or so until he was sure the car wouldn't be visible from the road. He took the macana, stepped out of the car, and stood quietly for a moment. Listening. The only thing he heard was the rustling of the pines and the faint sound of waves breaking on the shore. He opened the passenger door, stuck his hand in the bag, and took out the duct tape. He put tape over Svärd's mouth, untied him, and pulled him out of the car. He left the noose around his neck and ordered him to walk towards the sea.

After about a hundred yards, the forest became considerably more sparse and an open field spread out before them. Luke saw the top of what he believed was the bunker. He dragged Svärd a few yards backward and tied him tightly to a tall pine. Then he stole along the edge of the forest around the area to see if they were alone or if Svärd's partner was already there.

When he'd gone some distance, he saw a small wooden structure fifty-odd yards from the bunker. But no car, no sign that anyone was there. It was completely impossible to get to the bunker with a vehicle other than via the gravel road. Unless you came by boat, he suddenly realized.

He turned around and looked down towards the sea, which was only fifty yards away. There was no dock from what he could see. And it would be very difficult to moor a boat here because of all the rocks. He hurried back to Svärd, loosened the rope from the tree, and pushed him in front of him through the meadow and to the bunker. Concrete steps led down to a steel door that looked like it weighed several tons.

Luke took the macana out of its sheath, shoved Svärd down the steps to the door, and pushed down the handle. To his surprise, it swung open easily, and he propelled Svärd into the darkness. He realized there was a small possibility the partner was already in the bunker, waiting, but he had to take that chance. He went in and held the door open so the light would enable him to see inside. Svärd stood in the middle of the floor, waiting. They were alone. Luke took a stone and set it between the door and the doorframe. He didn't want to get locked inside.

Luke saw there was a button to turn on the lights just to the left of the door, and he pushed it. He looked around. He'd seen bunkers in pictures before, but never been in one. He'd been in jail at the police station in Williamsburg, though. This was more luxurious, even if it were spartan and had the same type of concrete floor. He saw the portholes, which someone had covered with boards. There were three, pointed in three different directions. He went towards them and, with the help of the macana's handle, he knocked the boards off so the openings were clear. He looked out through the one that faced west. He could see the whole coastline towards Tjurkö. He turned to Svärd.

"Are there any weapons here?"

Svärd shook his head. Luke looked at him suspiciously and searched quickly through the space. Didn't find anything. Then he took hold of Svärd and moved him to the radiator, which was affixed to the concrete wall. He forced him to sit down and bound the rope properly. He left the tape across his mouth.

Svärd was now sitting apathetic, cross-legged, leaning against the radiator. Luke stood up, took the macana, and quickly exited the bunker.

51.

Jonna sat in the car parked in the yard outside Karin Abrahamsson's dilapidated house on the outskirts of Sävsjöström. The visit didn't produce any results. Karin Abrahamsson hadn't been in contact with her son in over twenty years. Jonna searched through the house and then pressured the mom hard. The only thing she was taking away from it was a sulfurous sermon about the seven deadly sins, Karin's son's fornicating behavior, Sodom and Gomorrah, and that he would end up both in Gehenna and in purgatory.

Jonna was thoroughly convinced the woman's son wasn't hiding out at her house, drove out of town, and turned south towards Karlskrona. She took out her phone and saw that she had several missed calls both from Luke and Mattias, as well as several texts. She pulled into a rest stop and listened.

Dear Lord, she thought. He's completely unbelievable. How on earth did he find Jenny Eklund? She found Luke's phone number in her contacts and dialed. The signal didn't go through. Either his battery was dead or he had no coverage where he was. She tried to collect her thoughts. What should she do? She started the car and accelerated quickly. If she stepped on it, she could be back in an hour. She called Mattias, who said Luke had been in contact with him.

"When did you last talk to Luke?" Jonna asked.

"A half-hour ago. He said he'd find out which of the six bunkers they were going to. And then he'd call me."

"We have to get out to Sturkö, and fast," Jonna continued. "The problem is that it's the largest island in the archipelago. How does it look on the map you have? The bunkers aren't labeled on there, are they?"

"No," Mattias answered. "We probably have to find a historic defense map to be able to see where they are."

"Then I know who we should talk to," Jonna said. "Call you back in a minute."

"Meanwhile I'll check which cell company Luke uses," Mattias said. "If we're lucky, he has Telenor. Hansson, the tech, has an in-law who works there and can locate a cell phone position for us a little quicker than usual.

In that case, we can at least see where he was before his phone died, and then we can maybe eliminate a number of possibilities."

Jonna called information and got hold of the phone number of Olle Melin, a retired colonel with the Coastal Artillery and expert on the defense fortifications in the archipelago. Maybe he could quickly get them a map that showed where the bunkers on Sturkö were located.

She got lucky. He answered immediately and could answer Jonna's question. There were six artillery bunkers on Sturkö, he explained. Jonna had to interrupt him when he started going on about the Per Albin line and how the bunkers were manned.

Olle Melin promised to email the map to Jonna immediately, and three minutes later, her phone dinged. She opened the attachment and saw the map on her screen. The six bunkers were clearly marked. All lay on the coast facing southwest. And there were small paths down to them from the middle of the island, but none between them. If she chose the wrong bunker, she'd have to drive a long way to get to the next. She called Mattias to hear if he'd been successful with Telenor.

"Yes, Hansson's on it," he said. "What a lucky break. Luke has Telenor. It'll only take a few minutes and Hansson will have the positions. I'll email a map to you as soon as we've marked where he was."

When, twenty minutes later, Jonna got to the exit for Sturkö and turned south towards the islands, her phone dinged again. It was an email from Mattias and contained a map. She stopped her car at the first rest area and opened the email. The positions were marked with blue dots, evenly spaced until Bredavik. Then they stopped.

She took out the map she got from Olle Melin. Dammit. From Bredavik, you could reach all of the bunkers. If his phone held the signal for two more minutes, Luke would have been at Sturkö Mill, where there was a crossing. If Jonna could only find out which of the two paths Luke took, the number of bunkers would be reduced to two or three. Now, she had no help at all. They could have gone to any of the six bunkers. The question now was which one she should start with? There was less than a third of a mile between them so if the terrain wasn't too treacherous, she could get from one to the next quickly. The phone rang. It was Mattias.

"How does it look?" he asked. "Did the positions help?"

"Unfortunately not. From the last position, you can get to all six bunkers," she said. "I'll send Olle Melin's map over to you so you can also check it out. Could you contact dispatch and ask them to send as many cars as they have, as quickly as possible? Tell them they should contact me when they've arrived in Sturkö. By then, I should know which of the bunkers it is."

Jonna ended the conversation, picked up her service weapon, checked that everything was as it should be, put it back into its holster, and gunned it out of the parking spot.

52.

A single cloud covered the sun for a few seconds. Luke stood still outside the bunker. He looked around the terrain to find the best place to hide. He went quickly through possible scenarios. The man would probably come by car. He would find that Svärd's car wasn't there and believe he was the first to arrive. In all probability, he would go into the bunker. But that wasn't a sure thing. He could also wait in his car or get out of the car and wait outside. Luke wanted to have him inside the bunker.

He swore. If Svärd's car were parked visibly by the gravel road, the man would surely go into the bunker. He made the snap decision and ran through the forest to the car. He stopped it as far down the gravel path he could and sprinted from the car towards the bunker. He looked for a boulder that lay about twenty yards next to the bunker. He pulled out the macana and positioned himself. It was the perfect spot. He could lie down and simultaneously peer towards the entrance to the bunker.

After ten minutes, he heard a car approaching. He hoped it was Svärd's partner and not Jonna or one of her colleagues who figured out where they were. There couldn't be that many bunkers on this island, and they would surely drive around and look. Then it would all be over. If police were driving around, the man would be scared off and the police wouldn't be able to get hold of him. Shit.

The sound of an engine approached, and Luke moved to the other side of the boulder so he could see. He caught a glimpse of the car between the trees. A Volvo V40, not a squad car. He saw that there was only one person in it, but he couldn't see who it was. When the car came out of the woods, he had a clear view and saw that the driver was Anders Loman. He must have listened to Luke's message and been able to find the bunker. Luke ran up from his hiding place, pushed the macana back into its sheath, and rushed to the car that now stopped fifty meters from the bunker. Anders Loman stepped out of the car, caught sight of Luke running towards him, and waved.

"Damn, Anders. You can't stop the car here," Luke panted when he reached him. "I think the man we're after is on his way, and if we're going to catch him, he has to think no one else is around. You have to hide the car, quick."

Anders understood immediately, turned around and looked for a suitable spot.

"Okay. What do you think about behind the shed down there?" he said, pointing to the little storage shed.

"No, that won't work," Luke said. "Jump in the car. I know where we can hide it."

They hopped back into the car and Anders backed up a bit until he could turn around. Then he drove quickly back up the road into the woods.

"I have to apologize for my behavior the other day," Anders said. "I wasn't really myself. I've been having a tough time privately as of late. I hope you can accept my apology."

"Of course," Luke said. "No problem."

"I also have to say you've done a damn fine job," Anders continued, smiling. "You haven't considered applying to law enforcement programs, have you?"

Luke chuckled.

"No way. The thought never crossed my mind. I'm perfectly happy working with my teenagers."

"Where's the other guy you mentioned in your message?" Anders asked as they bounced around on the bumpy little gravel road.

"Thomas Svärd is his name. But his actual name is Magnus Abrahamsson. He's tied up with tape across his mouth inside the bunker," Luke said.

Before Loman had the chance to reply, Luke spoke again. "Are more officers on their way?" Luke asked. "If so, you have to stop them so they don't scare the guy off."

"Three squad cars are on their way," Anders answered. "But they've received orders to hide themselves up in town until further orders are given."

"How did you find your way here, anyway?" Luke asked. "When I left the message, I didn't know which of the six bunkers it would be."

"I took a guess that it would be the one furthest south," Anders answered. "If that was wrong, I would've just gone up the line."

Luke kept his eyes turned into the forest so they wouldn't miss the little path where they previously hid Svärd's car. Suddenly, he glimpsed it between the tree trunks. Anders turned onto it and drove a little bit so they were out of sight of the gravel path. They jumped out and ran through the forest towards the bunker. At the edge of the woods, they stopped and looked out over the open area. They stood still for several seconds, panting.

Listening for the sound of a car, but the only thing they heard was screams of gulls flying out over the skerries.

"I suggest we wait for him inside the bunker," Luke said. "He may very well be armed, and if we're in there, we could surprise him more than if we go in after him. We could keep an eye out for him through the embrasures that face west, those narrow slits in the wall. They were built for people defending this place to be able to see out while others couldn't see in, so they're perfect for us now."

"Excellent," Anders said. "Let's do it."

They dashed to the bunker. Anders went in first. Svärd lay down on the floor, still with his wrists tied to the radiator. His arms looked almost dislocated. When Luke and Loman came in, he sat up with a blank expression.

Luke pulled out the macana and immediately positioned himself by the embrasure, looking towards the gravel path. Nobody was coming. Luke turned around and saw that Anders had taken out his service weapon and removed the safety. He stood next to Luke and looked out.

"How long ago since you had text contact with the man?" Anders asked.

Luke looked at his watch.

"An hour and a half."

"I wonder why it's taking so long," Anders said. "It only takes thirty minutes to drive here from town." He leaned down and picked up the macana Luke had propped against the wall.

"Interesting weapon," he said, feeling the razor-sharp obsidian shards. "Good weight. I heard that the Incas could decapitate a horse with one of these. Is that true?"

Anders took a few steps backwards for some clearance and tested a few swings of the sword in the air.

"Be careful," Luke said. "In the hands of someone who isn't trained, it can be extra dangerous. Especially if that person also has a cocked Sig Sauer in his other hand."

He reached out his hand to receive the macana back.

Anders ignored Luke's outstretched hand. Instead, he took two steps back and aimed his pistol at Luke.

"Release him," he said, nodding towards Svärd.

53.

Luke stared at Anders Loman, examining his eyes to see if they revealed he was joking, but they were stone cold. His mouth didn't even give the hint of a smile. Only the hand holding the pistol revealed that he wasn't calm. It was shaking.

"You don't need to point a pistol at me for me to untie him," Luke said.

Now he's completely lost it, Luke thought. He saw signs of it earlier, in Loman's sudden fit of rage in the conference room. The cancer must be pushing him towards a breakdown.

"Why do you want me to let him go?" Luke asked.

"Do as I say," Loman said. "Untie him now! Quickly!"

He screamed the last words, and Luke realized he had to do as he was told. Loman seemed completely unbalanced. Luke went to Svärd, crouched down, and began loosening the knot that tied his wrists to the radiator. Luke fiddled with the knot for a few seconds, and then stood up. His legs felt weak under him, and his mouth was dry.

"It's you," he said to Loman. "You're the other man."

"For Christ's sake," Loman said. "I promise you, I'll shoot you if you don't do as I say. Untie that knot, now!"

Luke could see from Loman's eyes that he wasn't reachable anymore. The Anders Loman he talked with previously wasn't there now. Maybe that version of Loman was never there at all. Luke bent over and continued struggling with the knot, trying to breathe slowly and deeply to keep control of his body. If he panicked now, he wouldn't stand a chance.

Luke heard Loman move. He looked up and saw him stepping backward, still with the pistol aimed at Luke and Svärd, towards the embrasure. When he got there, he stood with his back to it, listening. Luke realized he was worried about whether Jonna or another unit might be on their way. He went back into the room.

"How difficult is it to untie that damn knot?" Loman shouted.

Loman stood along the wall, between Luke and Svärd, so that he could see what Luke was doing. Just then, Luke loosened the last bit of rope and Svärd was free. He stood up and pulled the tape from his mouth. He grimaced in pain as the tape came off.

"Thanks," he said to Loman and spat on the ground. "Be done with him and let's head out quick."

"Tie the American to the radiator," Loman said to Svärd. "He should be sitting exactly like you and the rope has to be tied just as well as when you sat there. Do it quick."

"Why's that?" Svärd asked. "Can't you just shoot him?"

"Do as I say!" Loman screamed.

"Okay, okay," Svärd said. "Take it easy."

He leaned over and picked up the rope he was tied with. Loman took a few steps away from Svärd, still with the pistol pointed at Luke.

"Now take off your jacket and walk nice and quiet over to the wall and sit where Svärd was."

Luke looked at him. He'd backed up so he stood in the middle of the room with his pistol cocked and pointed right at Luke. Luke wondered if he should throw himself at him, but realized the risk was too great. Loman was at least two yards away, and all his attention was focused on Luke. He'd never make it. He took off his jacket and walked slowly to Svärd.

"Why, Anders?" he asked when he got to the wall and sat down. "Why are you doing this? Why did you kill all these people?"

Loman didn't bother with Luke's questions. Instead, he gave orders to Svärd.

"Hurry up! Tie him up now!"

Svärd got moving. Loman stood so he could supervise the work. Wanted to be sure it was done properly and quickly.

"I assume you're going to kill me," Luke said. "Isn't it reasonable that, before you do, you tell me why you've done all of this? What's the justification?"

Loman didn't answer. He again went to the door and opened it, still pointing the gun at them. He listened.

"Did it feel good to kill little Agnes?" Luke asked.

No reaction from Loman. Svärd was done with the knot. He stood up. Loman bent down and felt it. Approved.

"How did your children die?" Luke asked.

"Damn, you Americans go on and on," he said at the same time as he switched the macana to his right hand, pistol to his left.

Without a hint of warning, Loman raised the macana and swung it with all his strength towards Thomas Svärd's neck. The dagger-like glass shards made contact just a bit from above, first cutting through the oblique neck muscle, then the small muscles and connective tissue, before cutting off the trachea at the same height as the larynx. The knife stopped at the cervical vertebra. Blood cascaded over the floor, soaking Luke's sneakers and forming a puddle at Loman's feet. He took a few quick steps backward so he wouldn't be covered with it. Thomas Svärd's dead body fell heavily on the bed, which immediately filled with the pumping blood from the open neck wound.

Anders Loman stood still for a few seconds, looking at Svärd's body. It was completely silent in the bunker. The only sound was Loman's panting. Luke looked at him as he worked with his hands behind his back. He tried to get hold of the knot. Hoped Svärd wasn't very good at tying knots.

Loman went quickly to the bed and carefully wiped the handle of the macana. Luke realized he wanted it to look like Luke slit Svärd's throat. But then he'd have to make sure he got Luke's fingerprints on the macana to prove he killed him.

Loman laid the macana on the bed and stood in front of Luke. He pushed the pistol into its holster, took a pair of thin black gloves from his pocket and quickly pulled them on, then slipped a black case out of his inner pocket. It was the size of an eyeglasses case. Now Luke understood why he wanted Luke to take his jacket off.

"This will go quickly," he said, as if to reassure Luke. "It'll only take a minute before you go unconscious and then you won't feel anything. Svärd was able to lure you here and give you the injection, and when you realized it, you cut his head off. Then you calmly fell asleep. And I was the first one here, but unfortunately arrived too late to be able to do anything."

He raised the hand holding the syringe to the light. He squeezed out a few drops of cloudy liquid. Luke gave up hope of untying the rope. He had to concentrate on warding off Loman, who approached Luke from the left. Luke aimed his left foot to the hollow of Loman's right knee. When Loman paused less than two feet from Luke and bent down, Luke acted. He kicked with everything he had against the hollow of Loman's knee. The kick was well-placed. Loman fell backwards against the bed and hit his head on its edge. Luke pulled the rope so he could get closer and tried to kick him more, but Loman ended up out of reach.

Loman moaned and held the back of his head. He sat up and looked for the syringe, which he dropped in the fall. Luke also looked and caught sight of it first. It was on the concrete floor next to Luke. He tried to crawl closer to the wall to be able to get to the syringe with his feet. But Loman saw what he was doing and threw himself forward, getting hold of it before Luke was able to stomp it to pieces.

Luke could see that Loman was furious. He stood in front of Luke and ripped his pistol out of its holster. But then he hesitated as he got his thoughts in order. Luke realized he couldn't use his pistol if he still wanted his story to hold water. Loman put the pistol away again. Took the syringe in his right hand and now went to the wall on Luke's other side. He approached more cautiously this time. Luke tried to kick him. He made contact, but the angle was too tight for there to be any force behind it. When Loman was just a foot or so from Luke, he had to try to knee him instead. But Loman didn't come close enough for Luke to have any impact.

"There's no point in trying," Loman said. "You aren't going to be able to stop this."

54.

Jonna heard someone talking and fought to muffle her heavy breathing from all the running so it wouldn't be audible inside the bunker. She sat with her back to the wall of the bunker, next to one of the embrasures.

Of course, she started at the wrong end. The bunker she started with was furthest north. The right one was furthest south. There was a third of a mile between them, and Jonna swore loudly five times, every time she saw that the bunkers were closed up tight. She ran the mile along the shore as fast as she could. There was a path along the shoreline between the first three bunkers. The rest of the way she ran on exposed stone, through thorny branches and over marshy soil. She began to doubt when she realized the fifth bunker also wasn't the right one and started wondering if Luke misspoke. Said Sturkö but meant Tjurkö. Not easy for an immigrant American to discern the difference between the initial consonants in the two words. But when she approached the last bunker and saw the two cars parked close to it, she sensed she had finally found the right one.

Jonna clearly heard someone inside the bunker say, "There's no point in trying. You aren't going to be able to stop this."

Jonna recognized the voice. It was Anders Loman. How did he get here? Wasn't he going through chemotherapy? How did he know which bunker it was? She couldn't piece it together. She leaned carefully forward towards the hold in the embrasure and looked in.

She had to bite her tongue not to make a sound when she realized what she was looking at. She pulled her head back. Tried to interpret the situation. She had to act quickly. At the same time, her brain was working on high to make sense out of what she just saw.

Why was Anders trying to inject Luke with something? Who killed that man? Luke? Was it Luke?

She didn't understand any of it, but she knew she had to stop what was going on in there. She knelt in front of the narrow opening of the embrasure, held her pistol with both hands, and aimed it right at Loman.

"Freeze! Drop the syringe and back up."

Loman stiffened in the middle of the movement that would have resulted in Luke's poisoning. He looked up at the embrasure and first saw the pistol, then Jonna. Luke saw his chance. This was the moment he was waiting for. In his last effort, he threw up his left leg and flung his foot towards Loman's head with all the strength he had left. The hit was powerful, but not completely clean. Loman's head jerked backwards and hit the concrete wall. He was knocked out and sank to the floor.

"The door's open, Jonna," Luke called.

Jonna sprinted around the bunker, down the steps, and opened the door. She held the pistol in front of her. Loman stood up and drew his own pistol. He aimed it at Luke's head.

"Release your weapon, Anders!" Jonna said.

Loman didn't react. He looked at Luke with distant eyes.

"Anders. It's over. Release your weapon before anyone else gets hurt," Jonna said, still not understanding how all of this hung together.

Suddenly, Loman whipped round towards Jonna. She cringed and aimed her pistol at his chest. Loman shook his head, took the pistol from Luke's temple, put it in his own mouth, and pulled the trigger.

55.

Jonna had never seen a person take their own life before. Nor had she ever seen anyone shot. The sound of the gun going off reverberated through her head, and with the image of half of Anders Loman's brain splattered across the concrete wall burned onto her retinas, she ran out of the bunker and threw up on the steps.

After a couple of minutes, she went back in. She couldn't hear her own footsteps. Her eardrums were deafened by the shot. The smell of gunpowder mixed with the strong smell of blood. She tried not to look at the wall or at Anders Loman's body, which was now half-lying on the floor next to Luke. He hadn't managed to get out of the knot Svärd tied. Jonna went over quickly and helped him get free. Neither of them said anything. When Luke got to his feet, he put his arms around Jonna.

"Thank you," he said. "Now we're square."

He took a step back and looked into her eyes. The gaze was empty, and her face was gray. Luke looked around for a place where Jonna could sit. Not the bed; Svärd's bloody body was there. Luke went to the table by the wall, took the chair, and put it in the middle of the floor. Then he led Jonna to the chair and sat her down on it. He opened the door to let in fresh air, and then crouched next to her. He took her hand. She leaned forward and laid her arms on either side of his head.

"Was it Anders who cut off the head of the man on the bed?" she whispered. "Or was it you?"

"It was Anders," Luke said. "It came as a complete surprise. I had no chance of stopping it."

Suddenly, they heard a voice call through the same opening Jonna just peeked in through.

"Hello? Do you have all of this under control?"

It was the patrol unit, which had arrived at the bunker.

"It's clear," Luke called. "You can come in."

"Gustafson! Is that correct? Can we come in?"

Jonna lifted her head and looked at the opening. Glimpsed her colleague Hansson's walrus mustache.

"Yes," she said. "Find someone who can take care of the bodies. Two of them."

Her phone dinged, and she pulled it out and looked. It was Mattias, texting to ask how it was going. Jonna stood up.

"I have to call Mattias and tell him what happened," she said, leaving the bunker. On the steps, she met Hansson and Elvenäs. She gave them a short description of what happened before going up and calling Mattias.

Two days later, Luke was called to the police station by Jonna to leave his statement of the course of events. Mattias, Jonna, and Luke sat in the same conference room where they sat together with Anders Loman just a few days earlier, when he had a fit of rage and stormed out.

"Nice that you could come, Luke," Jonna said. "We can start with Mattias and I giving an account of what we figured out. You are welcome to jump in with what you know as we go along."

She left the floor to Mattias, who said they primarily built their theory on how it all hung together using information from Jenny Dahl.

"How is she doing, by the way?" Luke asked.

"Quite well, considering the circumstances, as they say," Jonna said.

"She's incredibly upset about what happened, of course, but she has a good therapist and will probably get over it. She's also very thankful, by the way. I'm supposed to tell you that."

Luke nodded in appreciation.

"I can start by saying that Loman and Abrahamsson were able to take the lives of eight former Scientologists and a preschool teacher before you stopped them," Mattias said to Luke.

"A preschool teacher?" Luke said.

"Abrahamsson needed money, and he supported himself by selling pictures of children via an international pedophile website. He was able to lie his way into a substitute teacher position at a preschool in Kungsholmen at the same time as he was to kill Maria Palm. A couple of parents found the preschool director strangled in her office, and in the playroom were seven children, five of whom were naked. We found pictures of the children on Abrahamsson's camera."

"Judging from everything, Abrahamsson was the sole perpetrator of that murder," Jonna said. "We don't think Loman sanctioned it. Abrahamsson probably panicked when he was found out."

"And Loman must have murdered Max Billing alone," Luke said. "Maria Palm and Max Billing died the same day, on Wednesday last week."

Jonna nodded.

"Our theory is that Loman was stressed out by your inquiries and wanted a quick resolution to his plans. So he ordered Abrahamsson to head to Stockholm while he carried out the murder of Max Billing the same day."

"The remaining murders probably originate in events connected to the activities of the Church of Scientology in Karlskrona in the early 1990s," Mattias continued. "As you've understood, Jenny was a member of the church at that time. She had a boyfriend who was also a member. His name was Daniel Loman."

"Anders Loman's son," Luke said.

"Yep," Mattias said. "When Daniel was nineteen, he hanged himself a short time after his sister Åsa Loman, also a Scientologist, died tragically from a blood clot in her left lung. Åsa was only a year older than Daniel."

"And Loman laid the blame on the Church of Scientology?" Luke asked.

"That was clearly how he saw it," Mattias said.

"Jenny found Daniel, hanged on the bathroom door in their cabin on Trummenäs. On the record player was 'Return to the Mothership' with Chick Corea, and on her pillow, he left a sort of goodbye note."

"With the same quote found in the homes of the people Loman and Abrahamsson killed," Luke said.

"He wanted the people he saw as guilty of his children's deaths to experience the same thing as his son did," Jonna interjected.

"According to Jenny, Loman was right," Mattias continued. "Åsa Loman was psychologically unstable and ended up at the hospital. The Scientologists took her home and cared for her themselves. When she grew worse, they refused to take her to the hospital, and eventually, she died. Daniel was crushed, ended up in a deep depression, and took his own life."

"We've checked Anders Loman's story," Jonna continued. "A few months after Daniel's suicide, in January of 1994, Anders and his wife filed for divorce. Their marriage apparently didn't survive the deaths of both of their children. Loman applied for and received a job at the Swedish Security Service in Stockholm, where he worked until May 2012 when he applied for and received the job here. His wife was diagnosed with Alzheimer's five years ago and lives in a nursing home here in town."

"Loman got his cancer diagnosis in February 2012," Mattias said.

"Just about two years ago, then," Jonna said.

Mattias nodded. "The doctors gave him two years max," he said. "We

238

think that's when he made his decision. He has clearly harbored thoughts of revenge since his children died, and when he found out that he was going to die, he began planning his revenge."

"Wasn't there anyone here at the station who knew all this about Loman's children and the connection to Scientology?" Luke asked. "Someone should have reacted when Scientologists began being serial murdered and reflected over a possible connection to Loman and what happened twenty-three years ago?"

"Yes, you might think that in hindsight," Jonna said. "There are two people at the station who were around then, but they've been completely occupied by the Yara case, working day and night, so they missed the whole story, unfortunately. We maybe could've saved Maria Palm and Max Billing if these colleagues were properly informed."

"Doubtful," Mattias said. "It's only been a week since we realized someone was murdering Scientologists. I'm not at all sure that we could have stopped them even if we understood the connection to Loman immediately."

"No matter what," Jonna continued. "Loman planned this out thoroughly. We were at his apartment yesterday and found a whole lot of evidence. All nice and neat on his computer. General surveillance on all the old members, timelines, travel and hotel bookings, the purchase of the defense bunker on Sturkö from the Fortification Administration, orders for equipment. You name it."

"I've been wondering about the connection to Abrahamsson," Luke said. "How did he come into the picture? Why didn't Loman carry out the murders himself?"

"We don't really know," Jonna said. "My theory is that he became far too weak just physically speaking, both from the cancer itself and the chemotherapy. So he needed someone else to do the heavy lifting. He maybe didn't want to subject himself to the risks involved. He was going to kill ten people, and if he failed in this with one of the first and was found out and sent to jail, he wouldn't have had his revenge. By using Abrahamsson, he had a sort of buffer. If he went to prison, maybe Loman would have been able to carry out the rest himself."

"He might even have been thinking of his reputation after his death," Mattias interjected. "He maybe planned to kill Abrahamsson, too, once everyone was dead, and to be the one who solved the case. Then he could die with his name unsullied."

"So Loman hired Abrahamsson?" Luke asked.

"We don't think it's that simple," Jonna answered. "Abrahamsson was not a career killer. He was a pedophile and probably murdered before, but in that case, two of his victims were children. Abrahamsson was Loman's nephew, and so Åsa and Daniel's cousin, the same age as Daniel. We've talked to Abrahamsson's mother and found out that when he was little, he lived with his uncle and family for periods of time, and he was close to his cousins. He was released from prison in Kalmar in December of 2013 after having served a ten-year sentence for first-degree rapes of two children. The prosecutor wasn't able to produce the requisite evidence to charge him for the two murdered children. He moved to Karlskrona immediately, and on January 21, he was attacked in his apartment in Kungsmarken, assaulted and castrated by the leader of the Revenge Crew in Kalmar, Jörgen Gustafsson. One of the children Abrahamsson forced himself on was Jörgen's niece. Loman took care of Abrahamsson, arranged for protected identity, and let him live in the defense bunker on Sturkö in exchange for him helping Loman get revenge."

"Our IT-specialists were able to hack into Loman's Google account so that we could access the email conversations between Loman and Abrahamsson," Mattias said. "It was clear that Loman also threatened to reveal to Jörgen Gustafsson where Abrahamsson was if he didn't agree to help."

"Oh, right," Jonna said. "The two men who broke into your cottage. They were from The Force Soldiers in Spjutsbygd, and we're pretty sure Loman hired them to get you to stop digging around in this case. We haven't had the chance to interview them yet, but we found the email address of one of them in Loman's computer."

"And what about Viktor and Max Billing's trips to Russia? Did that have anything to do with this?" Luke asked.

"Not from what I could see," Jonna said. "They were probably just typical business trips."

The three of them sat silently for a moment. Luke considered the whole story. Loman staged a well-thought-out plan for revenge. Twenty-one years after both his children died. Twenty-one years of hate that built up and finally released in a wave of revenge possibly driven by the hope he would gain some sort of peace.

"I only have one more question," Luke said. "Agnes. Why was she killed?"

"We don't know," Jonna answered. "We can only guess. It seems to have been Abrahamsson who prepared everything. Tricked the victims into inviting him in, gave them an opiate, and got them into the noose. Arranged the music and the quote. When everything was rigged up, Loman came in to witness the final spectacle. It was probably that moment he enjoyed most of all—or didn't want to miss, in any case. Why Abrahamsson decided to kill Agnes is hard to understand. She couldn't have testified against him because she was only four years old. But he gave her the poison. After he molested her. Awful."

Jonna saw Luke's face turn white and realized he didn't know what Abrahamsson had done with Agnes. She cursed herself for being so insensitive. But before she could say anything, there was a knock at the door. Jonna called "Come in!" and a uniformed officer stuck her head in.

"The press conference starts in ten minutes. Are you coming?"

"We're coming," Jonna said. "Mattias, can you go ahead and I'll finish up the conversation with Luke?"

Mattias nodded, picked up his things, and left the room. Jonna looked at Luke. His eyes were black. His jaw muscles tense.

"I don't want to know what that piece of shit did," he said. "Not now."

"I'm so sorry I didn't say anything earlier, but–"

"It's okay, Jonna," Luke interrupted her. "I understand. I don't want to talk about it."

He stood up.

"Is the press conference about this case?" Luke asked.

"Yes, but we aren't going to be able to say much," Jonna said. "The investigation is far from over."

"Have you recovered after the bunker?" Luke asked.

"I haven't slept a full night," she said. "Nightmares take over. It's been a tough week personally, too, as you might have realized. When the investigation is over, I'm going to take a long time off. Get away with the kids. Alone."

"Is it that bad?"

"Yes, it's that bad. Married the wrong man."

"A bad investment?"

Jonna gave a half-smile. "Big time," she said, rising from her chair. "What will you do now?"

Luke shrugged his shoulders. "I'll keep working with my teenagers," he said. "They need me. And I need them."

They stood silent for a while.

"I need a little air," he said. "Give me a ring if you feel like enjoying the view from Björkholmen any time. I'll gladly give you a tour."

Author's Note

Kult is a work of fiction, but important parts are accurate retellings of true events.

I joined the Church of Scientology at the age of twenty, in 1978, in Hässleholm in southern Sweden, the city I grew up in. My descriptions of Jenny's time with the Scientology congregation – how she was pulled into the church, what she saw, how she was treated, the details of her studies – are all based on my own experiences. Jenny's thoughts, worries and fears at these moments are identical to my own reactions in those circumstances.

It sounds bizarre, but our group of Scientologists really did dig for the entrance to a spacecraft, exactly as I describe it. The leadership of the Hässleholm congregation had taken note of L Ron Hubbard's description of how the evil galactic ruler Xenu took a group of individuals to a prison planet in the outer edge of the universe 75 million years ago. Our leaders believed they knew exactly where their spaceship was buried – on the coast of southern Sweden – and so we started digging.

That extraordinary episode was one of the reasons why I decided to leave the cult. At the time I was twenty-five years old, with plenty of life in front of me. My experiences in Scientology affected me deeply, both in the short and long term. When I joined, I ended a promising sporting career and broke off contact with family and friends in order to devote my life to Scientology. It took a long time to repair these relationships. Some never fully recovered, I am sad to say.

Many years later, when I had my own family, I finally decided to explore what made me do those things, and so I started writing *Kult*. While working on the book, I was acutely aware that it is primarily young people who are vulnerable to the mental virus spread by destructive groups like Scientology and their leaders. These groups are the same whether it is a crackpot cult – which Scientology is – or a violent and extreme political or religious movement. My hope is that this book and the lectures I now give to adolescents will increase young people's awareness of and resilience to the temptations offered by those who claim to have found the truth and the solution to all problems. Such people are liars.

The scenes describing the death of Daniel's sister Åsa are closely based on true events which happened in Clearwater, Florida in 1995. A young Scientology Church member there, Lisa McPherson, died on 5 December of that year, having been isolated and 'treated' by members of the church for seventeen days. Some circumstances in my description of Åsa's death differ from Lisa McPherson's, such as Åsa's suicide attempt, which I added for dramatic reasons. But otherwise, the episode describes accurately the events leading up to the end of Lisa McPherson's life. More information can be found easily on the internet, and I would advise anyone reading this to seek it out.

Lisa McPherson did not have a brother who committed suicide. I created Daniel for dramatic purposes but also to make the point that suicide is far from unusual in Scientology. During the years I was a member and shortly after, two members of my congregation took their own lives, both talented young men who should have lived much longer. This is one of the great tragedies the Church of Scientology is responsible for – the devastating effects it has on young people who either join themselves at an early age, or whose parents join when they are children or whose parents are already members when they are born. It is worth mentioning that Quentin Hubbard, the son of the church's founder, L Ron Hubbard, took his own life at the age of 22 in 1976.

I was lucky to get out when I did. I have had a good life, and every day I am glad that I left. In the end, the person I have to thank most is Hanna, my wife and also my best friend, my sounding board and my companion during every step of this journey. She has listened to lots of bad ideas, understood how to bury them gently, and always recognized the good ideas when I was lucky enough to get them. She has also been prepared to watch me evening after evening, weekend after weekend, sitting in my armchair with the computer on the knee. Thank you, Hanna. I dedicate *Kult* to her with love.

Stefan Malmström
May, 2019.

Made in the USA
Middletown, DE
20 March 2020